BRIDESHIP WIFE

A Novel

Leslie Howard

Published by Simon & Schuster

New York   London   Toronto   Sydney   New Delhi

SIMON &
SCHUSTER
CANADA

Simon & Schuster Canada
A Division of Simon & Schuster, Inc.
166 King Street East, Suite 300
Toronto, Ontario M5A 1J3

This Simon & Schuster Canada edition May 2020

SIMON & SCHUSTER CANADA and colophon are trademarks
of Simon & Schuster, Inc.

For information about special discounts for bulk purchases,
please contact Simon & Schuster Special Sales at 1-800-268-3216 or
CustomerService@simonandschuster.ca.

Interior design by Alexis Minieri

Manufactured in the United States of America

1   3   5   7   9   10   8   6   4   2

Library and Archives Canada Cataloguing in Publication
Title: The brideship wife / Leslie Howard.
Names: Howard, Leslie, 1953– author.
Identifiers: Canadiana (print) 20190162864 | Canadiana (ebook) 20190162872 |
ISBN 9781508259350
(softcover) | ISBN 9781508259367 (ebook)
Classification: LCC PS8615.O899 B75 2020 | DDC C813/.6—dc23

ISBN 978-1-5082-5935-0
ISBN 978-1-5082-5936-7 (ebook)

This book is dedicated to my mother,
the novelist Blanche Howard (1923–2014),
who encouraged me to write fiction.

The
BRIDESHIP
WIFE

Prologue

September 16, 1862

The solitude of the upper deck was perfect for me. I suspected that many people on board the ship were having trouble sleeping this night, but unlike me, they sought comfort from their fellow travellers. I didn't want to trouble the others with my fears; they had their own to come to terms with.

From the time the captain had sounded the horn to signal our entry into British-held territory, excitement and anxiety had run high. Some chose to toast the news with glasses of champagne, while others huddled in small groups, their heads bent close together in murmured conversation. Tomorrow we would dock in Victoria on the northwest coast of North America, about as far away from my home as I could imagine.

Like pebbles tossed upon the beach, we would scatter, trying to make our way as best we could. Most of us would marry; some would not. All of us hoped for a better life than we could ever have found in England. As Charles Dickens once described us, we were the deserving unmarried—unemployed factory workers, Lancashire cotton mill labourers, orphans, the destitute. And a few, like me, were impoverished gentlewomen, unable to prevail upon our male relatives to support us for the rest of our days. To the best of my knowledge though, I was the only one who had been forced to flee England as a social outcast.

At the age of twenty-one I was about to start my life over. It is said that we are born alone and we die alone. And that certainly described me now. When I set foot on the foreign shore, I would have no loved ones to support me and no money to help me find my way. But I also would not have the same strict rules dictated by Victorian society, the rules that had been my downfall.

I had been told that the colonies offer women more opportunity. Despite the staggering uncertainty now before me, I couldn't wait to taste freedom.

PART ONE

England

Chapter One

"One look at you tonight and George won't stand a chance. Not that he ever did, once it was decided that he was the one for you. But this evening, you'll dazzle him, seduce him, make him beg for your hand."

It was an order, not a compliment. My sister, Harriet, leaned closer to me as we sat side by side at her dressing table. I could smell her sweet breath and a hint of lilac water coming from her long, elegant neck.

"And what a relief you've put on a proper corset for a change," she half whispered in my ear.

I tugged absentmindedly at the wretched garment, looking forward to the end of the evening when I would gleefully fling it into my bureau, where I expected it would remain for some time. It had been agreed that I needed to wear a full whalebone corset only when I was in proper society, which was thankfully not a daily event for me.

"Tonight you'll get George alone, allow him to steal a kiss or two, light a bit of fire in him. Give him a taste of what he can expect in married life."

"I think I would stir more passion if I talked about duck hunting," I said. "Maybe I should rub rendered duck fat behind my ears. That might stoke the flame a little."

Harriet flushed. "This is serious, Charlotte! George Chalmers is a brilliant match for you. He's your third suitor, and there's not exactly a line forming behind him."

"Not fair," I said, holding up an index finger to make my point. "Alfred doesn't count. He must be fifty if he's a day and he's more interested in a nurse than a wife. Surely I have the right to pick a man who offers me a little romance, some excitement even. And we both agreed Reginald isn't a real contender—he rarely leaves his mother's side. Thirty years old and he still makes faces at children during church service."

"You can't afford to be choosy," she said. "If it weren't for Papa's troubles, you would have had a decent dowry and plenty of prospects. But now we have to be realistic."

Hari's abigail drifted silently into the room carrying the black-lacquered jewellery box that housed Hari's newly polished earrings and brooches. Setting it on the dressing table, she bobbed a curtsey before busying herself with the white cambric day dress that had been tossed on the four-poster bed. I flipped open the box lid and began rummaging through, looking for the perfect jewelled pin for the bodice of my gown. Picking up the box, I wandered over to the window for better light.

In a low voice Harriet muttered, "Time is running out."

I looked up to see Hari twisting her string of pearls into a ball around her neck.

"Time?" I echoed.

Hari turned from the mirror and peered at me, the bright

6

light from the window making her eyes water. "It's just that, after I pushed him to find someone, Charles went to great lengths. If this doesn't work out, I can't keep asking him to help you. George is the best of the lot."

But that's not saying much, I thought. *It was a pretty narrow field, and Charles didn't dig very deeply.* I wasn't really surprised. Harriet's husband, the Honourable Charles Baldwin, MP, was much more interested in politics than finding a good marriage match for me.

"That will do, Jane." Hari waved dismissively at her abigail, then waited until she left the room to speak again. "There are more complications."

"What?"

"It's his uncle Lord Ainsley. He told Charles that he's ready to declare him his heir and to pass on his seat in the House of Lords to him. So Charles wants to be very careful not to attract gossip of any kind. Nothing that could affect Lord Ainsley's decision."

"What does that have to do with me?" I wanted to ask why everything had to revolve around Charles and his ambition, but I didn't.

Hari let out a sigh. "Women of a certain age need to be properly married with children or settled in a suitable position for a spinster—a governess, for example."

I shivered at the thought of being a governess and the exhausting boredom it entailed. I wanted something more exciting. Someday I would marry, of course, but I was just twenty-one. Surely I had time to make a match. Harriet was twenty-five and had only wedded three years ago. She and Charles hadn't even started their own family yet. I knew that unmarried women attracted gossip—that while seldom true was always malicious—but I doubted people had much of anything to say about me, certainly nothing that would influence Charles's aspirations negatively.

"But George?" I wondered aloud.

"You should be pleased," Hari said. "Many women would consider George a prime catch. He's just been appointed chief whip, an enormously powerful position. Everyone in Charles's circle fawns over him. He can make or destroy a parliamentarian's career with just a word to the prime minister."

I flopped back on the bed. "I grant you that George seems an attractive-enough fellow in a balding, middle-aged sort of way. Just the sort of very respectable husband women yearn for. But I don't know if we would be happy together. I'm not even sure I'm ready to marry."

"I've just said you have no other option!" Harriet cried.

The sudden sharpness in her voice startled me, and I sat up. "What do you mean? What's wrong, Harriet?"

"I'm sorry." She came towards me and took one of my hands in her own. "But I do worry about you sometimes, Charlotte. One hears such dreadful tales. You remember Mildred Winthrope? Really quite a lovely little thing, wellborn but certainly poor. By her third season she still hadn't found a husband and was forced to beg from relatives. She died last winter. Caught a cold, and in her weakened state she was gone in a fortnight." Hari dropped my hand. "They had to bury her in a pauper's grave!"

I couldn't help but laugh. "Do I look like I'm about to fade away from lack of nutrition? If George doesn't make me an offer, I have another thought." It was hardly formed, if I was being honest, but Harriet seemed to think that this marriage was my last chance for a good life, and I wanted to reassure her. The intense setting sun emerged from behind a tall tree, sending an unforgiving light through the three west-facing windows. Was it a sign?

Harriet leaned towards me, brows raised. "Don't tell me someone else is dangling after you. Someone wealthy? Connected? You are full of surprises. Do tell."

"No, nothing like that. It's something else entirely." I'd seen an advertisement posted in the broadsheets for a new veterinary program just yesterday and it had piqued my interest. I had always loved animals, whether it was barn cats, hunting dogs, or the majestic racehorses my father bred. As a girl, I spent my daylight hours tramping around our estate. Mama was always so preoccupied with making social connections, going to parties, and working to find the right match for Harriet, I don't think she noticed, or if she did, she let it go. When our estate was in arrears and we'd had to let most of the help go, I tried to keep the animals and livestock in good condition until they were sold, but we'd had to get in Dr. Boyd, a veterinary surgeon, to tend to the racehorses, one of whom was pregnant. Harriet had seen the work as beneath me, but in truth, I'd enjoyed it.

I gave Harriet's hand a gentle squeeze. "I had a thought about applying to the inaugural veterinary apprenticeship course."

Harriet dropped my hand as the vein in her temple began to throb. People often assumed that a beautiful woman would have a sweet temperament to match her angelic looks, but that was rarely true.

"Do not for one moment think that you are a candidate for this ridiculous scheme. Because if that is where this conversation is headed, you can stop right now. Besides, I'm certain they would never accept a woman."

"Not as a veterinary surgeon, no, but perhaps as an assistant. It would be something to fill my days. Something besides social calls and parties."

"I can't imagine what sort of woman would apply for this, certainly no lady of quality." Harriet didn't seem to realize how loudly she was speaking until I shushed her. Maids always seemed to be lurking about this vast house. She lowered her voice. "There are things happening that you are not aware of. Wheels are in motion. We have no input and no control over them. And time is running out for us, for you. You must marry, and soon, or Charles will create your future for you, one I doubt you would choose for yourself."

Her humourless eyes worried me. We often liked to gently tease each other, but not today. She was like this when she was trying to shield me from trouble. She did it when Papa was struggling with the estate, and she was doing it now. I took her hand in mine again. "It was just a thought. Nothing to get upset about."

"Of course." She got up and walked towards the window. "But honestly, Char, I think you have a lot of our father's romantic recklessness in you."

Her last comment was like a blow to the stomach, but before I could respond we were interrupted by a sharp knock at the door and Charles entered. It was his routine to visit Harriet's room before any social event. The inspection, I called it, which Harriet hated. He was obsessed with what others thought of Hari and revelled in the admiration that she attracted from other men.

As usual, Charles was dressed immaculately in perfect evening attire created for him by one of the most expensive tailors in London. When it came to himself, he spared no expense. His gentleman's gentleman had done wonders covering his new bald spot, combing the sides of his straight blond hair into position and using some sort of oil to hold it in place. His neat, short beard had not a whisker out of place, and I couldn't be sure, but it appeared that powder had been applied to his cheeks and the end of his thin nose.

"Charlotte," he said. "That shade of green is most becoming, a perfect match for your reddish-blond colouring."

"Thank you," I replied, a little stunned at the rare compliment. Perhaps I was in the habit of judging him a bit too harshly.

"I was delighted when George told me he was looking forward to seeing you tonight. Don't disappoint me."

He turned his attention to Hari. "The hair is all wrong, Harriet. Send for your abigail. Curls, not straight. And what were you thinking with the pearls? Something an old maid would wear." His glance strayed in my direction for a moment. "Don't forget Lord Ainsley and Lady Margaret are coming. It's important that you make a great fuss over them. I want them reminded of how much I value their endorsement. And hurry, the guests will be arriving soon." With that he turned on his heel and was gone, no small kiss on Hari's cheek, no goodbye, nothing.

The discordant, confused sounds of the string quartet warming up on the outdoor stage below the open window wafted into the room.

"Is he always that sharp with you?" I asked Hari quietly.

"Charles is under a lot of pressure these days," she said, but I could hear a trace of irritation in her voice. "He's not completely himself. You know how short-tempered he can get when something's weighing on him."

Charles was usually short with me, and I was happy to avoid lengthy conversations with him. I'm sure he felt that it was one thing to generously take me in after Papa's death but quite another to acknowledge my presence.

"We are closer than most sisters, wouldn't you agree?" Harriet said, turning to face me. By the fading light, I noticed the beginnings of the tiniest of crow's-feet in the corners of her eyes. "In some ways I think we are more like mother and daughter. I was always there for you when you were growing up. I had to be; Mama wasn't. I've looked out for you and steered you in the right direction, haven't I?"

I nodded, feeling a lump in my throat.

"Then hear me now." Her grip on my hand tightened. "Do whatever it takes to get George to propose to you tonight or we will both suffer the consequences."

Chapter Two

Harriet's words played over and over in my head and left me feeling uneasy. I found refuge in my third-floor bedroom and immediately sought out the one thing that always brought me comfort: my red-lacquered jewellery box, a twin of Hari's black one. I picked it up and wound the crank on the bottom before lifting the lid. Tinkling musical notes filled the small room, and I sat down and closed my eyes, allowing myself to be soothed by the lilting notes of "Greensleeves."

Harriet's played a Brahms lullaby. The small chests were a gift from our father from before, when he still had most of his fortune, and they were the one thing Hari and I had saved from our childhoods. We had come a long way from those days, but when I checked myself in the mirror, I saw that same uncertain girl staring back at me. I leaned forward and dabbed my face with powder in a vain attempt to cover the freckles.

The veterinary-assistant idea had been a foolish thought. Hari was right—ladies of my station would never be accepted into the program. Marriage was my only real option. But I didn't want to marry and leave my sister, not yet and not for George. I barely knew the man, let alone felt anything resembling affection. Would I even make him happy? Would he make me?

One of my clearest memories of my mother was her lamenting her own fate as a country squire's wife. She could have done much better, she declared—a gentleman with a comfortable income, a city house in London and another for the season in Bath. At the very least, she might have had a senior military officer from a prominent family. But a full year since her coming-out party, she'd had not a single proposal. (There had been an offer from a charming but poor clergyman, but she didn't consider it serious.) Filled with doubts about whether other, better suitors might come along, she had panicked and jumped at my father's proposal. He was a man of good social standing, due to inherit his father's profitable estate near London.

I heard the familiar refrain in my head: "I was the daughter of a decorated cavalry officer. I had a decent dowry and pretty-enough looks. I could have married a man with a larger inheritance and a lot more common sense, but instead I settled for your father, who loses every cent he ever has."

Even as she lay dying from consumption, she belaboured my father's faults. He dismissed her complaints. She would eat her words, he insisted, when his next investment made us rich and famous. Perhaps if he hadn't had the accident and later died, he would have proved himself.

It made me sad to see them that way. Neither of them were saints, but I loved them both, in different ways. All they wanted was the best for Harriet and me. Still, my parents were miserable together. Theirs was a life I had no interest in emulating, but did I have a choice?

A knock on the door brought me out of my reverie.

"Come in," I said.

Jane entered and handed me a letter on a silver tray. I ripped open the seal and had to stifle an unladylike cry of joy. It was from our beloved governess, Miss Wiggins. As a very young child with a lisp, I had struggled to say Miss Wiggins's name correctly, and it often came out sounding more like *Wiggles*. Hari, of course, burst into fits of laughter every time I said it, but our teacher smiled tolerantly and suggested I address her simply as Ma'am. But for Hari and me, she would always be Wiggles.

My dear Charlotte,

It's been ages since we had a nice cup of tea together, and I'd love to spend an afternoon with you if you can prevail upon the Baldwins to let you borrow a coach. I hope you can visit soon as I have something very interesting to tell you about. Best to talk in person.

I had no inkling about what was on Wiggles's mind, but I was happy to have a good excuse to call on her. In the three years since I moved into Harriet's home, I'd seen her less and less, and I missed her dearly. She was always the calm voice of reason, something I could definitely use right now. I scribbled a note of acceptance to Wiggles and passed it back to the abigail for delivery.

"Your sister is ready for you downstairs," Jane said.

"Thank you, Jane. Tell her I'll be right down."

After she left, I looked at my face one more time in the mirror. I thought of Harriet and Charles. I owed them a great debt. Harriet and I did not inherit our father's estate, and I had nowhere to go after Papa's funeral. Hari and Charles had immediately taken me in. As much as I complained about Charles, he had shown me great kindness when I needed it most. And now I must return the favour. I just wished I had more time. I closed the jewellery box and steeled myself for the night to come.

Chapter Three

I caught my breath as the butler flung open the doors to the stone patio, and Hari and I stepped through the glass-paned French doors and took in the rolling lawn, formal gardens, and Lake Lily. My sister was always one to make a grand entrance. Her smile was wide, and her face glowed without a trace of our earlier fraught discussion.

Harriet had christened her glittering Mayday evening soirée "A Fairy's Garden Party," and I had to admit, it was fair billing. Her reputation as a brilliant hostess was well-earned.

Delicate lights shimmered about the grounds and glowed throughout the formal gardens. Long glass cylinders each housing a candle hung on the acacia trees dotting the lawn, and small lanterns wound around the garden pathways, from the patio to the lake, and along a hundred or so feet of shoreline, creating what looked like laneways for wood nymphs. Harriet, with an ever-present eye for detail, had directed the gardeners to row over to the small island, just offshore, and place lights along its dock. It made me want to visit the island to see the view of the party from there.

I squeezed Hari's hand. "You've outdone yourself."

"You can have a home like this too if you play your cards right," she said, already surveying the crowd of guests, nodding and exchanging smiles. "Oh there's Lady Persephone Fitzwilliam, the prime minister's cousin. Good! I wasn't sure she would come. I'll be sure to sit with her during the midnight supper."

The idea of my own elegant home *was* a bit seductive, I thought, as I inhaled the intoxicating aroma of fresh-cut grass, lavender, and camellias. Nearby, the string quartet struck up a Mozart minuet. I reached for a flute of champagne from a passing tray. It was tart but delicious, and the tiny bubbles burst and tickled my nose.

Just as I was beginning to lose myself in the fantasy of Hari's make-believe world, I noticed the patio tables that were set up for games of cards and chance.

"You're your mother's daughter," I told Hari. "It's not a party without card games."

"But you were the one most like her when it came to cards. You always won," she said with a laugh.

Mama gambled, in a very ladylike fashion, of course, but she taught herself strategies and became an expert in games of chance. Tea and cards games at our home always involved small bets. She taught me as well, so that I could be a fourth when needed, and I loved to play. It was one of the few ways my mother took interest in me. A brilliant marriage for Hari was all she had focused on. "Hari is our one great hope," she'd say. "She will restore the fortunes of our family and save us all." It was too bad Mama hadn't lived to see her wish come true.

I didn't notice Charles until he was standing next to us.

"There you are, Charlotte," he said. "Perfect timing, and I'll say again, you do look exceptionally lovely this evening." He took my elbow and propelled me forward. "I just saw George chatting with a group of men over on the lawn. Follow me."

Hari took my other arm, and I allowed myself to be led, still reluctant to seal my fate with George. I couldn't quite put my finger on the reason why, but something nagged at me. Of the handful of times I'd seen him, he seemed like a perfectly good sort, but dull as dishwater.

Our progress was slow. It was always like that when I tried to walk anywhere in public with Charles and Hari. As we passed groups of guests, they broke apart, the men approaching us to shake Charles's hand and the women nodding respectfully to Hari. It seemed everyone wanted a word. Charles took it all in good humour; in fact, he revelled in it.

The only one who didn't step forward to shake Charles's hand was a very distinguished man I recognized as Lord Ralston, a grizzled old warhorse in a top hat and tails. Charles didn't move to greet him either.

Beside me, Harriet whispered, "Don't they remind you of a couple of stallions fighting for control of the herd?"

Lord Ralston stood very still, taking the measure of the up-and-comer. I could see that he was reluctant to cede the turf Charles was moving into, but after a moment, he tipped his hat and Charles acknowledged the gesture with a slight, smug nod.

Harriet fit well into Charles's political circles, looking every bit the part. Her gold taffeta gown fell in soft folds over her statuesque figure and set off her pale, patrician face with its high cheekbones, square jaw, and long, thin nose. The final touch was a tiara expertly entwined in her artfully constructed blond curls. Our mother would have been so proud. Harriet was everything I was not, and I suspected people thought that she was the one beauty of the family.

"Poor, dear Charlotte," I could imagine them saying. "Her star can never hope to burn as bright as her sister's. Such a pity she didn't inherit the tall, willowy frame and the taste in clothing to show it off."

I caught sight of our destination, a group of men engaged in an animated discussion, and my throat went dry. I knew I would be expected to make witty small talk, something I dreaded. As we neared the men, there was a burst of raucous laughter at some shared joke, but it faded when Harriet held out her hand. The group parted to make room for the three of us, and each man gallantly took Hari's hand, bestowing a small kiss, an homage to her beauty and to her place in society. I tried to stay back, but Charles pushed me forward once again.

"Gentlemen, I am sure you all know my sister-in-law, Miss Charlotte Harding?" he said.

George was the only one to reach for my hand. His was large and fleshy with surprisingly soft skin.

"Of course, the lovely Miss Harding," he murmured as he held my hand to his lips and brushed it with his sticky-wet moustache. "A delight to see you again. I hope you'll do me the honour of stepping out with me tonight. Perhaps a walk along the shoreline to admire the lanterns?"

"Charlotte will be flattered to join you, George," Charles said with an ingratiating smile.

"Yes, I'm sure I should enjoy that," I murmured dutifully.

George seemed pleased, and Charles nodded to Sandwell. His butler snapped his fingers at one of the servants carrying champagne, and within seconds, we were offered fresh glasses.

I took a glass and held it to the light, pretending to examine the colour and lustre of the wine, while I looked anew at the man with whom I might spend the rest of my life. He was clearly beginning to show the first signs of oncoming middle age. His gold hair was thinning but still no sign of grey. The cheeks of his jovial face were rounding, the neck thickening. A slightly bulbous red nose was crisscrossed with spider veins, the telltale signs that he drank to excess. His throat bulged over the tight, high collar of his dress shirt, while his stomach strained against the confines of a cummerbund. Clearly not the Prince Charming of most young girls' dreams, but he had a comfortable, solid look.

As the servant bent forward to offer a delicate flute of champagne, I heard George quietly mutter, "Have you got anything more substantial? I'm not a big fan of the bubbly." The man nodded and headed off discreetly.

"I distinctly heard a peal of laughter as we approached your group," Harriet said, commanding the group's attention. "And I demand to be let in on your joke."

"Ah, that. We were making light of the petition brought to the House of Lords demanding the vote for women," George explained on behalf of the group. "Someone suggested that getting the vote would surely encourage women to become involved in politics, a soul-destroying enterprise if there ever was one. Another countered that it wouldn't be a problem because he wasn't sure women actually have souls." He sputtered with laughter and the rest of the group joined in. The servant returned with a tray carrying a large tumbler of Scotch for George, who drained it within a few seconds.

What a bunch of buffoons, I thought, but I kept a polite smile on my face. Charles would not appreciate me looking at George like he was an unbridled idiot.

Harriet fluttered her ivory-and-feather fan. "I am more than happy to leave the politics in the family to my husband. It's his passion, not mine. My one role is to be his hostess."

"But you're forgetting your other, more important role, that of a wife and mother," George said.

A shadow seemed to flit across Harriet's face.

"My wife would never forget those obligations, would you, dear?" Charles's look held little affection.

I felt embarrassed for Harriet and struck up the courage to change the topic. "Charles tells me you are the government's whip, Mr. Chalmers. I know little of what that role entails. I imagine it's very challenging?"

"Yes, indeed. It seems the prime minister doesn't wish to make a single decision without my input, and on the other end of things, I have to ride the junior members of Parliament very hard to keep them in line. Long hours with no time off, but I don't complain. It's for the good of the nation and the empire."

"If you'll excuse me," Charles interrupted. "I'll leave you to get better acquainted while I attend to some of the other guests."

As he moved off, the conversation shifted to the questionable thrills of foxhunting. George then began telling a dull story that had something to do with the construction of the perfect duck blinds. Stifling a yawn, I glanced longingly over at the card games, and when I turned back to the dwindling circle, I caught Harriet scanning the crowd of a hundred or so people.

"Who are you looking for?" I asked under my breath.

"Just making sure everything is as it should be," she replied, but I saw her eyes rest on Charles. He was speaking with a young woman I knew to be a recent widow.

"Excuse me," she said, and raised her eyebrows towards George as she brushed past me.

I nodded, then drained my glass. Fortification for completing the task before me. Eying my empty drink, George stepped forward and offered his hand. "Shall we?"

He took my arm and steered me in the direction of the lake. As we walked along the well-lit path that wound through the flower gardens and acacia trees from the house to the lake, he talked about his speaking engagements. It seemed that all the best men's clubs in London were perpetually begging him to enlighten their members regarding the state of the empire. Then, when I stopped to examine a rose, he took the opportunity to lean close to me.

"You look ravishing tonight, Miss Harding." I felt his lips brush my ear. "Good enough to get a man thinking thoughts he ought not to. Do you know you torture me?"

I focused on the flower in front of me, unsure how to react. Part of me wanted to wave him away, but another part wanted to hear more. I felt a small fluttering thrill to think I could have this effect on a man. It would make marriage to him so much more palatable if he was truly captivated by me.

"Look here." George pointed through the twilight to the shoreline. "A rowboat. How about we take a romantic ride over to the island and see what the party looks like from that vantage point. A fine treat for us both, don't you think?"

"Yes, I would love to do just that." I smiled, pleased that we shared a certain sensibility. Perhaps he had just been trying to impress me with his self-importance. He was probably feeling a bit nervous, as I was. Maybe we would find we had much in common as we got to know each other better. "I've never actually been to the island before," I said as we neared the dock. "Hari only has the boats brought out for parties."

"Charles and I used to row out there when we were children and swim all day."

The thought of Charles as a young, carefree boy made me laugh. As an adult he was always so serious, so bent on his future in politics.

With surprising dexterity, George helped me step off the short dock and into the boat, then settled himself easily onto the opposite seat. He pushed away from shore and started to row with determination. When he began to perspire, he asked my permission to remove his jacket.

"Certainly," then catching sight of a cluster of lily pads, I said, "Oh, look, let's row over there. I can pick a flower for my hair. The yellow ones are especially lovely, don't you think?"

"My vision is already filled with a picture of loveliness," he said, gazing intently at me. "A mere water lily can't compete."

I smiled sweetly at his attempt at gallantry. I imagined us ten years on, a couple who had grown very fond of each other. We would have pet names, and I could see us stepping out in matching tweed outfits for our daily strolls. Comfortable, if unexceptional.

George did not stop to pick a flower but continued to make a beeline for the island. As the boat rammed the dock, I lurched forward in my seat and fought a wave of nausea. I closed my eyes and took a deep breath, and when I opened them, I saw that George was already up and out of the boat, securing it to the dock.

"Come along, my dear," he said.

"Just a minute." I struggled to untuck my feet from my long skirts and clamber up beside him. As I was brushing my gown, I felt his hand on the small of my back.

"Look up," he said softly.

"Oh! It's gorgeous." From where we stood together on the dock, the lights and sounds of Harriet's party were truly a thing of beauty. The starry sky above the haloed lights, the soft lilting notes of the string quartet occasionally interrupted by happy shouts of laughter, were even more appealing with distance and perspective.

It was enchanting, and rather romantic, and I moved to lean into him, thinking this was the moment he might propose. But he was twisting away, scanning the topography of the island.

"There it is." He gestured to a tiny cottage tucked away in the trees. "The old summer bathing house. Its front porch has a large swing chair just big enough for two. Let's give it a try."

"But what about the party?" I asked.

"We'll go back. Don't worry," he said, giving me a sheepish look. "I'm afraid I'm not as young as I used to be. I just need a moment to rest before rowing again."

I hesitated for a moment, then remembered Harriet's and Charles's admonishments to not let them down. The swing chair sounded like the perfect spot.

As we moved inland through the looming trees, the yellow light from the lanterns along the shore faded into a muted grey and the tinkling music and giddy laughter from the party dulled into flat noise. It was difficult to see in the increasing darkness, but George guided me over the ground brush. We stumbled a little as we went, and a thornbush snagged my bare forearm, leaving itchy pricks in my skin. When we finally mounted the wooden steps of the porch, I felt a surge of relief. There was a charming old swing, just as George had described, though the unmistakable sweet odour of rotting wood hung in the air. With a sigh, I dropped into the chair, leaving ample room for George, but he immediately went to the cottage door and gave it a resounding kick with the heel of his boot to open it.

"You must see this first, my dear. It's quite exquisite—a lovely representation of the arts-and-crafts style of interior design. Charles's family never did spare any extravagance."

I reluctantly got up and peered in. "I can't quite make it out now. Perhaps we will have to come back to see it in the light of day."

"No, no. Just move inside a little ways while I light this old lantern from the porch."

Darkness enveloped me as I stepped over the threshold, then a light flared behind me, just bright enough for me to make out the room. The space held nothing more than a large metal-frame bed with an old, stained mattress, pushed up against one wall.

My earlier nausea returned with a vengeance. This was not decent. Surely George knew that. What was he thinking? Before I could turn to leave, I felt a sharp blow to the base of my neck. A bright yellow light exploded in the back of my eyes, and hot tendrils of pain flared upwards from the bottom of my skull. I tried to cry out, but I couldn't breathe. I felt myself falling, and then all went black.

Chapter Four

When I came to, my first clear thought was for air. I gasped, taking long jagged breaths as the scene before me came into focus. In the half-light of the lantern, George was pulling at his clothing, his face flushed a deepening shade of red. My head throbbing, I looked down at myself. My skirts were lifted to my waist, garters broken, stockings sagging. My bloomers were torn and at my knees. Panic washed over me, a dizzying wave of nausea and fear.

"George!" I cried, reaching for my underclothes. "You're Charles's friend. He would be shock—"

"Shut up, you silly bitch!"

A slap stung my face and I tasted blood. Who was this man before me? My body began to tremble as my heart thumped in my chest. How could I stop him?

George cursed as he struggled with the tiny clasps that held his cummerbund in place. "Stupid goddamned monkey suit." At that moment, the final clasp on his cummerbund gave way and he flung it to the floor, then shed his trousers, revealing his undershorts. His manhood bulged beneath the thin fabric.

"No, no, no!" I protested, tears springing to my eyes.

George knelt on my legs, pinning them down. "It's always much more civilized if you just lay still. I'll be done in a minute."

With sickening dread, I realized this wasn't the first time he had done this. I began to scream, but he covered my mouth with his hand. "If you breathe a word of this to anyone, I'll tell them you seduced me in order to force marriage. Whose version do you think people will believe?" His words stung like the slap. I knew his story would be unquestioned. "There's no future for you if you talk. No one else will want my leavings. Do you understand?"

I nodded, and he removed his hand from my mouth.

"Please, don't do this," I pleaded. "Charles said—"

"What? You think just because you are Charles's sister-in-law that makes you something? You have nothing to your name. Everyone knows your father was just a feckless dreamer who lost his fortune. If I marry anyone, it will be an heiress, not some penniless old maid like you."

My fear hardened into a burning anger as the failings of my family were once again thrown in my face. I was so sick of people's judgements, the mocking, the entitlement to treat me however they pleased. I felt feverish as a deep animal rage stirred within me. It propelled me to action.

I let out a fierce yell and drove my head deep into George's soft, protruding belly.

"Good Christ, what are you doing?" he wheezed, clutching for my hands, but I wrestled them free and grabbed the fleshy area below his male organ.

He gasped. "Oh, God! Oh, God! Stop it, you stupid cow."

I squeezed hard, and he shrieked and clawed at my hands, but I held fast, twisting further. He continued to flail until we both tumbled off the bed and onto the floor, my grip broken at last.

I struggled to my feet, but George remained curled on the floor, whimpering. I pulled at my clothing and stumbled out of the cabin into the dark night, breathing hard. In spite of the warm evening, I felt a cold shiver down my spine. How long had we been here? Surely people would begin to notice our absence, if they hadn't already. My reputation, my one thing of value, was in grave danger. One hint of what had occurred tonight would be the ruin of me. And Harriet. I had to get back to the party.

I heard George moaning inside the cabin as I set off running in the direction of the dock, tripping over low bushes and uneven ground. A sharp stick pierced my shoe, burying itself in my big toe, but I pushed on, limping, until I found the boat. I began to untie the rope, then pulled myself up short. If I attempted to row myself to the main dock, people would see me with my torn and dishevelled clothing. There would be no disguising my misadventure.

Hot tears threatened to overwhelm me, but I fought them back. Turning towards the cottage, I peered hard into the darkness, looking for any sign of movement, but I saw and heard nothing except the distant sound of the party, where the guests' lives continued on, untouched by the evil that threatened me. I caught a snatch of sound, the echo of my sister's voice, calling cheerfully to an old friend.

Then I remembered something Hari had said about the

boats and why she only brought them out at parties for the guests to use. In summers, there was no need of boats; the island could be accessed on foot by a narrow land bridge that snaked from the northernmost point of the island to a spot on the mainland around the back of the house, near the servants' entrance. This time of year, the land bridge was covered with a few inches of water.

The festive lanterns that had delighted me at the beginning of the evening were now my godsend, and I used their light to find the beginning of the land bridge, a line of large, flat stones protruding from the lake. I managed to hop from one to the next until, landing on one that was partly submerged, I lost my footing and flipped backwards into the bracing water. I struggled to my feet, standing shin-deep in the lake, my hair ribbons plastered to my nose and chin, and continued on, taking great care with each step not to repeat my plunge.

It was not long before my foot struck the mainland shore. Hoisting my sodden skirts around me, I moved quickly across the slippery grass path that led from the water to the back of the great house. Light poured from the windows of almost every room in the vast mansion, forcing me to hide in the shadows of a holly hedge. From there, I could see the back end of the servants' wing, but how would I get in unnoticed?

As I watched, the large wooden door by the kitchen opened and Sandwell emerged on his way to the patio, but a doorstop prevented it from closing all the way behind him. I shrank back into the darkness, waiting to see if anyone followed him, testing a story in my mind.

If I were discovered, I would make light of it all. I'd tell them that I had been out for a rowboat ride with Charles's dear friend, Mr. Chalmers, that I insisted he row me over to pick a flower from a lily pad, but I leaned too far over the water and I upset the boat. I'd paint George gallantly, and excuse myself to get cleaned up.

If I can somehow carry this off, I thought, *I'll marry whatever suitor Harriet wants me to.* All would not be lost.

I pressed on with renewed confidence. I knew the back staircase was just off the kitchen and would be a hive of activity as the servants prepared the midnight meal. Lucky for me they would be focused on their work.

I could hear the clanging of pots and pans by the kitchen, then: "Look here, who's out there?"

I froze. It was Harriet's chief of housekeeping.

"I don't care who you are, or if you think yourself too fancy to help out in the kitchen. Get yourself an apron and get to work. Be quick about it!"

How did she know I was there? I realized too late that the light in the hallway cast my shadow on the nearly opaque glass of the kitchen door. I made a run for the stairs, just rounding the first landing when the kitchen door creaked open.

"You upstairs maids think you're too bloody good for us, don't you?" she called after me. "Mr. Sandwell will hear about this, be sure of it!"

What was left of my shoes and stockings was wet and slippery, and I gripped the bannister as I vaulted the stairs two and three at a time. I thought of my mother, scolding me for this habit. "You don't behave as a lady should, what with running wild on the estate all day. You've not learned polite manners."

If I was to remain a lady, sacrifices had to be made, I decided wryly, as I sprinted in a most unladylike manner down the hall to my room. I opened the door and flung myself inside. I had done it. Leaning back, I shut my eyes and caught my breath. I had made it back without encountering a soul.

"Oh, miss, it's you. You gave me quite a start!"

My eyes flashed open and I saw Jane, Harriet's abigail, standing at my dressing table, my paste-glass necklace hanging limply from her hand, a candle in the other. A bright crimson flush rose quickly up her throat to her cheeks.

"I . . . I was just tidying up your dressing table," she said, quickly depositing my jewellery into my red-lacquered box. "I didn't expect you back from the party till much later."

With her back to me, she made a show of straightening the few objects on the dresser top, but I didn't care. I just needed her to go.

"That's fine, Jane," I said. "You can leave that for now. I heard the kitchen is looking for help, so perhaps you should see what you can do there."

"Surely I can be of some assistance to you here, miss. Do you need your hair brushed or perhaps a dab of powder on your face?" She turned towards me, holding the candle high. A look of shock crossed her face. "If you don't mind me saying so, miss, you could do with more than just a dab of powder."

"I must look frightful, but a quick change of clothes and I'll rejoin the party," I said as lightly as I could. "I had a small accident with one of the rowboats, my own silly fault, leaned too far out to pluck a lily flower. You can fetch me a new gown. The lilac one will do nicely."

"But your face, miss—there's . . ." She motioned to the mirror.

We stepped forward, she beside me, observing my reflection, the candle close. The angry imprint of a hand was clearly visible on my face. I saw the light come into her eyes as it faded from mine. She knew my story was false. The whispers would start soon. How far they would go, I didn't know.

Chapter Five

Two days after the party, the mark on my face had faded and I had concealed any remaining evidence with powder. My head was still sore, but that wasn't what troubled me most. George's face haunted my dreams, and I was afraid to close my eyes at night because I would see him looming over me. In my waking hours, my mind kept replaying what had happened. Where had he gone afterwards? Had he said anything?

I'd seen no sign that the story of my ragged appearance had gone further than some of the servants' pointed looks my way, and I held on to the fantasy that if I didn't say anything, it hadn't really happened. I wanted everything to be normal again, for life to go on much as it had before, though I didn't know what that meant for Harriet's plans to wed me to George. Even if he did want me, I could never marry him after what he'd done.

As if sensing my internal turmoil, the weather changed dramatically. A heavy, cold mass of air had crept in while we slept, pushing out the balmy hint of an early summer that we had enjoyed the night of the party. I thought of Wiggles's letter. It was a godsend, a chance to get away, even for an afternoon. Desperation was new for me, but I felt it now. Maybe there would be something to what Wiggles had to tell me, a light or a hope I could cling to. I asked Hari to come with me, but she demurred as she had an appointment with her new doctor in town, Dr. Randolph, though I knew she wouldn't have come anyway. She often said that I should limit my social engagements to women of our class.

The morning was chilly, and as Hari and I settled in her coach, I was grateful for the heated bricks that the footman had set out for our feet to rest upon and for the fur-lined rugs we pulled across our laps.

"Thanks for letting me tag along," I said as I snuggled deeper under my wrap. "Once you are at your doctor's, I'll head directly to visit Wiggles. I haven't seen her for ages." I patted my purse to make sure I had brought a book for the journey. I often felt a bit anxious if I didn't have one with me.

Harriet mumbled something indistinct and stared unseeing out the window. It wasn't like her to be so quiet. In fact, now that I thought about it, she had been rather subdued since the party. Had she heard any gossip from the servants? Or did her mood have anything to do with our fraught conversation before the party? In an attempt to draw her out, I asked her about her new doctor. All she had said was that he was from the Continent and up on all the latest medical advancements.

"You've seen quite a lot of Dr. Randolph lately," I said lightly. "That's not like you. You've always avoided doctors like the plague, ever since that awful time you broke your leg as a child. That was the worst of Papa's failed investment schemes, don't you think—the hot-air balloon? I don't think Mama ever forgave him."

Hari shrugged. "I don't know if that was the worst—just one in a long line."

I peered into Harriet's face. "I hope everything is all right with you."

"I'm fine, and I expect to be even better. I'm hoping for good news soon." She rested a hand on her stomach.

So that was what was weighing on her. Charles and Hari were finally starting a family, and she was clearly anxious to share glad tidings with him.

After a pause, Harriet turned to me. "Sandwell came to me this morning."

My stomach dropped. "Oh?"

"He felt it was his duty to inform me of what the servants were saying about you—not to his face, of course, but what they were saying when they thought he wasn't listening." Hari searched my eyes intently. "What in God's name happened between you and George? Did you get carried away with your seduction?"

"It wasn't my fault, Harriet. Nothing went the way I expected."

"Your instructions were so simple. A kiss, a proposal, not . . . not whatever it was you did."

"I didn't do anything. It was George." I felt so ashamed—for getting myself into such a situation, for letting both Hari and Charles down, and for my own vulnerability. "He attacked me, Harriet," I whispered. "When we were alone together, in the cottage on the island."

"How on earth did you end up there? How could you let yourself get into a compromising position like that?"

"I know. I shouldn't have, but it all happened so fast. I didn't have time to react. It was almost as if . . ." I hesitated. "He planned it."

Hari's face flushed a deep crimson.

"He said he would never marry a penniless old maid like me." My throat tightened as I repeated his hateful words.

"This puts us in a terrible predicament. According to the belowstairs staff, you are of questionable virtue, a woman who wouldn't hesitate to affix her garter in public, as they say. If this gets around, your reputation will be in shreds. How we'll find you another suitor, I have no notion."

"Does Charles know?" I asked anxiously.

"No, thank goodness, and we certainly can't let him get wind of it. He would be furious, and there's no telling what he might do." She gripped the blanket and wrung one end into a knot. "Why did this have to happen with George, of all people? It could be disastrous for Charles."

"I'm sorry, Hari." I tried once more to explain, but she just held up the palm of her hand.

"It doesn't matter what actually happened. All that matters is that we manage the repercussions. I asked Sandwell to make enquiries, and he reported that George changed his plans and didn't stay over that night as he intended but left quietly for his country house before the midnight meal was served."

I felt new stirrings of hope. "He must want to avoid scandal just as much as we do. Perhaps it will all just blow over if no one fans the flames of gossip."

"I am not going to simply cross my fingers and pray it all works out," Harriet said. "Early in our marriage Charles told me that I am one of the most astute strategists he's ever known. I've already persuaded him to take a few days to unwind at his hunting lodge, where the gossip can't reach him. But Charlotte, I must know. Did anyone see you?"

"Jane. She was in my room when I made it back from the island. She's the source of the rumours."

"She will be sent packing immediately. The rest of the staff will take note. And you"—she frowned at me—"will do nothing that could cause the tiniest hint of gossip from now on. You will be the very model of propriety."

"I promise." On this, I was committed.

"If all goes well, we will weather this storm, and in time I'll find someone else for you."

I knew I should feel grateful, but I felt a twinge of resentment as full control of my future passed to my sister, and part of me was wounded that she showed so little concern for my well-being. Her only real focus seemed to be how this could affect Charles and his political prospects, but I was starting to realize that my welfare was wrapped up in Charles's. Hari was looking out for me, just as she'd done after our parents' deaths and through all the family's financial troubles. I had to trust her now.

Chapter Six

An hour later, I arrived at our old family estate after dropping Harriet off at Dr. Randolph's. My mood lightened at the prospect of an afternoon of tea and a chat with my dear governess Wiggles. She had no family, so our father had given her a life interest in a small cottage in return for her years of service. We were passing the rose garden, about to make a right-hand turn off the main driveway towards the cottage, when I spotted my cousin Edward, pruning shears in hand. He waved us down.

I had vowed not to visit Edward. I knew I wasn't being fair to Edward and his wife, Prunella—that my distaste for them was influenced by the fact that, after my father's death, Edward had inherited my childhood home: the twenty-room manor house and surrounding three-hundred-acre farm, the formal gardens, the stables, and all the livestock.

In my heart, though, I knew my feelings were unfounded. I continually avoided blaming the one person whose actions were behind the downfall of my family: my father. He was the one who squandered his large inheritance and left our estate to

Edward. His actions drove my mother to gamble, created the need for Hari to marry well, and forced me to try to make a decent marriage with no dowry. The sight of Edward, in what should have been my garden, was a painful reminder of all of that. My coach came to a halt.

"Why, Cousin Charlotte! Just the person I wanted to have a word with. How perfect. This saves me sending for you."

"Lovely to see you, Edward, but I'm on my way to visit Miss Wiggins—not much time."

I hoped my apologetic smile would carry the day, but he opened the coach door and held it firmly. "This will only take a minute."

I could see no alternative than to step out with him into the garden. It annoyed me to see that he and I resembled each other. There was a look that ran through our family: freckled, reddish-blond colouring, tall, with long limbs and a tendency to carry a little extra weight.

At least I have all my hair, I thought.

Edward's prize roses had been smartly clipped in time for the warm growing season ahead. It was hard to imagine the feathery beauty that these prickly stumps had so frivolously exposed to the world last summer. Now the severely pared-back bushes stood in neat rows like little soldiers at attention, awaiting further orders.

"You know I'm not one to mince words," Edward began. "I'll get straight to the point. I've been told you haven't garnered a single marriage proposal since your coming-out three years ago. You know you're getting up in years, don't you? Not much hope now, I reckon."

I opened my mouth to respond, but he kept talking.

"Prunella's been at me. 'We have a duty,' she says, 'a Christian duty, to offer charity where it's needed, especially when it's family.' I don't hold much with that sentiment, mind you. I've never asked for a handout, but the wife won't let it rest."

I studied his face, looking for some awareness that he had inherited all that should have gone to Hari and me, but found none.

"The wife wants me to offer you a place here," he was saying. "This could be your home for the foreseeable future."

Despite my feelings for Edward, it was a kind offer, and I said as much.

"Don't think you won't earn your keep," he went on. "Prunella's been having trouble keeping nannies. With two sets of twin boys plus little Bess, she's run off her feet. You can be the help, and when the children are older we'll promote you to governess, in exchange for room and board. Your dear father saw fit to tie my hands by giving the dowager's cottage to Miss Wiggins for as long as she lives, otherwise I could have offered it to you. The old governess is too long in the tooth to be of much use to me, and yet I can't turn her out."

In others words, I would work like a servant for little monetary reward, I thought, but bit my tongue. I had promised Hari I would be the very model of propriety. "I don't know what to say, Edward." That was the truth.

"Don't get any fancy notions in your pretty little head, now." He turned our path back towards the coach. "You'll not live like one of the family, attending dinners, parties, and such, and your room will be on the top floor, in the attic, not your old room on the second floor—Bess has that."

My smile froze on my face. Nothing about Edward's offer even remotely appealed to me. I'd take marriage, even to an old senile man, over Edward's ungovernable children any day.

"Thank you for the offer, Edward," I said, stepping into the coach. "I'll think about it and let you know."

"Better hurry! You're not getting any younger," he added as he shut the door.

As we pulled away from the gardens, I looked back at the house where I had grown up, as it receded into the distance. I could never stand to live as the beholden relative in a house that had always been mine, and I blinked back a few unexpected tears. The sight of Wiggles's cottage a few minutes later calmed me, and I quickly descended from the coach and went to her door.

"Charlotte, how lovely to see you," she said, welcoming me in.

"It's been too long, Miss Wiggins." I presented her with a large jar of strawberry preserves I had pilfered from the kitchens.

Wiggles's eyes lit up as she took the gift. "Charlotte, dear, I think it's high time you called me by my Christian name, Hortense."

She had changed since I last saw her. Age had begun to turn her bright blue eyes to a milky grey and her soft, dark hair to a salt-and-pepper brown. The port-wine stain on her right cheek—a disfigurement that had cost her all chances of a good marriage, my mother had often said—had largely faded from existence.

The cottage was as cozy as only a spinster could make it.

Framed embroidery and needlepoint samples hung on the walls and a colourful quilt covered the settee. True to her vocation, Wiggles had a well-stocked bookshelf that ran the length of one wall and a large globe that stood on a pedestal in a corner. I recognized *Gulliver's Travels*, *Pride and Prejudice*, and *Great Expectations*. These were the books that I had loved so well growing up.

The intoxicating aroma of fresh baking hung in the air, and my stomach groaned with anticipation. A perfect tea had been set on the small wooden table: chocolate biscuits, scones, preserves, tea, clotted cream, sugar. A stickler for etiquette, Wiggles had drummed the fine art of formal tea service into Hari and me.

"Hari sends her very best, but she has an appointment with her doctor in the city today. She said she'll be up to see you again as soon as she can." It was a lie, and I suspected Wiggles knew it. If she was hurt, she didn't show it.

We sat at the table and Wiggles poured our tea. "What are you reading these days?"

"I've nothing new at the moment. Perhaps I can borrow something from you. You know how I love a great adventure story."

"Of course," she said, looking thoughtful. "You remind me of your father. He was always reading that sort of thing. He was a bit of an adventurer himself, wasn't he?"

Papa loved investing in new inventions. Nothing seemed to excite him more than to underwrite the development of some new labour-saving mechanism or other.

"Mama often said she dearly wished he would live as a

gentleman should, but he swore he would die of boredom." I sighed and set my teacup down. "But look where it got him."

My mind drifted back to that unhappy time. Papa had put money towards developing a steam-powered tricycle. He was riding it when it blew up. He was hit in the head with shrapnel and spent a month with dreadful headaches and vertigo. I helped tend to him, but when he finally emerged from the sickroom, he was not the same person, either in mind or body. He could not remember things that should have been fresh in his memory. He began to live in the past, as those were the only memories he had easy access to. His judgement was impaired and he became an easy target for all sorts of unscrupulous charlatans and fraudsters.

Wiggles didn't respond. "Enough about the past, let's talk about cheerier things. What have you been up to lately?"

"I'm afraid I don't have much to report. No new marriage offers and no plans if I don't receive one. I expect I'll have to persuade Charles to support me until my dying day." I said it with a forced laugh. I didn't want her to pity me, and I didn't want to inform her of Edward's offer. How could I tell her that the idea of a governess position filled me with dread?

She paused for a moment, then said, "The question of your future is one of the reasons I wanted to see you today. There is a new movement I've heard of. The Columbia Emigration Society. They're sending ships of unmarried women—brideships, they're called—to the colonies. They have some very distinguished backers for the plan."

I almost choked on my tea. "Is this what happens to women who can't find a husband here? They're sent off to the colonies like the shiploads of transported convicts and political prisoners bound for Australia?"

"Not quite, Charlotte." Wiggles offered a small smile. "The idea is to give the women a chance to marry or live independently in the colony of British Columbia, where there is more opportunity. It's for the poor, the unemployed, and impoverished gentlewomen." She pressed a pamphlet into my hand. "There's to be an organizational meeting at the London Tavern. You should go."

I glanced at the paper. "That's Charles's club. They don't let women in, and besides, Hari and Charles want me respectably married, not travelling to the colonies in search of a husband."

Wiggles set down her cup gently. "There's precious little here for women like us, Charlotte."

I winced at the truth of her statement, but I didn't see how this brideship plan changed anything for me. Charles and Harriet would never hear of it.

Wiggles used the table to push herself to her feet and shuffled over to a locked cupboard in the tiny sitting room. Taking a key from a chain around her neck, she unlocked the door and withdrew a blue velvet box. With great care, she set the box on the table, released the metal clasp, and flipped open the lid. I gasped. Inside was a necklace, a single emerald hung by a gold chain. I gingerly picked up the necklace and held it to the light. The colour was stunning—sparkling chartreuse in natural light but more of an absinthe colour when I returned it to the box. I would never have expected that Wiggles would own anything like this.

"Where did it come from?" I asked.

"It was my mother's—an engagement present from a

wealthy, much older man. He died two weeks before they were to be married. She cared for him deeply and was still in grief when her family pushed her to accept an offer from my father, a country pastor. Theirs was not a happy marriage. After my father died and she was on her deathbed, she passed the necklace on to me. She knew I would never marry." As she spoke, Wiggles unconsciously stroked the side of her face, where the bright red splash of a birthmark once dominated. "It's the only thing of my mother's I have left. I was close to selling it before I found work with your family."

"I've never seen you wear it," I said.

"On what occasion would I ever wear something like this? I spend my life in this tiny cottage or at the church in town. Jewels are not de rigueur." She laughed, but it was hollow. "Besides, I'm just a governess. I will never be anything more."

I had always seen Wiggles through the eyes of a child—she was my adored, devoted governess. It never entered my mind that she might have wanted something else for her life. Perhaps she and I were more alike than I realized.

"Do you remember our lessons on ancient myths? The word for emeralds comes from the ancient Greek *smaragdos*."

"Green stone," I said.

"That's right. The Egyptians thought they signified something. Do you remember what?"

In the deep, dark recesses of my mind, there was a spark of light. "A sign of rebirth?"

"Very good, Charlotte." She slid the box towards me. "I want you to take the necklace."

"I can't possibly! I would never dream of it."

She closed her hands over mine, as if to hold me still and make me focus. "You must take it. I have no one to pass it on to. Nothing would give me greater pleasure. Sell the emerald when you get to the New World. Use the money to make your own path and live the life I never had."

I felt tears well up. The bond I felt with Wiggles touched me deeply. Perhaps we had found something in each other that had been missing in our own lives. She was the doting mother figure I never had, and in turn I was her only family. The thought made me open my mind to what she was proposing. For one brief moment it felt as though a door had opened, and I caught a glimpse of another world. It was an untamed place full of light and colour and as different from the streets of London as I could imagine. I briefly saw myself there, living as an independent woman. But just as easily as it opened, the door swung shut. I had no skills or training, and even if I did, no one would hire a gentlewoman. It was not to be. I had obligations to live up to, and life had suddenly become full of urgency and uncertainty. I pulled my hands from beneath hers to dab the corners of my eyes.

"At least go to the meeting and hear about the plan," she said. "They're letting women attend just this one time. Give it a chance."

I didn't want to spoil Wiggles's dreams for me. Not yet. As much as I loved and respected her, a future in the colonies was her fantasy, not mine. I had no real interest in sailing to the other side of the earth and starting a new life, but I would leave that news for another day, a day when I was betrothed and could return her beautiful necklace. Of course, that would depend on Hari's plan working.

Chapter Seven

As I left Wiggles's cottage, it began to rain, but by the time I arrived at Dr. Randolph's, the deluge had abated to a fine drizzle that coated the streets with a slick film. When Hari emerged from the building, she was leaning heavily on the doctor, and his arm moved to her waist as he guided her to the coach.

He was a slim man, pale, with intense dark eyes and a neatly trimmed moustache. Handsome, I thought, but there was an aura of vulnerability about him. Before he closed the door against the damp, late-afternoon chill, he took Hari's limp hand and pressed it to his lips, holding it for some time before letting go.

I hoped his attentions meant there was good news, but Hari wasn't smiling. She slumped against the cushioned seat of the coach and closed her eyes. I had thought to tell her about Wiggles's idea, even as I discounted it, but her expression made me think twice.

"How did it go?" I asked tentatively.

Hari just shook her head.

I remembered George's thoughtless comment at the party about her responsibility to give Charles children. She must be under so much pressure, I reasoned, and I certainly wasn't helping.

"I hope you know that if there's anything you need, you just have to ask."

"I'm fine, really, Charlotte. It's you that we have to worry about." She straightened a little. "I've been thinking that I should send George a note—an expression of regret that there was a misunderstanding between the two of you. Something conciliatory."

"A misunderstanding?" I was ready to protest, but the world-weary look on Harriet's face stopped me.

Harriet sighed. "If he thinks you might publicly accuse him of wrongdoing, he'll go on the offensive, do everything he can to destroy your reputation and limit Charles's political power. But if we appease him, he won't feel threatened and may just let the whole thing drop."

The carriage continued its creeping progress through the winding, congested streets of town, but my mind would not quiet. I knew what she said made sense, but the very thought that we should have to be the ones to come grovelling to him made my skin crawl. I couldn't stop Hari from sending a note to him, but I was certain I would never put my signature to it.

"George is a bully," I said. "And the only way to control a bully is to stand up to him. If he senses weakness, he'll be emboldened."

"Will you leave this to me?" Hari's jaw was tight.

"Can't we at least discuss—"

The coach came to a skidding stop, vaulting me forward, and I put out my hands to brace myself. A high-pitched shriek cut through the air.

"What on earth?" We peered out the side window to see a horse sprawled on the damp ground in front of our coach. The carriage on the other side of the street must have skidded on the wet stone and dragged the horse off its footing. The poor creature had run into a wooden lamppost and broken its leg. In spite of its injury, the horse was desperately trying to stand, crying out in fear and pain, its eyes white with panic.

Harriet uttered a soft cry and covered her mouth with her hands. I desperately wanted to help the unfortunate animal, but as I reached for the door handle, a man stepped forward with a pistol.

"No!" I cried.

It was too late. In one swift motion, he had fired his pistol at the horse's head. A sticky-sweet smell filled the air as a dark mixture of blood and brain matter began to ooze from the shattered head of the horse onto the cobblestone streets.

I sat back, fighting an urge to cry. A beautiful creature lost in such a terrible accident.

Harriet turned away, her handkerchief pressed against her nose.

Her footman's head—a ruddy, deeply lined face topped by a brown derby hat—appeared at the side-door window. "I'm right sorry you had to witness that," he said. "Not a sight for ladies. Sit back 'n' keep warm, the coachman'll get us out of here in a jiff, soon's they clear the road."

Harriet nodded, and he touched his hat and disappeared from view.

I couldn't watch. In an attempt to block out the sounds and smells as they carried out their task, I focused my attention on the view from the opposite side of the carriage. It was a vast town house, its windows elegantly appointed with rich brocade tapestries. Inside I could see a young woman and three little boys seated at a great oak table laid with a silver tea service and candles. This was clearly the city home of someone, as Hari would say, in the first circles.

I nudged her and pointed to the window. "Do you know who lives here?"

She shook her head, but just then, a new figure entered the room. Harriet gasped. The man was unmistakable. It was Charles.

"Isn't he supposed to be at his hunting lodge?" I asked.

She didn't answer, but remained focused on the scene before us. The children were looking adoringly at their mother as she poured tea and offered cakes, while Charles, dressed in formal attire, watched the elegant family with clear admiration. A casual observer would have easily assumed he was the children's father and the lady's husband.

I studied the woman. I had seen her before. The carriage jerked forwards, and Harriet fell back against her seat.

"That's the young widow who was at your party, isn't it? Charles was talking with her. Why would he be having tea with her?"

"There are four perfectly good reasons, actually," Hari said in a resigned voice. "The first is the vast sum of money Mary

Sledge happily inherited from her late husband, and then there are sons one, two, and three."

With a shaking hand, she removed her gloves and searched through her velvet handbag, withdrawing a small green vial. Unstopping it, she dropped her head back and swallowed its contents. I couldn't read the label, but whatever was in the tiny glass fingerling had an instant effect on Hari. Her shoulders relaxed and her gaze lost its focus.

"Surely Charles isn't having a . . . romantic assignation with this woman. He wouldn't be sitting with her whole family." I shook Harriet's arm. "Hari, you must tell me what's going on."

But she ignored me, burying herself in her wraps and closing her eyes.

My mind ran over the possible explanations for what I just witnessed. Was Charles having an affair? Not when he was so concerned about his public image, surely. Was it money? He seemed to have ample income. Well on the path to success, he would no doubt be in cabinet soon and possibly prime minister one day. He was a man who was ruthless when it came to his ambition and wanted nothing short of perfection from everyone in his professional circle and, of course, Harriet. I thought she was living up to his demands, but she seemed to know something that I didn't. But why would he risk it all?

What she achieved through her marriage to Charles was an unattainable dream, according to the gossips. Many expected that Charles would choose money or status over beauty, but he hadn't. Harriet had no dowry, like me, and said it was love and mutual respect that drew them together. But now a new thought occurred to me. Had Charles expected to inherit our estate instead of Edward? Was he now after the widow's money? But then, what did the widow's sons have to do with that? I pulled anxiously at the rug over my lap as the carriage brought us closer and closer to home, but instead of a refuge, Charles's estate now felt like a hostile environment, full of traps and pitfalls that had to be avoided, if I could just figure out what and where they were.

Chapter Eight

The visit with the widow had been a campaign-donor call, Harriet told me the next day. She came to my bedroom rather late in the morning, still looking peaked. "With everything on my mind, I completely forgot that Charles had some business to take care of before he left for the lodge."

There was something about the casual way she spoke that left me doubting I had heard the whole truth, but I sensed she needed me to accept her answer and let it be for the time being. When she was feeling better, I would sit her down and make her tell me what was going on and see what I could do to help.

Harriet turned her attentions back to my problem. "Jane has already been let go," she said, then placed a piece of paper in front of me.

"What's this?"

"A very carefully crafted note to George for you to sign. I want it delivered today."

"Delivered by whom?"

"By you."

"No, Hari! I never want to see that man again, ever."

"To make this work he needs to see that you are not a threat, that you are genuinely making a peace offering."

She was right as usual, but I could barely stomach the idea. I went over to my writing desk, and as I rummaged through it looking for pen and ink, I spotted the brochure Wiggles had given me. The date of the meeting was today, I realized. If I decided to go, I could put off the dreaded visit to George until after.

I paused, my pen hovering over the paper I was expected to sign, feeling somewhat of a traitor to myself. I once fancied that I had some of my father's independent spirit in me, but I doubted that now. I imagined the sort of women who would be attracted to the brideship resettlement scheme. They would be bold and adventurous, not afraid to stand up to the "Georges" of the world. What kind of life would await them? I sighed and reluctantly signed the bottom of the fine, elegant paper, applying my red wax seal before tucking it into my bag.

I told myself that I couldn't seriously contemplate resettling in the colonies because Hari and Charles would never hear of it, but there was more to it than that. Hari was the only family I had left, and I couldn't bear to leave her. The more I ruminated about it, the more I could see that she was going to need my support in the coming months. I had always depended on her, but perhaps the time had come for her to lean on me. I would be the one to take on the role of the big sister for once. But after Wiggles's selfless gift of her most prized possession, I felt obligated to attend the Columbia Emigration Society meeting as she had asked. *I will at least go through the motions so that when I return her necklace I can honestly say that I gave her idea some thought.*

It was unusual for me to set out for London two days in a row. I seldom came to the city—its charms were lost on me—and when I did, I was rarely alone. But today my shoes made a lonely echo on London's cobblestone streets as I stepped out of the carriage across the street from Charles's club. A watery sun broke through the clouds, gracing the grand white marble building before me with elegant light. I had to squint and lower my eyes as I advanced towards a group of men making their way up the steps to the front door. Despite my firm resolution that this venture wasn't for me, a heady exhilaration filled me at the thought of thumbing my nose at society's rules about ladies requiring escorts.

I felt a hand firmly grip my arm and pull me sharply to one side. A man hissed in my ear, "What in blazes are you doing here?"

I wrenched my arm away and looked up at my accoster. It was George. Bile rose in my throat at the smell of him, the touch of his hand. "Mr. Chalmers! Why are you here?"

"Are you planning to make trouble for me at my club, of all places? I will make you very sorry if you even try."

"I'm attending a meeting. Women are being admitted to the club just for today." I remembered the letter. I opened the drawstring on my purse and pulled the sealed paper out. "This is for you. We have to come to some sort of agreement about what happened . . . settle things once and for all."

"What is this? Some sort of legal summons? I won't accept

it, I tell you." We were attracting some curious glances from the group of men lingering by the door. "Get away from me." He began to pull back from me, but I tried to push the letter into his coat pocket. I just wanted to be done with this man, for Harriet's and my sakes.

"Just what do you think yer doing, little missy?" a new voice said.

I dropped the letter as I spun around to see a bearded policeman looking me over.

"Unaccompanied ladies ain't welcome here," he said. "Ply your trade in the back alleys like the rest of 'em."

He picked up the letter and handed it to George. "This looks like it belongs to the gentleman. Here you go, sir. Sorry you were bothered by the likes of her."

George took the letter and almost stumbled in his haste to get away. The policeman gripped my arm and leaned in on me. The sharp tang of chewing tobacco made me recoil.

"I'm here for the meeting. I have every right to be here."

"Ah, it's yer rights yer after, is it?" He put his sweaty, black-whiskered face too close to mine. "You don't look the part of a working woman, you're too well dressed. You're not one o' them women's rights types, are ya, trying to force your way into places where you've no business? You get yerself home, lass, before I'm forced to arrest you for trespass."

After everything I had been through in recent days, this felt like the last straw. I searched for my pamphlet and waved it in his face. "I have legitimate business. You can't stop me."

I backed away but lost my balance, falling backwards off the low curb and landing hard on the cobblestone street. Two well-dressed young women in large bonnets, clearly out for an afternoon stroll, giggled behind lace handkerchiefs while their male partners strained for a better view. A burning flush crept from my chest to my cheeks. The last thing I needed was to be at the center of more gossip. I struggled to untangle my skirts when a man stepped forward from the gathering onlookers and offered me his hand. "Charles Dickens, at your service."

One of the young women gave a small gasp, and a hushed silence descended on the crowd. In the moment, I forgot myself, so entranced was I at the prospect of England's favourite author standing before me. I wanted to tell him how much I adored him and that I had read *Little Dorrit* ten times at least, but I simply stared. I was glad that Hari wasn't with me. She often adopted her husband's opinions on social issues, and I had heard him refer to Dickens as "a bloody socialist who pandered to the uneducated masses." I cared little for Charles's politics.

"Are you all right?" Dickens asked as he pulled me to my feet. He was dressed in a long black frock coat with a flowing neckerchief tied loosely under a high-point collar. He was handsome in his own way, a soulful artist with long hair and dark, searching eyes.

"Yes, thank you." I let out the breath I'd been holding. Hopefully any gossip would be about him, not me.

He addressed the policeman. "Unescorted young women are welcome, even encouraged, to attend today's meeting. It's their future we'll be discussing." He raised his voice and turned to face the crowd. "Ladies and gentlemen, step inside with me and be witness to an historic event: the launch of the brideships destined for the far-off colony of British Columbia."

There was a smattering of applause and a rush for seats. I was swept up in the crowd, propelled forward through venetian-glass doors into the grand ballroom. Ladies were only admitted into the spectators' galleries on each end of the vast marble-pillared room, and I had to squeeze my way into a seat at the very back, but I was relieved. From this obscure corner, I wouldn't attract attention, and I could still see the head table and hear much of what was said. My fluttering stomach soon settled, and I cooled my flush by fanning myself with the speakers list that had been placed on the chair.

"That's wha' I heard, Gertie," one of the ladies in front of me was saying to the woman next to her. They both looked to be about my age, but their clothes, rough calico cotton dresses with matching bonnets, told me they were working class. "There's hundreds o' thousands more women than men in this country 'cause o' the wars and such. So I ask you, how's a lass to find a husband when she's not a fancy-looker and has no money?"

I found myself nodding in sympathetic agreement. *Not to mention when she's the centre of a scandal*, I thought.

A hush fell, and I recognized the Lord Mayor of London, William Cubitt, as he rose to speak. "Gentlemen, and, ah, ladies, we are here to discuss a bold proposal to send shipments of marriageable women to the colony of British Columbia. This plan has the strong endorsement of Mr. Charles Dickens and, I say, what could be better than to support our fellow countrymen who are facing great hardship as they carve a foothold for the empire in every corner of the world?"

Several of the soberly dressed gentlemen in front murmured, "Hear! Hear!"

The mayor took his seat, and a dandy in a yellow-striped knee-length coat with a ridiculously large handlebar moustache stepped to the front of the room. I resisted the urge to giggle at his dress. He proceeded to read a letter from a Reverend Lundin Brown, whose congregation included the gold prospectors in a town called Yale. Reverend Brown was "appalled by the number of illicit relationships conducted with both Native and white women" and said that frontier prostitution would "ultimately ruin religion and morals in this fine country."

Two very different pictures were emerging here, one of a land of lonely upstanding men in a fruitless search for good Christian wives, and the other? Not so charitable. I wondered at the truth of it. How would these women get on in such a society? Would they be the recipient of many worthy offers, free to take their time and choose carefully, or would they be forced to fend off endless unwanted advances? I suspected the answer would be somewhere in the middle. But the New World offered hope for a better future, and there was a stir of excitement in the crowd as the bishop of Honolulu spoke with passion on the need for British women to emigrate to all regions of the far-flung empire.

I tried to imagine what life would be like in a colony on the other side of the world. It would be a physically rigorous existence, I expected, where ladies dressed for a day of riding or hiking, not social calls. I briefly saw myself striding out in a long split skirt with high boots, my corsets a thing of the past. But in truth, the more I listened to the speakers, the more assured I was that my place was in England with Harriet. I was not made for this sort of thing. While the other ladies were clapping with enthusiasm, I shrank back. The concerns being discussed were for a world completely foreign to me. Why should I care about North America and the problems there? I had enough to worry about right here.

There was a buzz from the crowd as Charles Dickens stood to speak, and he held up his hand to quiet the crowd.

"Let us send those confined to working in cotton mills and workhouses. Surely some of these women would have better lives in the colonies with a chance to marry and raise good Christian families."

"But what should we do with our upper-class old maids?" someone shouted from a far corner of the room.

A roar of laughter went up, and I sank deeper into my seat.

Another voice responded, "Send them to the lonely gold miners too!"

The cheers grew even louder, and a few men tossed their hats in the air.

The chairman stood up and demanded order. Banging a gavel, he introduced the next speaker, Miss Angela Burdett-Coutts. I knew that name. Miss Burdett-Coutts was the talk of all the society pages in the broadsheets. At age twenty-four, she had inherited the vast fortune of her grandfather's bank. It was said she was blessed with high energy and a serious mind and that she had dedicated herself to a life of philanthropy. If I had such a fortune, I thought, I would see to it that Harriet and I were always comfortable and safe. Perhaps I could even convince Edward to sell our estate back to me.

I strained for a better view as Miss Burdett-Coutts rose from her seat at the head table. She was an elegant woman, wearing a green silk day gown with pagoda sleeves and the very latest fashion of a slim-fitted skirt.

"Gentlemen," she began. "I propose we send two ships of impoverished single women, of varied classes and backgrounds, to the colony of British Columbia with the express intent of providing our lonely sons with good Christian wives. I will fund this project with a gift of fifteen thousand pounds."

Three cheers went up from the assembly, and the two women in front of me jumped to their feet and hugged each other. I slouched in my seat. Would life be better for these women in the colonics? Charles Dickens, a man I greatly admired, seemed sure of it. But I had seen firsthand what could happen when a man feels he can do as he wishes, sure that the law won't touch him. I couldn't imagine what liberties he would take in a lawless land. No, everything I heard here today confirmed that this wasn't the path for me. I would tell Wiggles as much once Harriet found me a suitable staid Englishman to marry. I just hoped that I hadn't made matters worse with George and that the letter would smooth everything over.

Chapter Nine

A week after the party, the house was a hive of activity as preparations were underway for a dinner with Lord Ainsley. Charles was due back from his hunting lodge that day, and as much as Harriet denied it, I knew she was just as anxious as I was to see what kind of mood he would be in. George had not yet responded to our letter, but we sensed no gossip at church on Sunday. I hoped it was a good omen, that he had been placated by what he had read.

The one solace was the weather. Spring had reasserted itself once again. May was out in all its glory, and I sat on a rug in the garden in the warm afternoon sun with *Little Dorrit*. I'd had an inclination to reread it after meeting Charles Dickens. My experiences of late had opened my eyes to many things, and I found new meanings in the narrative. I was startled when something warm brushed my arm. I dropped my book just as a small ball of fur darted across my lap and began nipping playfully at my fingers.

"A puppy!" I cried happily, scratching its ears. "And just who might you be?"

"Belle. A little gift I brought back for Hari." I looked up to see Charles coming towards me. He must have just returned. "She's a Pekinese. I want you to train her. I won't have any puddles on the carpets."

Charles was always keeping up appearances, and these adorable dogs were all the rage after the Chinese Dowager Empress Cixi gave one to Queen Victoria to cement relations between our two countries.

"I'd love to train her," I said. "I'm good with animals. I always trained the dogs on our estate when I was a girl."

I smiled, expecting Charles to leave having entrusted the pup to my care, but he remained where he was. "Did you have a nice trip?" I asked uneasily.

"Never mind my trip. I had expected that you and George would have announced your engagement by the time I returned. Didn't the two of you wander off at the party? I should have thought a little private tête-à-tête would have moved things along. Lord knows I've done everything in my power."

So George hadn't spoken to him. That was good. But how could I get Charles to stop pushing for the marriage? I decided to be partially honest with him. "I don't think he's really all that keen on me."

Charles took a step towards me. "I thought Harriet explained this to you. I need to be in George's good graces if I'm to get into cabinet. He rewards those who treat him with deference and respect. He lets everyone else wallow in political oblivion. It would be best if he and I were related through marriage. Is that too hard for you understand?"

"I understand," I choked, determined not to let my inner

fury show. Was Charles so desperate for political favours that he would use me as a pawn in his grand plan? Belle sensed the tension between us and did what puppies do. She nervously urinated on Charles's shoe. He gave me a look that suggested I was to blame for the dog's indiscretion and stalked off.

I let out the breath I had been holding. I was quite sure Charles could not convince George to marry me, and if he tried, what would George say? I cringed at the thought of the story that he had threatened to tell. I knew whose version Charles would believe, but what I didn't know was what would happen to me. I held the puppy close and prayed that Harriet wouldn't be punished for my trouble.

When I returned to the house with Belle, I found Harriet in the small family parlour. One look at her agitated pacing and I could tell she was in a mood. Perhaps it was better I not mention my conversation with Charles just yet.

"Why Charles thought a dog would please me, I have no notion." She dabbed her cheeks with one of her elegant white lace handkerchiefs.

"Are you feeling all right?" I asked, reaching up to touch her forehead.

She pulled away from me. "I'm fine."

I looked closely at her face. *Not fine*, I thought. *Sallow skin, dark circles under her eyes.*

"Are you sure? Do you need to go back to the doctor?"

"I'm seeing him tomorrow, but never mind about that now, Charlotte."

"Has Charles said something?"

"He's done something. He has invited that ridiculous

widow, Mary Sledge, and her three children to supper. He just told me."

"First the tea with her and now this. Hari, something's going on. You have to tell me. I can help. Please."

"I don't know for sure, but I can guess," she said, her voice weak. "I'll bet it's no coincidence that Charles's uncle is the guest of honour tonight."

"Charles wants Lord Ainsley to meet Mary?"

"It's not about Mary; at least I don't think so. It has to do with her children." She said no more, as a housemaid came in to light the candles and fire. After a few moments, she spoke in her usual calm, authoritative voice. "Charles has asked that you be seated here in the family parlour to supervise Mrs. Sledge's children. Since we have no governess, someone needs to keep an eye on them and help them with their meals."

I didn't understand why Charles had taken such an interest in these children, but this was not the time to ask in front of the maid. "Anything I can do to help."

"Thank you. Now, I must change my gown." In a flurry of lace and perfume, she was off. The maid followed her out, leaving me alone with Belle.

"What a mess. What are we going to do?" I asked the little pup. She didn't answer, just looked at me with her big brown eyes and licked my cheek.

After I freshened up my gown, I went to the small dining room and studied the name cards on the table so I could greet my charges by their Christian names. A friendly gesture, I thought, and one that would help make the evening run smoothly. Positioned at the head of the little table was Master James. Master

Donald's chair was on James's right, and Master Neal, clearly the youngest with an extra pillow on his seat, was on the left. The fourth spot—mine, I realized—was a dark corner beside the glass-panelled French door that led off the main dining room.

The boys soon came tumbling in, along with their mother.

"You must be Mrs. Sledge," I said. We had not been formally introduced, so I was not sure of the proper etiquette. I cautiously offered my hand, and we briefly shook.

I took the opportunity to study her closely. She was small and dark haired with a flawless, milky complexion and an open expression on her face. Young to be a mother of three.

"And you must be Miss Harding," she said with a slightly apologetic tone. "Charles, I mean Mr. Baldwin, told me you were good enough to offer to watch my children during dinner. I was happy to leave them at home with their nanny, but Cha—Mr. Baldwin insisted I bring them. He's so terribly fond of them."

Her earnest manner caught me off guard. Still, I wondered at the impropriety of her having had tea alone with Charles. "You've brought them here before, then?"

"Well, no, Mr. Baldwin has met them on other occasions." She looked down at her children and kissed each of them on the forehead, admonishing them to be good little boys and eat their dinners. She turned back to me. "I'm sure your sister will become fond of my boys in time too."

I didn't have time to dwell on what she meant, as other guests began to arrive and she was drawn into the dining room. I surveyed the brood of boys with some misgivings. Master James, with dark curls like his mother, immediately assumed an air of authority, directing the other children to their seats.

"How are we to address you, madam, and when will dinner be served and what is for dinner?" he asked, all in one breath.

"You may address me as Miss Charlotte, and in answer to your other questions, I don't know."

They appeared slightly put out that I couldn't provide the prized information regarding dinner. Little, fair-haired Neal decided to take me on.

"Why are we to call you Miss? Why aren't you a Mrs., like Mama? Only little girls are called Miss, aren't they? And you're not a little girl, that's for sure. How old are you anyway?"

"I'm a Miss because I'm not married, and it is not polite to ask a lady her age, Master Neal."

"My mama isn't married anymore because Papa died. He was much older than Mama. He was very old, and that's why he died. Are you going to die soon?"

"For heaven's sake, Neal. Don't be such a dolt," James said. "You can't ask people that."

"Why?"

"It's rude."

"Is not."

With that, Neal got up from his chair, walked over to James, and hit him in the shoulder. James punched him back, and Neal burst into tears. This was what it would be like all the time, I thought with a shiver, if I took care of Edward's five children. I said a silent prayer that I would never be forced into that position.

"Boys, boys, settle down," I said as I pulled them apart and reseated Neal on his chair. The last thing I needed was for Charles to hear the commotion and come to investigate.

Thankfully, Cook had had the presence of mind to feed the

children first, and moments later the servants arrived bearing a wonderful array of food specially prepared to appeal to small boys. There were little pork pies with images of bunnies and ducks carved into their crusts and battered cod with slices of deep-fried potatoes, a new culinary trend. During their meal, the silence was interrupted only by their occasional requests for help cutting or buttering bread.

Meanwhile, the noise level from the dining room had risen to a steady hum. Crystal glasses chimed as the servants cleared away the first course and set down the roast pheasant, but I could make out Charles's voice. It was slow and careful, verging on pedantic.

"I have a clear vision of the path this country and the empire should be on," he was saying. "We can't yield to the bloody isolationists. Colonization is the only way forward. We do the world a great favour. What could be better than British know-how? We are superior at most things, by far."

Who was he talking to? I peered through the gap behind the door. The backs of those at the head of the table were only a few feet from my hidden seat. I recognized the back of Charles's head, of course, with its bald spot carefully combed over. On his right, I saw the grizzled silver hair of his uncle, Lord Ainsley. I leaned forward to catch a glimpse of the lady on his left; I couldn't quite make her out at first. I thought it likely to be Lady Margaret but was startled to see the thick black hair and milky skin of Mrs. Sledge. Why did she have such an honoured seat? And where was Harriet?

I leaned back, a little precariously, on two legs of my chair, scanning the faces at the far end of the table. There she was.

Instead of chatting to the guest on her right, as etiquette would dictate, she was staring, unabashedly, at the head of the table. She looked even paler than she did before dinner.

"Miss Charlotte!"

I almost lost my balance and overcorrected, the front legs of my chair landing on the floor with a loud thud. There was a pause in the main room before the conversation resumed.

"Yes, Donald. What is it?"

"What are we having for the pudding course? And when is it coming?"

"I don't know, but we can find out." I made my way over to the writing desk in the corner where the capsule pipeline was installed. "Let me show you the very latest in technology that our host has installed for our comfort." I scribbled a note on a scrap of paper. "You see, all I have to do is write my question, put it in the round cylinder, and . . ." I opened the small brass door in the wall beside the desk and placed the canister through the opening. With a loud swoosh, the canister was snatched from my hand and sucked into the vacuum.

"Ohhhh," the boys said in unison.

"Cook will be sending her note back directly."

The three sets of small eyes grew rounder as we waited in hushed silence for a few moments until a rattling in the tube told me my return note had arrived. I opened the little brass door and the cylinder popped out into my hand.

Opening the note, I read, "'Thank you for your note, miss. The pudding will be chocolate, and there'll be apple cake with caramel sauce. Paul will bring it up directly.'" I added my own postscript: "Dessert is reserved for those little boys who have eaten at least half the food on their dinner plates."

The boys dove for their seats and attacked their plates.

It was not long after the dessert course that, with immense relief, I welcomed the presence of our butler, Sandwell. He ceremoniously entered our little den and, bowing, announced that the carriage had arrived to take the boys and their mother home, as it was long past the young masters' bedtime. He ushered them into the main dining room to say their good nights.

I watched through the door crack as Mary rose from her seat and herded her sons over to where Lord Ainsley sat. Charles stepped in and formally introduced them to his uncle. Each child, the perfect model of propriety, bowed slightly and shook the older man's hand. After a few minutes of observing from afar, Hari stood and walked the length of the room to join the group. With what seemed an afterthought, Charles introduced her to the boys. I saw her nod to each in turn, a forced smile on her face. Mary and her brood soon left, and I watched Hari wander back to her seat. I wished I was there to console her.

Settling back down, I noticed the youngest, Neal, had left part of his apple cake, and I didn't hesitate to pull it across the table towards me.

"Lovely young lads, a credit to their mother," I heard Lord Ainsley say. I put down my fork. Now that the children were gone, I could hear the conversation at the head of the table even more clearly.

"They're fine boys. I know them well, and I wanted you to get a chance to meet them," Charles replied.

"Three healthy sons. Some women are blessed. How I wished my Margaret would have been. How long have you been married now?"

"Three years."

There was a pause before Lord Ainsley spoke again. "You know I'm ready to make my will and pass the baton on to you. No other real choice since your cousin Jeffrey married the daughter of a merchant, of all the idiot things."

I heard Charles chortle.

"But surely your wife understands? She won't become Lady Harriet until she does her duty by you."

Charles's voice dropped to just above a whisper. I gingerly rose from my chair and stood next to the gap in the door. Scanning the room for Hari, I wondered if she had observed the two men with their heads bent in serious conversation. She was oblivious, I saw, her attention taken up by the butler who was asking for direction on some matter.

"Uncle, I've just had a thought," Charles said. "We could go about this another way. If Harriet doesn't give me a son, what if I were to adopt those boys as my own? I've seen this sort of thing done in other aristocratic families. Would you be satisfied? An heir and two spares."

The last comment was like a splash of cold water in my face. So this was why Charles was having tea at Mrs. Sledge's. Oh, my poor sister. I felt my heart ache for her. She had enough of her own problems without adding mine into the mix.

"I could see that the boys' mother would likely agree, but you might find yourself married to a scorned woman," Lord Ainsley said. "Harriet could make you very unhappy."

"Harriet would see the light. She's as ambitious as I am."

Lord Ainsley studied Charles for a moment. "If something should ever happen to you, dear boy, I would rest easy knowing the line of succession for my legacy had been established, but the title is another matter; the successor must be blood, unless we could successfully petition the Committee of Privileges."

"I know that, Uncle, but one step at a time. First the adoption and then the petition—and I do have connections on the committee, by the way." Charles gently touched his glass to his uncle's. "To our heirs."

"To our heirs," Lord Ainsley replied.

My heart was thumping in my chest as I ran up the back stairs to my room. I had no idea what committee they were speaking of, but Charles had clearly been working on a plan to make these boys his heirs for some time. How much did Hari know? I thought over her comments that day in the carriage. She must suspect. No wonder she looked unwell. If Hari was not the mother of Charles's heirs, she would become a grass widow with a tainted title. No doubt Charles would want to launch these boys into society and take them everywhere he could, and the children would want their mother by their side. They would form a family with Hari and me on the outside. I couldn't let that happen.

Chapter Ten

"N o!" I awoke to the sound of my own voice and sat upright in my bed. I blinked hard several times, and the image of George's face evaporated in the darkness of my bedroom. It was just another dream. Belle stirred next to me, then settled back down.

I lit a candle to check the timepiece that hung from a clasp on my chest. Midnight. I must have fallen asleep waiting for Harriet to return to her room—I was still fully clothed. The memory of Charles's words to Lord Ainsley came rushing back along with a new, more intense anxiety about the future, both mine and Hari's.

I needed to have a long heart-to-heart with my sister as soon as possible. Surely she would become pregnant before long, especially with the help of her new doctor, but in the meantime, we had to find a way to buy more time. If I could make a decent match with someone else with political influence, perhaps that would please Charles. In a benevolent mood, he would be more patient, and I suspected that a happy, relaxed couple would be more likely to conceive a child. Then he would have everything he wanted—a title and a place in cabinet. And Harriet's position would remain unchallenged.

My mind swimming, I stood up and wandered to the window. A bold full moon hung low on the horizon, defying the night's darkness by casting light where none would normally be. The estate's beautifully manicured lawns, which ran from the front gate to the house, stretched out in gentle, light-frosted waves before me. This really was the most splendid home in the county. Was Charles planning for the boys to live here? Hari had so much to lose if Charles decided he had no more need of her and sent her to live in one of the cottages.

There was a movement in the distance. The moonlight reflected off a polished surface that appeared to bob and weave with slow but steady progress. It must be a carriage. But at this hour?

As the vehicle rounded the semicircle driveway it came to a stop, not at the main door to the house but off to the right, and a rather stout figure lowered himself stiffly to the ground. I strained to make out who this nocturnal caller was but shadows obscured his face. He walked towards the seldom-used side entry, just as a light came on in Charles's study.

"No rest for the wicked," I murmured under my breath.

What business did Charles have at this hour? Was it something to do with Harriet? Or was Charles planning something else? I padded downstairs to see what I could find out.

I stopped outside the closed double doors leading to Charles's study, careful not to let my feet cast a shadow, and listened intently, but the solid oak doors had been built with someone like me in mind. I couldn't hear a thing. After a few minutes I gave up. In frustration, I shoved my hands in my pockets and found the note that Cook had sent me earlier. I stared at it for a moment. The capsule pipeline. It was worth a try.

As quietly as I could, I made my way down the back stairs to the kitchen. The full moon bathed the room in sufficient semi-light that I didn't need candles. I saw the bright copper cylinder lying on Cook's desk, and I glanced up at the small brass door in the wall above. The opening led to a network of vacuum hoses that connected the kitchen to the dining rooms, the morning room, the main drawing room, and Charles's study. If the vacuum door was open in the study, I might be able to hear some of his conversation. As quietly as I could, I opened the kitchen vacuum door.

Charles's voice filled the kitchen instantly. He had to be sitting at his desk, right next to the opening.

"She did what? I knew nothing of this."

My heart skipped a beat. Was the stranger a messenger from George? I couldn't tell. His voice was muffled, as he was some distance from the open vacuum-tube door.

"After all I've done for that family! I've given them everything." I could almost feel the heat of Charles's words, see his red face deepening into an unhealthy shade of purple.

The other speaker must have moved as his voice came through clear as day. It was George. I felt dizzy all of a sudden and gripped the edge of the desk. He must be telling Charles everything.

"This will be your downfall, Charles. You must take care of it once and for all if you hope to have a political career with a seat in cabinet."

"Of course. You're right." Charles's voice was subdued, pleading almost. "She has a cousin outside London, I could send—"

"She's only part of the problem." George continued to speak at length, but he'd moved off, and I couldn't make out what he was saying.

"I understand what must be done," Charles finally said. "It's the only way. Thank you for coming directly to me with this. I'll be forever in your debt."

I stood there in the kitchen for a long while after I heard the men leave the study. My fate had been decided. I only hoped that I could persuade Charles that Harriet was innocent in all this. As for me, I would ask to go live with Edward. It was the only way to protect Harriet from my scandal.

After a fitful night, I rose and knocked on Harriet's door, but she was gone. To the doctor's, I remembered. Perhaps it was better that she wasn't here to see Charles's anger. With a sense of foreboding, I went downstairs for breakfast. Charles was planted at the head of the dining table, the *Times* spread out in front of him.

"Good morning," I murmured.

I sensed him watching me as I made my way along the sideboard dabbing a spoonful from each platter. My mouth felt like I had just bitten into a lemon, and my stomach tightened at the sight of the food. I kept my eyes lowered as I sat down. The feathery white bread that I slathered with chunks of melting butter tasted like cardboard. Charles eyed my plate and moved the butter crock to the far side of the table.

"I've received some news about you that has deeply troubled me."

I knew it was hopeless, but I had to at least try and convince him of the truth. "Charles, let me explain," I said.

"What were you thinking?" His voice rose an octave as he set his teacup down with force. "Inviting George's physical affections so you could threaten him and claim he took advantage of your innocence. Force the marriage through blackmail. How gullible do you think George is? How stupid are you?"

It was exactly the lie George said he would tell, and yet I was still surprised. "That's not what happened. I wasn't trying to blackmail him."

"Don't try to deny it. I saw the letter, and he told me how you ambushed him at the club, demanding an agreement to settle the whole affair once and for all."

"No, please, hear me out."

He ignored my protests. "And I question Harriet's hand in this whole affair as well. How could she go behind my back like that?"

"Harriet has nothing to do with it. She's been unwell and spending time at her doctor's," I said quickly. "And George hasn't told you the truth."

"Do you really think I should believe you, my penniless sister-in-law with no connections, over George, the esteemed government whip and pillar of the community? Don't be ridiculous. There is no longer any room for you at my table."

Anger bubbled up inside me at the echo of George's heartless words about my family and me. We had our faults, to be sure, but we were honest, and we treated others with respect and caring, no matter their position. It seemed to me that those seeking the highest levels of society lost their humanity on the way to the top. "I can go to my cousin Edward's. He's offered me a position as a governess."

"I would feel honour-bound to tell him of your behaviour and there's no way to keep a lid on the rumours, anyway. Edward would never take you now. George is outraged by your attempts at blackmail and is demanding action." His eyes were as cold and grey as the pewter tableware in front of him. "No, I have other plans for you. You have to go. There is simply no other way to deal with your situation, no other course open to us."

I felt the pulse in my temples begin to throb. "Go where?"

He presented me with a piece of paper torn from the *Times*. "George brought this to my attention last night."

STEAM to the GOLD FIELDS of BRITISH COLUMBIA—Notice to passengers and shippers— For VICTORIA, Vancouver's Island, (calling if required at San Francisco), the iron screw steamship TYNEMOUTH, A 1, 9 years at Lloyd's, 1,650 tons register, and 600-horse power indicated, ALFRED HELLYER Commander: will load at the Jetty, London Docks, leaving punctually on the 24th of May.

"You have a short time to prepare for the journey. I have purchased passage for you on a steamship leaving for Victoria, in the colony of British Columbia. No doubt you will end up a governess or even a servant, but there is also a possibility of marriage."

He launched into a short lecture on how I needed to be

industrious and work hard to make a better future for myself, but I stopped listening. There it was. I sat rooted in my chair, unable to move, as if someone had placed a heavy weight upon my lap. I was to be sent to a lawless land full of unruly men. Out of the frying pan, into the fire. I was flooded with cascading emotions—intense shock at the suddenness of it all, a nebulous fear of the unknown, and, worst of all, a profound feeling of homesickness at the thought of leaving my dearest Hari forever.

PART TWO

The Voyage

Chapter Eleven

I caught my first glimpse of the *Tynemouth* anchored off-shore. Its freshly painted exterior appeared as a constant dark mass on a watery horizon where ocean and sky were indistinct. I had been dreading this day for so long that I felt numb now that I was here, leaving my old life behind. Wiggles was the only person excited by the adventure before me, and I wondered if it was fate that made her give me that pamphlet that day. I hadn't had the heart to explain the circumstances of my departure to her, but promised her I would write. I patted my carpetbag, feeling the jewellery box buried deep inside where the emerald necklace was stowed. I needed it now, as never before.

I tried to imagine what life on the northwest coast of North America would be like. I reasoned it must resemble the paintings I had seen of Lower Canada in a gallery in London of voyageurs, their snowshoes strapped to their backs, driving teams of sled dogs over rolling, snow-covered hills. I had read library books about explorers freezing to death in frigid winters and drowning as they tried to navigate uncharted rivers, and heard tales about swarms of blackflies in summer that can turn an exposed face to a swollen pulp. The New World didn't sound like a place for me. It was a land of gold-crazed adventurers from every corner of the earth, I remembered with a shudder.

At least I would have my sister by my side for a little longer. I turned to study Harriet. She looked miserable, wet and shivering.

"Almost there," I said. "We'll be out of this drizzle soon and settled in our cabin."

She gave me a stoic smile, but her face was deathly pale. "Is that supposed to comfort me?"

It was my fault she was here, and I wore the guilt like a hair shirt.

My earlier fear of being parted from her hadn't lasted long. When she'd returned from the doctor, Charles had summoned her to his study. He had taken her actions as a betrayal, she'd told me later in her room. Because she had kept him in the dark, he had been forced to bend to George's demands for justice and was now forever in his debt. Charles wanted her out of his sight. Publicly, he explained that Harriet was suffering from exhaustion and would be taking an extended holiday to escort her sister to her new life in the colonies. Privately, she was a banished wife, sent away to do penance for her sins by her once-adoring husband. He would send word when the whole sorry mess was long forgotten by polite society and she could return.

I had been shocked by his reaction and had said as much to

Harriet. "What about trying for a baby? You certainly can't do that halfway around the world."

"I think he may have given up on having children with me," she'd told me softly.

I didn't have the nerve to tell her what I had overheard Charles say to Lord Ainsley, but the conversation played at my heart. Despite Charles's plan, it was I who was responsible for her tragic fall from grace, and I had to try to make it up to her. If only I could find an acceptable husband willing to support us both, if need be. When the time was right—when we knew our next step—I would tell her about Charles.

Huddled next to Hari in the chill mist, I felt love and affection for her, and much concern. I put one arm around her. In spite of the calendar, the weather was more like winter than spring. Cold, stinging spray, kicked up by the boat's plunging bow, threatened to soak our travel clothes as the tender shoved its way through the dense Atlantic waters towards the *Tynemouth*, our home for the next three and a half months—106 days, to be exact. The closer we got, the better I could see the vessel. With all its patches and repairs, even I could tell that she was past her prime.

It was still raining when we boarded the main deck, where a lively crowd of people from every station and class were preparing to embark. Sailors hoisted large trunks with a makeshift crane, and peacoated officers shouted instructions from the deck above. When a small barrel broke loose and burst open, molasses oozed across the deck and the tangy smell of sweetness mixed with the smoky aroma from the aft coal burners.

Black soot swirled in the air before depositing a thick film over the lower-deck portholes. It was dirty and chaotic. I looked around for the purser, who would direct the first- and second-class passengers to their cabins.

Some gentlemen adventurers appeared to be setting out for the gold rush in the colony; they were outfitted with rucksacks and various outdoor equipment. Second and third sons with no inheritance, most likely, with their passage funded by families anxious for them to find their way in life. As we made our way past these men, they turned with admiring glances. I knew the stares were directed at my sister, still beautiful in spite of her current state of poor health, still dressed with elaborate care in the latest fashion.

"Do you know where we can find the purser?" I asked the group.

"Do not engage with them," Harriet murmured.

One of the men pointed to a uniformed man with a notepad conferring with a young couple farther down the deck.

I nodded a thank-you and we moved towards the purser just as a flurry of activity caught everyone's attention. A group of young women were making their way along the main deck towards the stairs that led to the lower decks. Like a gaggle of geese, they were led by a stout woman in front and an even stouter man took up the rear. There must have been almost sixty of them, I thought. As they shuffled dutifully along, some dabbed handkerchiefs to their tearful faces while others giggled with excitement.

They must be the unmarried women who were spoken of at the Columbia Emigration Society meeting, I realized. Orphans, unemployed workers from the cotton mills in Lancashire and London factories, the dispossessed, and a few gentlewomen unable to cover the cost of their passage. Their keepers shooed the women towards the stairs. One woman stumbled in the confusion, and I moved to help her, but Harriet held me back.

"It's not your place, Charlotte."

The woman managed to get up on her own, moving slowly and carefully, as if protecting herself from a previous injury. She was striking. With her golden-brown skin and thick, silky black hair, she stood out from the other emigrant women. I couldn't help but wonder what her story was, but Harriet was pulling me away, towards the purser.

In short order, he directed us to our cabin, one of twelve that opened directly off the top deck. From what I could see, one row was occupied by men, the other, by women and couples.

I followed Harriet into our quarters. In his characteristic concern for saving money, Charles had purchased one first-class room for Hari, with an adjoining maid's room for me, which proved to be a tiny, windowless chamber with just enough space for a bunk. I noticed it had a hinged board that could be pulled into place to prevent one from falling out of bed. No doubt a precaution for children. I couldn't imagine adults needing such a contraption.

But there were a few simple delights in the main room. Two comfortable-looking chairs, a white porcelain washbasin with its blue stencil depicting the *Tynemouth* and a matching water pitcher, a light blue velveteen coverlet on the bed, hooks along one wall for hanging clothes, and a sculpted mirror bolted to the opposite wall. I allowed myself a small smile.

"It doesn't take much to please you, does it?" Hari said as she felt the bed before sitting gingerly on the edge. "How soon you forget the luxuries we once had. I had hoped for something much grander. Thank God it's only temporary. Governor and Mrs. Douglas's residence will be a welcome respite after this."

The governor, I knew, was a high-ranking man in the Hudson's Bay fur trading company. Charles had sent letters of introduction for us until we could find suitable lodgings elsewhere, but what was next? Hari would starve before she would consider a paid position, and I had no employable skills. Harriet saw the concerned look on my face.

"Don't worry. Charles will call us home. He needs me far more than he realizes. I did everything for him, even wrote some of his speeches. And if you marry respectably, I'm convinced all will be forgiven and forgotten."

Her optimism weighed me down. I had to tell her now. I sat next to her and took one of her hands in mine. "There's something I need to tell you. I overheard a conversation Charles had with Lord Ainsley." I had kept the awful story bottled up inside me for so long it poured out of me now. I told her everything, how Charles had suggested the adoption of Mary's boys and his uncle's tacit agreement, the one concern being the need to get permission to pass the title to an adopted child. I didn't add that Charles was fairly confident about his petition to the Committee of Privileges. As I spoke, Hari's eyes widened, then a heavy sadness fell around the corners, but she kept up a defiant chin.

"Well, there you are, my perfect opportunity," she said once I was done.

"I'm sorry?"

"If permission is not granted, then Charles will have no choice other than to try to have a child with me and he'll have to forget about Mary Sledge and her boys." She reached into her handbag and withdrew a green vial and pulled the stopper. "This is great news," she said weakly.

"Wait a minute." I pulled the vial from her hand. In the weeks leading up to our voyage, she'd been taking the medication with more and more regularity, but she only seemed to be getting sicker.

"What exactly is this, Harriet?"

"Something Dr. Randolph gave me to settle my nerves. Give it back."

She reached for it, and I noticed her dry, yellowing nails. She had a hungry, feral look in her eye, and I let her take it. I watched with a sinking heart as she took a long swallow.

"Are you sure it's wise to take so much?" I asked.

But the medicine was already taking effect. Her dark-shadowed eyes glassed over and she lay down on the bed. I picked up the tiny glass container and sniffed. There was an acidic smell, like vinegar. I didn't recognize what it was, nor could I make a guess based on its amber colour. Something in the pit of my stomach told me that it wasn't good for my sister.

A sharp rap at the cabin door made me leap to my feet. I quickly smoothed my skirts and answered. Two sailors stood on the other side.

"Baldwin, Harding cabin?" one asked.

"Yes."

"We have your luggage."

"Please come in." I stepped away from the door and stood in front of Harriet in an attempt to block their view of her. "My sister is just resting."

The sailors paid her no mind, anxious to deposit our trunks and be off to their regular work. After doing so, they handed me a card, then, with a touch of their caps, escaped the cabin.

I shoved the card in my pocket and dragged my small trunk into my room, but I didn't feel like unpacking. My mind was racing. I had the sinking feeling that Hari was using the medicine to cope with her situation. Since she'd been taking it, she only looked paler, and it was almost as if she'd come to rely on it. What I should do, I had no notion. I felt overwhelmed with all that was going on. Beneath me, I felt the ship begin to move. I needed air. With one last look at Hari, I left the cabin and stepped out onto the main deck.

The rain had stopped, and a warming sun fought the clouds for dominance. Others were emerging from the cabins to enjoy the change in weather and see the ship off. As I approached the railing, I caught my breath. The full mast of sails was catching the wind at just the right angle, their expanse of white cloth snapping taut in the centre while their edges fluttered like delicate white-gloved fingers over piano keys. The deck under my feet surged forward, and I had to grip a handrail to steady myself.

In the distance, the English coast began to recede. A feeling of profound sadness swept over me as I watched the only home I had ever known fade from sight. My father would have loved this, I thought. I could hear him now: *A grand adventure, my dear girl, a grand adventure.*

I felt for the card inside my pocket.

Captain Hellyer wishes to welcome you aboard. The Tynemouth *is of the barque class of seagoing ship boasting three masts and a steam engine with screw propeller. At 250 feet long she can carry up to three hundred passengers. First- and second-class passengers are welcome on all three decks, while steerage passengers are asked to restrict their movements to the third deck. Have an enjoyable voyage.*

Flipping the card over, I found the imprint of a map on the other side. With my index finger, I traced the course our ship would take. The route crossed the English Channel before hugging the coasts of France, Spain, and Portugal, and then taking a sharp right turn to Bermuda and on down the coasts of Brazil and Argentina to our first stop, the Falkland Islands. Then it went around Cape Horn, up the west coasts of Chile, Peru, and Mexico, all the way to the new American state of California and the city of San Francisco before it continued north to the colony of British Columbia and the town of Victoria on Vancouver Island. I resolved to include the card in my first letter to Wiggles.

What awaited us on our journey? I wondered. I had heard of diseases, like smallpox, that carried away half the passengers on a ship before it reached its destination. And then there was the dreaded Cape Horn, the gale-ridden point of southern-most land that was home to countless shipwrecks. If we survive all that, what then? North America was a lawless land teeming with wild men. How would Hari and I make our way?

I didn't know. All I knew was that Harriet needed my help. That was my goal. First, I would find a way to nurse her back to health, and then I'd figure out how to make things right for her. *The little sister taking care of the big one, for a change.* As the coastline grew smaller and smaller, I realized that the distance between me and Charles, and George too, for that matter, was growing greater, and the thought eased the fear and worry that had weighed on me for weeks. Whatever came next, it wouldn't involve them. I knocked three times on the wooden railing for good luck.

Chapter Twelve

When I returned to the cabin, Hari was sitting up in one of the reading chairs and examining what looked like an invitation. She still looked unwell—perspiration dampened her brow—but she had an air of frenzied energy about her. Four or five of her best dresses were laid out haphazardly on the bed. "What's that?" I asked.

"An invitation to the captain's private dining room—only fitting, considering my place in society. Nice to know that proper decorum is being observed on board." She handed me the invitation, a feverish excitement in her eyes. "It's a very interesting guest list."

I scanned the list, curious as to what had improved her spirits. "How so?"

"Sir Richard and Lady Persephone Fitzwilliam. She's the prime minister's cousin, and he's a diplomat. They were at my party. Remember?"

I acknowledged a dim recollection.

"Charles would do anything to be close to them," she said.

"If I can befriend them and build a relationship while on board, he'll hear of it. This can only help our cause."

I saw the logic, but there was one problem. "If she was at the party, perhaps she's heard the rumours about me."

Harriet got up and, taking one of the gowns off the bed, held it next to her, admiring it in the mirror. "We'll learn that soon enough. Either way, you must behave impeccably whenever you are in her company, as I will. Follow my lead."

I held up my hand as if making a vow. "Only my best behaviour." And I meant it.

"She'll refer to the prime minister as Pam, so don't ask who Pam is."

"Pam?"

"Short for Lord Palmerston. Those in the know call him Pam." Without a maid, Hari was forced to dress herself. She started the laborious process, stepping into the first of several layers of petticoats. "No doubt they will be wined and dined royally by Victoria's elite. I wonder where they're staying in Victoria. It would be perfect if they were also staying with Governor Douglas and his wife. Perhaps they'd be willing to introduce you to some eligible gentlemen. Ideally, if we could arrange a match for you quickly, we could go straight from the Douglases' to your matrimonial home."

"That quickly?" I felt a small flutter in my chest but ignored it. I remembered my promise. "Of course, I can see how that would solve a lot of problems."

"Yes, it would, but it's more than that. I want to see you well looked after and taken care of. After that awful business with George, this could be a second chance to have it all. We mustn't waste it." She gestured to her back where the strings of her corset dangled limply. I braced my feet and pulled them as hard as I could, knowing how tight she liked them. "So you must make a good impression. I'll help you with your corset. We'll make a game of it. Who can tie them the tightest."

It was not my idea of fun, but I finished hers, knotting the strings in a neat bow, and stepped over to my trunk. Opening it, I looked down at the folds of fabric and instantly regretted my decision to leave my unpacking till later. My one good evening dress was terribly wrinkled. I tried it on and admired myself in the mirror. Despite the wrinkles, I thought I looked rather fine in the pale yellow-and-green tartan dress. It had wide accordion-pleated sleeves and a matching pleated midriff that flattered my figure. It would look even better once Hari tied me into my corset, I conceded.

Hari, of course, looked magnificent dressed in the very latest style from one of the finest shops in London, a dark green velvet off-the-shoulder affair with small puffed sleeves and two rows of satin ruffles at the bottom of the skirt. The one flaw in her deportment was her jewels. They were fake, paste glass like most of mine. Charles had insisted she leave her diamonds and other precious gems with him for safekeeping. I had planned to keep the emerald necklace locked in the bottom of my trunk for the duration of the voyage, but making Hari happy seemed a priority at the moment, and I dug my red-lacquered jewellery box out of the trunk.

"You can wear Wiggles's beautiful necklace, if you like," I offered. "You'll want to impress Lady Persephone."

"Oh, yes, I would love to," Hari said, her eyes lighting up

in a way that reminded me of our days as children. She loved to dress up in our mother's old discarded gowns and pretend we were having a fine tea in high society. It was not a game I enjoyed so much, but I went along with her then, just as I did now. Seeing her smile was my reward.

As I helped her with the clasp, I hoped I wouldn't have to sell the necklace right away. It was a beautiful piece, and Wiggles wanted me to do something meaningful with it.

"When we get to Victoria, will we have enough money to live on?" I asked Harriet.

She stroked the green pendant at her throat thoughtfully. "Charles gave me a modest allowance for the journey. Our needs will be taken care of."

"But what if we can't find a match for me right away?" I hoped she couldn't hear the slight optimism in my voice. "How will we live? Will I need to find employment?"

"That won't be necessary. I've found an alternate source of funds." She turned away from the mirror.

"From where?"

"I've always taken care of you, so try not to worry about money. We'll be all right." She clasped one of her paste-glass necklaces around my neck. "There. Exquisite. Now, you just focus on delighting Sir Richard and Lady Persephone tonight."

As we walked to dinner, Hari briefed me on the other invitees. Two clergymen, Reverends Burk and Crossman, Mrs. Burk, and Dr. Carson, the ship's surgeon. I murmured the names to myself, anxious to avoid any faux pas.

When we arrived at the captain's small dining quarters, the other guests were already there, and a waiter was serving predinner drinks. He handed Hari and me each a glass of sherry. I took a sip and looked around.

The chamber, panelled on both walls and ceiling in dark wood, doubled as the chart room by day. The cramped space was barely large enough for the dining table, so the chart tables had been pushed hard into corners to make room. Four men lounged with their Scotches over a card game at one of the chart tables. I easily picked out the captain in his dress uniform, and another slim man in a less formal uniform I guessed to be Dr. Carson. The other two men, undoubtedly the reverends, were only remarkable in how different they were from each other, one round and short, the other lean and tall.

When he saw us enter, Captain Hellyer left the game to welcome us. He was a man of average build about fifty years old, and his eyes were framed by starburst wrinkles—the aftereffect of years of squinting into the sun over reflective water.

"Let me introduce you to the other ladies," he said, and gestured towards two women in the centre of the room. One was short and plainly dressed, but the other was a regal woman with silver hair piled high on her head, a long prominent nose, and large blue eyes under heavy brows. She was dressed in elegant black, but her silk gown was decidedly staid with its high round neck, wide sweeping skirt, and raglan sleeves. Diamonds sparkled around her throat and wrists.

"Lady Persephone," Hari whispered in my ear, then turned to the captain. "Don't worry about making introductions, Captain Hellyer. The lady and I know each other."

He smiled and returned to his game as Harriet made a

beeline for Lady Persephone. Recognition dawned on her face when she saw Harriet.

"Harriet Baldwin, what a treat," she said. I saw warmth in her eyes, but her reaction to the surprise was controlled, as if any overt display of genuine affection would be unseemly. "Wait till Richard learns that you and Charles are on the voyage; he'll be so gratified to hear. He won't be joining us tonight, hasn't quite got his sea legs yet, but this news will cheer him."

"It's a delight to see you again, Lady Persephone." Hari reached over and gently touched the older woman's arm. "I'm afraid I shall have to disappoint your dear husband. Charles was unable to make the journey. So busy with his work at home."

"Oh?" A wrinkle appeared on Lady Persephone's brow. "Richard tells me that issues in the colonies should be made a priority if the empire is going to continue to thrive. Perhaps we can persuade Charles to join you for a while? He can gather some firsthand knowledge. I'm sure I could get Richard to write and urge him."

"A wonderful idea," Hari said, and I could tell she was delighted how easily her plan was falling into place. "I don't believe you've met my sister, Miss Charlotte Harding?"

"Miss Harding, yes, I've heard of you." There was a pregnant pause while Lady Persephone looked long into my face. I could only hope she hadn't heard the gossip.

"How do you do?" I said.

She nodded in reply, then turned to the other woman in our group. "Allow me to introduce Mrs. Gertrude Burk, wife of Reverend Burk."

She gestured to the card table and the short, round man

seated there, and I realized that the Burks were the very stout couple I had witnessed directing their flock of young women to the lower decks earlier in the day. They had the look of two people married a long time, such that they closely resembled each other. Both were plump from every angle, and their bulbous flesh in various shades of pink strained the seams of their clothing. I thought of the crate of pigs I had seen loaded on the deck when we boarded.

Mrs. Burk shook mine and Harriet's hands. "Happy to make your acquaintance," she said with a north England accent. "I'm sure we'll all become good friends before this voyage is through."

"Yes, indeed," Harriet said.

The dinner chime sounded, and we all made our way to the table. Hari and I consulted the name cards and found our seats on either side of Captain Hellyer. He appeared and seated Hari while one of the other men pulled out my chair for me. I looked up over my shoulder to thank him and met the gaze of a very tall man with startlingly blue eyes.

"Th-thank you," I stammered as I sank into my chair.

"You're welcome," he said, then took a seat opposite me.

I pretended to examine the menu on my plate while surreptitiously glancing across the table to read his name card. Reverend John Crossman. He didn't remind me at all of Reverend Smithson back home. Everything about him seemed larger than life. His head was covered in thick, wavy black curls that extended uninterrupted into wide muttonchop sideburns. Dense whiskers ran down his cheeks into his jawline. The darkness of his hair and eyebrows made his cobalt-blue eyes all the brighter, while his Roman nose added just a touch of the patrician.

On my left was Dr. Carson. Of average build, the doctor had very short, sandy hair with just a hint of matching facial hair. His face and body were wiry, the skin pulled tight over its frame with little or no fat to pad it. I guessed him to be in his late thirties, still young enough to be considered youthful, but something about the way he held himself, the back straight enough but with shoulders and neck pulled forward, suggested age beyond his years.

"Will you do the honours, Reverend Burk?" Captain Hellyer said once we were all seated and the last of the introductions had been made. "The cook gets in a foul temper if we don't stick to schedules."

We lowered our eyes as Reverend Burk cleared his throat and in his broad northern accent began what was to be a very lengthy beseech of the Lord to guide us through the perils that lay ahead. He did us the service of naming and expounding on each and every jeopardy one could possibly imagine afflicting our voyage. While I had plenty of things I was very fearful of, Burk's endless list, delivered in his melodramatic style, soon began to seem a tad overdone.

"Save us, Lord, from the frightful, savage gales that threaten to overturn our sturdy ship and toss us into the boiling hell of the sea. Save us, Lord, from disease and pestilence, small-pox, diphtheria, yellow fever, scarlet fever, rubella, dengue fever, polio, and cholera. Find it in your mighty power, Lord, to prevail upon the trade winds to blow so that we may not rot in the doldrums of the midlatitudes and finally die of scurvy. Bless our food so that weevils and worms do not spoil it and leave us, your devoted flock, to shrink to nothingness from malnutrition and eventual starvation."

As if to punctuate this last comment, the aroma of freshly roasted mutton wafted from the kitchen, but the reverend droned on, showing no sign of letting the meal begin. I peeked up at this harbinger of dire misfortune. I reckoned that he, and Mrs. Burk, could rest easy. Any threat of starvation was a long way off for them. I caught Reverend Crossman's eye and saw the corners of his mouth twitch.

"And what of the innocent young women you have entrusted into our care, dear Lord?" Burk continued on. "What evil lurks at every turn if, by your good grace, we should survive this voyage and reach the foreign shore? Spare them from the twin demons of drink and lust, Lord. If one or two of your flock should succumb to the devil's temptation, fling them from your bosom, Lord. Fling them, Jesus, fling them from your heavenly heart. And I say, leave them be where Jesus flung them! We will only care for the pure of heart."

Burk paused for air, and Captain Hellyer took advantage of the moment and interjected a quick "Amen." Then added, "Reverend Crossman, we don't want to play favourites. Would you do the honours next time?"

"Of course," Reverend Crossman replied with a straight face.

As the food was brought in, the captain warned that bad weather should be expected as long as we were in the northern Atlantic. He politely suggested we eat less than usual, especially if we were prone to seasickness. I noticed the dining table had developed a slight motion along with the ship and, with some trepidation, took a bite of the mutton in front of me.

"Tell me, Reverend Crossman," Harriet said. "Are you and Reverend Burk fellow travellers? Will you be working together when we reach the colony?"

As always, my sister was at home in any social setting, and I was glad to see that she had regained some of her usual calm, self-assured demeanour. Both Lady Persephone and Mrs. Burk looked to the reverend for his response, but before he could, Reverend Burk spoke.

"*Reverend* Crossman and I do not share the same philosophy when it comes to the Lord's work with the heathen. I firmly believe that the European civilization has defined the correct and only true path to salvation through worship. It is my role to bring light to the Natives to the extent that they are capable of understanding it."

He smiled at everyone around the table, inviting comment, but no one spoke, though Mrs. Burk was nodding. I looked to Reverend Crossman to hear his point of view, but he kept his head down, staring at the mutton and applesauce on his plate. I wondered if his frown was for the food or the last comment.

Reverend Burk reached across the table for the wine bottle the waiter had left and poured himself a glass before he went on. "The burden I carry is a heavy one, and I say with all sincerity that I am relieved that the Lord did not see fit to trouble John with the same burden. Some of us are free to enjoy our earthly existence, whilst I must wait for my heavenly reward."

Reverend Crossman looked up then, his blue eyes twinkling. "The good Reverend Burk has me there. I do enjoy my time in the colonies. Fishing, trapping, hunting. I've even tried my hand at panning for gold. But, there *are* a few things I take very seriously."

"Such as?" I asked, curious enough to speak.

He turned his intense focus on me. "My luggage is filled with tools I plan to offer to the Natives for their fight against smallpox. They are dying in startling numbers, and the government does little. I've read of awful things, whole villages wiped out in a matter of days." A cloud passed over his face. "Once we land in British Columbia, I'll head up the Fraser Canyon and visit as many villages as I can, offering training and supplies. That's what's important to me."

"I'd like to see how to administer those vaccinations," Dr. Carson said from my left. He spoke in a strong Welsh accent.

"I'd like to see how they're done, as well," I said, moved by the reverend's impassioned speech. "I have a long-standing fascination with medicine. Most of my experience is with animals. I've presided over the births of some calves and foals on our family estate—"

Harriet kicked my leg and I stopped short. Lady Persephone was studying me with raised eyebrows.

"My sister had a childhood infatuation with animals, but it's an interest she's long outgrown," Harriet said quickly.

"You must show us how you convince the Natives to let you give them the pox, John," Reverend Burk said, oblivious to any tension. "Your story would make for fine entertainment some evening. If our Miss Harding here is so impressed, you'll be all the rage with the sixty single ladies on board."

"I would be very happy to show Miss Harding and Dr. Carson

how I do smallpox vaccinations," Reverend Crossman said simply, returning to his mutton.

Dr. Carson turned to Reverend Burk. "How are the emigrant women faring so far? Are they in reasonable health?"

"There are issues I can't discuss in front of the ladies, Doctor. It seems some of them are not the innocent maidens they had presented themselves to be for the resettlement plan. I find in my line of work that many low-class females will happily lie in order to cover their sins, but the truth always comes out."

I lowered my eyes to my plate, but my appetite was gone. Outside the weather was picking up. The lantern that hung from the ceiling began to sway with the rolling ship, casting strobing lights and shadows about the room. The wind whistled through tiny cracks and openings in the outside wall of the room.

"Captain Hellyer," Lady Persephone said, delicately dabbing the corners of her mouth with her napkin. "My chef could do no better with a humble dish of mutton. My compliments to your cook." She turned to Hari. "Sir Richard and I are looking forward to our time in Victoria with Governor and Mrs. Douglas. We have been told they are wonderful hosts. I'm sure Mr. Baldwin sent letters of introduction?"

Hari could hardly suppress a smile. "Yes, of course. Charles only ever thinks of our comfort. We'll be joining you and Sir Richard at the governor's. Will you be staying long?"

"A few months. Richard is bringing a special dispatch from Pam. There's great concern about the horde of Californian gold seekers flooding north now that their own gold rush has run dry. There's even talk of an attempt at American annexation. They want the whole western coast, all the way to Alaska, and it's said they are even trying to buy Alaska from the Russians. More British emigration is the only way to halt the erosion of British sovereignty."

Lady Persephone's words reminded me of what I had heard at the emigration meeting. It seemed to me that the empire was getting rather far-flung; there were so many colonies and Britain itself was far away from most. Perhaps it was more prudent to focus on remedying the problems within our existing colonies closer to home.

"I wonder," I said tentatively, "how Britain can effectively manage so many territories." As soon as the words were out of my mouth, I realized it was the wrong thing to say, especially to the prime minister's cousin. I didn't need Harriet's kick under the table to tell me that.

Lady Persephone's eyes narrowed. "We do very well. We British were born to be rulers of lesser peoples. It's God's will." She raised her wineglass. "To the empire, may the sun never set upon her."

There was a cacophony of scraping chairs as we all rose to our feet. "The empire," we cried, raising our glasses in unison.

"What draws *you* to the colony, Miss Harding?" Lady Persephone asked when we'd sat down again.

I didn't know how to reply. I wasn't so much drawn as forced, but I couldn't tell Lady Persephone that. "I . . ."

"My sister is selflessly stepping forward to do what is in the best interests of the empire," Harriet said. "She's willing to settle in one of our furthest outposts in order to make a respectable marriage with one of our native sons and raise a good Christian family."

"Hear! Hear!" Reverend Burk said, raising his glass to me. Lady Persephone echoed the sentiment. I felt Reverend Crossman's eyes on me as he raised his drink with the others, and I desperately wanted to sink into my seat, but I sat erect, my chin up, and pretended to be the woman of conviction that Hari just described as the wind howled outside.

Chapter Thirteen

I awoke in the night feeling as though I had dropped through a trapdoor into Dante's nine circles of hell. The third circle, to be exact. I had heeded the captain's advice and hadn't eaten much at dinner, but clearly that wasn't enough. I gripped the headboard of my bed, trying desperately to brace myself against the endless plunging and lifting motion of the ship. I was thankful that I had snapped the bed's side plank into place before retiring despite thinking it childish earlier. It was all that held me from being tossed painfully from my bunk onto the cabin's cold wooden floor.

The howling gale brought with it a pungent seaweed-smelling dampness that seeped through wall cracks and permeated the cabin. My hot, dry lips tasted of salt, and my stomach cramped painfully as bile began to percolate up my throat. Sliding from my bed onto the floor, I crawled towards the washstand in Hari's room in the faint glow of the moonlight. I grasped the lovely porcelain washbowl that I had so admired and I retched, my stomach desperate to rid itself of its contents.

"Sorry, Hari," I croaked, sure I'd woken her, but she didn't respond.

As I clutched the bowl, I regretted my cynical view of Reverend Burk's long-winded supplication and prayed that the dreadful motion of the ship would stop. I vomited again until there was nothing left.

I didn't know how much time had passed, but eventually the endless gyrating motion that consumed my world subsided and my gut ceased its violent purging. My white flannelette nightgown was damp and clung to me. Slowly, I stood and looked over at Harriet's motionless body. How could she sleep through all of that—the storm, my sickness?

I ignored the shivers that ran over me and went to her bed. Even in the poor light, I could see that she was deathly pale.

"Harriet?" She didn't move. I scanned the bedside table and saw the remains of two spent vials of her medicine. *Oh no,* I thought. *What has she done?* I put my ear to her chest. Her breath came in short, shallow puffs. For a moment I was lost in panic. I couldn't lose my sister. "Hari, wake up." I shook her. She moaned but didn't stir. "Harriet," I said louder, gently slapping her cheek.

Her eyes fluttered open.

"Thank God," I murmured.

"Wha—? What are you doing?" She was groggy and confused, but awake.

"You took too much of your medicine."

"No, no—one, jus' one."

"You took two vials—two, not one."

"I—I can't h-have taken two." She struggled to sit up and

sort through the items on her table, stopping when her hands landed on the two empty vials. "I can't afford to take two! I don't have enough."

"Enough for what?" I asked. "Hari, you were barely breathing."

Pushing me aside, she threw back the covers and got to her feet. She staggered across the room to her trunk and rummaged through it until she found a velvet drawstring bag. "Six left, only six. What am I going to do?" She sank to the floor, a stricken look on her face.

"It will be all right," I said, wrapping us both up in the blanket from the bed. Her shoulders were shaking. I thought at first that she was cold, but then I realized that she was crying. I was shocked. Hari never cried. On many occasions, she told me that she didn't believe in giving in to one's emotions.

"What's wrong, Hari?" I asked, rubbing her back.

"I need my medicine. I can't do without it. It's the only thing that calms me."

"You've never needed anything like this before. What exactly is it? Did Dr. Randolph prescribe it?"

She nodded. "It's laudanum, and if I don't get more, I won't be able to hold myself together. What will Lady Persephone say?" She gripped my hands. "You must help me get more, Charlotte. You must."

The fevered look in her eye frightened me. I had heard of laudanum. Mama's friends had talked of it. Some called it "wife's best friend"—they couldn't get through their loveless marriages without it. But they also spoke of women who had overindulged to the point of ruining their health. What had it done to my poor sister?

She continued to cry, rocking listlessly back and forth. I pulled her close. "There, there. We'll figure this out. Don't worry."

Even as I said the words, I wasn't sure they were true. I had no idea how to get laudanum and, when it came down to it, I was frightened by what it had done to her tonight. The ghostly image of her lying on that bed wouldn't leave me for a long time. All I did know was that my sister was in desperate need of help.

I cradled her until she fell back to sleep, then at dawn, I dressed, pocketing the empty vials, and ran to find Dr. Carson.

Chapter Fourteen

D r. Carson didn't appear surprised when I knocked on his surgery door. "Are you poorly after the storm last night?" he asked, inviting me in.

The middle-deck room was small and dark with one window, a porthole that gave off a heady smell of mouldy dampness. I noticed it was just above the waterline and bolted closed against the swells and the grey, turgid water that threatened to swamp it. A lattice of small drawers, each labelled with a brass plate, covered one whole wall. I squinted, trying to read some of the labels, hoping that one of these little wooden cubicles housed the drug I sought.

"No, I'm fine," I replied. "It's my sister."

He sat and gestured to an old wooden chair on the other side of his desk. "Please, take a seat," he said in a lilting Welsh accent. "What can I do for you, Miss Harding?"

"Please call me Charlotte." I squirmed in my chair, uncertain how to begin. "My sister's regular doctor, Dr. Randolph, put her on some medication prior to our departure, and I'm afraid she doesn't have enough to see her through the voyage."

"What is she taking?"

"This," I said, holding out the two empty vials. "Laudanum."

Dr. Carson grew very serious as he took the vials. "Laudanum is a powerful drug made by combining opium and alcohol, and I take great care in who I give it to. It's very effective for pain in the short term, but over time it's highly addictive."

"Harriet says it calms her nerves. She hasn't suffered an injury, so I can't begin to understand why her doctor would have prescribed this for her in the first place." I remembered the way Dr. Randolph had helped Harriet into the carriage that rainy day. He'd seemed so attentive, but had I misread his intentions?

"I've heard that it is becoming quite commonplace with physicians who administer to the wealthy," Dr. Carson said. "But in my opinion they are playing with fire."

"How so?"

"The drug opium slows the heartbeat. Breathing becomes shallow. Heart attacks are not uncommon. Overdoses are often fatal. Those addicted can rarely focus on anything other than their next dose and the first symptoms of withdrawal are enough to make those trying to quit give up."

As he described exactly what I had just witnessed in Harriet, my throat felt dry and I swallowed hard. "May I be frank?"

"Please."

"My sister has been taking a full daily dose of laudanum for nearly a month now. I believe she's addicted. I'm terrified of what will happen if she continues to take it . . . but I'm also afraid of what might happen if she suddenly stops. She just needs enough to see her through the voyage, then we can get her proper help. Would you be able to prescribe her a few more doses? I'll monitor her closely."

His shoulders drooped and he slumped forward on his desk, as though the ills of the world hung heavily on him. "Miss Charlotte, you need to understand that accidents happen all the time on ships. This is dangerous work. There'll be broken bones, cuts, and coal-fire burns. There's no knowing what lies ahead, but I do know that the poor crewmen will suffer, and laudanum is the only drug I have to help them. I have none to spare." He raised his head and looked at me hard. "I won't lie to you. Withdrawal from the drug will be one of the hardest things your sister will ever do, but she will survive."

"Couldn't we try to wean her off of it? Do you have enough for that?" I couldn't bear the thought of going back to Harriet empty-handed.

"It's possible," he said after a moment. "But you will have to get her to commit, and it's not easy to cut back. The addiction is powerful. As long as they have a full dose available to them, most addicts will give in to the pull of the drug."

"I'll convince her, and I'll get her to turn over the last of her supply to you so she can't backslide," I said, my resolve building. Yes, this was what I could do for Harriet. "Of course, we would pay you so you can buy more laudanum. I wouldn't want the crew to be without. But my sister is also in great need."

The doctor straightened. "I'm forgetting my oath. The crew and passengers on this ship are *both* my patients, and I must do all I can to help you."

Relief washed over me like a wave, and I let out a breath I didn't know I had been holding.

"But I don't want your money," he said, then paused, deep in thought. "Let me propose something. I recall from the captain's dinner that you have some experience with veterinary medicine. I desperately need another set of hands. If you assist me on my daily rounds with the crew, I would be willing to use some of my supply of laudanum to help wean Harriet off the drug. She could reduce her daily dose to zero in a few weeks' time and I will restock when we stop in Bermuda. What do you say?"

I knew Harriet would balk at the idea of me working on board the ship, but I would have agreed to anything in order to help her. "Yes, I'll be happy to. Thank you, Dr. Carson."

"Don't thank me yet," he said. He searched the drawer of his desk and handed me a tiny container. "This is a half dose. Go give it to your sister, then come right back. Bring me any of her unused vials. Your new job starts in one hour."

∽

Harriet was sitting at her dressing table brushing her hair when I entered our cabin. In the mirror, I could see that she had dark circles under her eyes and a yellowish tinge to her skin.

"Hari, look what I've brought you." I opened my palm to reveal the vial in my hand.

She quickly came to me. She held the tiny glass cylinder up to the light of the window so she could see the amber liquid inside, then searched my face. "You found more. Where?"

"Dr. Carson. I explained your plight, and he's willing to help. Go ahead, this is today's dose."

Hari didn't hesitate. She pulled the stopper and swallowed the tincture. Her cheeks immediately flushed red, but her eyes remained flat, the whites tending towards grey. "This isn't the same. There's not enough."

"It's half your usual dose. Dr. Carson is going to help wean you off."

"But why? I'm perfectly fine taking it. The only problem is when I run out."

I drew her to the chairs and we sat down opposite each other. "You know that's not true," I said quietly. "Last night, you scared me, Harriet. I thought I might have lost you. And you . . . you were . . . I've never seen you so distraught."

She looked away, clearly uncomfortable at the recollection.

"You have to try to quit, Harriet," I continued. "The drug is dangerous. From what Dr. Carson told me, laudanum is used to manage severe short-term pain. Why did Dr. Randolph prescribe it for you in the first place?"

"It was to relax me, make me more likely to conceive. That's what Dr. Randolph said. I was desperate." She closed her eyes. "After three years of marriage, I had not been pregnant once, and it was all Charles would talk about. 'My uncle won't make me his heir and pass the title on until the line of succession has been established,' he told me time and again."

"Did you ever think the problem conceiving could be with Charles?" I asked. "Did he ever see a doctor?"

Harriet let out a harsh laugh. "How little you know of men. A man would never admit to that. Don't be ridiculous." Seeing my face, she softened. "I know you're just trying to help. I'm sorry for being such a witch lately."

"I know you don't mean it." I remembered something Wiggles said to me a long time ago when my father was caught up in the fever of his latest project and I had complained of his dismissive behaviour. "Sometimes we take our frustrations out on those we love the most," I told Hari now. "They're the only ones we can truly trust."

"It's always been me giving you advice. When did you get to be so wise?"

"If you think me wise, then listen to me now. You need to take this opportunity. You don't want to permanently ruin your health, do you?"

Harriet frowned, studying the floor. "You're right. I can see what it's doing to my physical condition, but when I'm on it I haven't a care in the world. When it wears off I feel anxious for more. It's as if it is a living thing inside me that's taken over my body and my will. How can I possibly mange without it?"

"Dr. Carson and I will help you manage your doses so the panic isn't unbearable. Don't worry. The first thing we need to do is give the last of your supply to Dr. Carson."

Harriet stiffened. "No! You can't leave me with none. What if I can't do this? I need some of the drug just in case." She had the eyes of a cornered animal.

"You can do it, Hari. I will help you every step of the way. Trust me. Now, where are the other vials?"

"They're in my chest, in the velvet purse," she said finally.

I went over to her trunk and found six vials, just as she said, and when I turned back, she was watching me, or rather watching the vials.

"It will be okay, Harriet. I promise."

"How much will this cost?" she asked.

"He doesn't want any money." I filled Hari in on the bargain I had struck with the doctor.

"You can't be serious—traipsing after him on the lower decks. A woman of your breeding should never step into the crew's quarters. It would be a disaster if Lady Persephone heard of it, especially after the weak impression you made at the captain's dinner. No, go back and tell the doctor I won't allow this. We will buy the medicine from him and that's that. I have sufficient funds."

As if to prove it, she slowly rose and went to her dresser, where she pulled out several coins.

"He won't take the money, Harriet."

"Of course he will. Everyone wants money. I won't be a charity case."

She thrust the money into my hand. As I fingered the coins, an idea came to me. "Fine, I'll do as you ask. But first, I'm going to change into my walking outfit and take a tour of all three decks. I need the fresh air after being sick last night."

Harriet nodded her assent, then returned to her bed. "I'm afraid I can't join you. I don't want Lady Persephone to see me like this."

I lifted a blanket over her. "I'll return a little later with something for you to eat. Rest for now."

She finally closed her eyes, and I stayed for a few minutes watching the slow, rhythmic rise and fall of her chest, comforted in the knowledge that her breathing seemed normal once more.

I quickly dressed in one of my older, simple cotton day

dresses with a full skirt that allowed ease of movement. If Harriet did leave her room, she would never go to the second or third decks. I could help Dr. Carson, and she need never know. It would be only for a few weeks. As I tucked the laudanum into my pocket, I tried not to doubt Hari's commitment to this new plan. Or my own. Harriet was right—it wouldn't do for those in our circle to know I was Dr. Carson's assistant and socializing with the lower classes. After all I'd been doing to try to salvage my reputation, I was taking a risk, but I had no other choice. I tried to ignore my queasy stomach. With luck, I would never be found out.

Chapter Fifteen

"This is everything," I said, handing Harriet's vials over to Dr. Carson.

"You're doing the right thing, Miss Charlotte," he said, meeting my gaze. Then he produced a large skeleton key from his pocket and went his desk. "One day your sister will thank you." Once he had locked the vials away, he pulled an aging frock coat on over his yellowing white shirt. "Let's get started."

I hesitated. "About my work with you . . ."

"Yes?"

"Could we keep it between us? It's just that it would be frowned upon by our circle of friends, if you know what I mean. I admire what you do, but there are certain . . . expectations I have to meet."

He gave me a world-weary look. "I know too well what you mean. I promise to keep this arrangement between us."

"Thank you," I said. "Now, what would you like me to do?"

"You can carry my instruments," he said, handing me a black leather bag. It was much heavier than it looked, and I had to carry it with two hands. He gathered up two other bags himself. "Your job will be to hand me items as I need them, but first you will clean each instrument with a disinfectant. I'm one of the new breed who believes in absolute cleanliness."

I nodded as if I knew what he was talking about, then we set off. He walked briskly, and it was all I could do to keep up with him as he headed to the staircase that led to the engine room deep within the ship's bowels.

"The worst injuries are the burns," he called over his shoulder. "They're the most likely to get infected and kill the patient. We are off to see Sam, the coal stoker. Nasty burn. Hope you have a strong stomach."

The heat and roar of the engine room hit me like a solid wall. I caught my breath and pressed back against a rough wooden post for support, taking in the hellish scene. Flames flared from the huge open furnace, casting sepia-orange light across the walls and low ceiling. The air, heavy with black, choking coal dust, made my lungs ache and my throat so dry I couldn't swallow. The sharp odour of male sweat mixed with old stale leather and unwashed linen was so thick I could almost taste it.

Everywhere men, stripped to the waists, grunted as they dragged carts of coal from the hold in the foredeck to the bunkers aft. After dropping their loads onto the floor in front of the burner that fed the throbbing, percussive engines, they pulled their carts back to the hold for yet another load. I felt sorry for them, but the stokers had it worse, standing as they were in front of the open furnace. They endured the intense heat and backbreaking work of feeding the hungry engines.

I had never seen anyone work in conditions like these. It

seemed no thought had been given to the health and well-being of the men, and I wondered at those who had agreed to take it on. What drove them to accept such work? Was there no other option?

Dr. Carson signalled to one of the stokers, who set his shovel aside and came to us. He was short heavyset man. His shirt-sleeves were rolled to his elbows, revealing arm muscles that resembled the thick ropes used to tie the sails down. A bandage covered in coal dust was wound around his left arm.

"This is Sam," Dr. Carson explained over the noise.

There was no real space to administer to Sam, but we made use of a few empty crates. Dr. Carson settled beside him and gestured for me to do the same, then set about unwinding the bandage on Sam's lower arm. I gasped at the sight of the large, fluid-filled blisters, but the clamour in the room was such that no one heard me. Dr. Carson pointed to the bag I carried and I opened it.

"A lance," he shouted.

I looked at the collection of instruments and reasoned that a lance would be some sort of piercing or cutting tool. Unfortunately, there were several that fit the bill. I held them up one at a time until Dr. Carson nodded. He indicated that I dip it in a jar of fluid. The disinfectant, I remembered. I did as he requested and handed the lance over.

As he began to slice open each blister, the smell of putrid flesh filled the room. I swallowed the bile in my throat, thankful there was nothing else in my stomach after last night. This was not anything like assisting the veterinary surgeon back home on our estate, and for a moment, I wished I had never agreed to help Dr. Carson. Working with the animals had been a fun adventure. I helped make them feel better, and they rewarded me with licks and snuggles. This felt like I had ventured into a battlefield where men suffered dreadful injuries in nightmarish conditions. Then I remembered Harriet, and I pushed my self-doubts away and willed myself to carry on.

A spasm of pain passed over Sam's face. I placed a gentle hand on his healthy arm. "Does it hurt very much?" I shouted.

"Nay, just a wee bee sting." He tried to smile, but his eyes were wet with tears.

"Dr. Carson," I said. He looked at me, and I pointed at the laudanum. Wasn't this the time to use it?

"Save it for the really bad cases."

There are worse ones than this? I thought with a shudder.

After dressing Sam's arm, we headed down the hall to a tiny room—the sick bay, Dr. Carson called it. It was a hot, window-less area with three bunk beds jammed so close together they almost touched. The place was meant to be where the injured and ill crew sought refuge, the closest thing to a hospital on board the ship, and it was in miserable condition. For their part, the men seemed grateful to see a nurse in their midst and nodded respectfully to me as I passed by.

Dr. Carson bent over one of the bottom beds, where a man was groaning in pain. I looked down to see his leg. While it was set firmly in a wooden splint, it was purple and swollen to twice the size of his good leg. Stiches had been sewn into the skin where it appeared a broken bone had once protruded.

"Casper broke his leg during the storm," Dr. Carson explained. The sailor had been at the animal pens, using a rope to secure the cow and prevent her from sliding across the deck with each roll of the ship, but the rope had become tangled around his leg. When a huge wave hit the vessel, the cow lost her footing and landed on top of him. "I set his leg last night, but he needs something for the pain. Can you pass me the laudanum?"

"Of course." I fumbled for the bag, my cheeks burning with shame as I realized just how badly these men needed the laudanum. I hoped Hari would be able to wean herself off quickly before Dr. Carson's supply ran out.

I handed Dr. Carson a vial, and he administered it to the seaman, and within seconds, he quieted. His eyelids briefly fluttered then closed, and I was glad we could bring him some peace.

"We'll check on him again later to see how he's doing," Dr. Carson whispered, then he beckoned me to follow him. We moved into a small private examination room next to the sick bay, where a young woman in a large cloak waited.

I had seen her before when we were boarding—she was the woman from the Columbia Emigration Society who had stumbled on the upper deck. She was quite lovely, with dark hair and eyes, and a clear golden-brown complexion. I guessed her to be of French or Spanish ancestry, her family likely from Breton or perhaps they were Basque.

Dr. Carson shut the door behind us. "You must be Sarah Roy," he said. "I'm Dr. Carson and this is Miss Charlotte Harding."

"Hello," I said. "I remember seeing you on deck yesterday. It's nice to meet you."

As she turned towards us, her cloak fell open, revealing her late-stage pregnancy. I tried not to let my surprise play on my face.

"Thank you for seeing me privately, Dr. Carson," Sarah said. "You see, to get on the brideship, I didn't tell the whole truth, and now the Burks are trying to make an example of me."

So this was what Reverend Burk was referring to at dinner. Was she unmarried? Or widowed? I wondered. I didn't see a ring on her finger. A thought struck me. Perhaps she had been attacked like me but hadn't escaped. I shuddered to think how close I had come to being in Sarah's shoes—alone and pregnant headed for an unknown world. My heart went out to her.

"How are you feeling?" Dr. Carson asked, bringing me out of my reverie. "Having any light contractions yet?"

"Yes, a few," Sarah said.

I tied to appear nonchalant as Dr. Carson gently ran his hands across her belly. "Ah, there's a fine kick. This little one's getting ready to make an entrance—any time now." He looked up at me. "Good thing I've got your extra hands."

I felt my knees weaken—I had seen Dr. Boyd birth foals on our estate, but I knew little about human births.

Sarah gave me a small smile. "Thank you ever so much, ma'am."

She must be so nervous, I thought. I placed my hand on her arm. "Please call me Charlotte."

"Charlotte, then," she said, and her shoulders relaxed.

"Come here the same time tomorrow. I want to monitor you daily so you can be as prepared and comfortable as possible when labour starts," Dr. Carson said. I nodded to Sarah and then followed Dr. Carson out and on to the next patient.

By the time we got back to the surgery, I was hungry and exhausted, but I felt a warmth from within at the thought of all the men I had helped that day. This was honest work, and I got much more enjoyment out of tending to the patients than making polite conversation with ladies of society. I looked down at my dress—it was a bit dirty and creased. I hoped Harriet wouldn't notice. All I wanted to do was find something to eat and crawl into bed, but waiting by the surgery door was John Crossman with a well-worn brown leather satchel in his hand.

"Dr. Carson, Miss Harding!" He smiled, displaying a fine set of strong white teeth. "I didn't expect to find you both together."

I felt my palms dampen and ran them across the folds of my gown, smoothing the lines and wrinkles. What if the reverend mentioned something to Lady Persephone at dinner one night? "Dr. Carson has been good enough to give me a few lessons, first aid and that sort of thing."

John's eyebrows shot up. "I'm impressed. Everyone else in first class is having a good long lie-in after last night's storm. You're very serious about learning more about medicine, then?"

"Purely as a point of interest," I said. "I doubt I would ever be called upon to put what I learned to practical use for anything other than a few scraped elbows and cut fingers."

"Well, I've stopped by with my smallpox vaccination supplies." He tapped his bag. "Are you up for a demonstration?"

"Definitely," Dr. Carson said, still full of energy. I reminded myself he didn't spend half the night spilling his innards into a washbasin. "How about you, Miss Charlotte? You did express a curiosity."

In spite of my exhaustion I didn't see how I could politely refuse. John's timing was terrible, but I really was keen to see the demonstration and I doubted I'd get a second chance. "Count me in."

Dr. Carson ushered us inside his small office and cleared a space on the desk for Reverend Crossman to work. John opened his bag and took out several small scalpels, glass plates, jars, and cloths, then set about demonstrating the latest vaccination technique.

"We make the serum from the sores that cows develop from a related disease, cowpox. Much safer than using a live pox like in the old days," he explained, tapping the glass jars. "I won't open these here; we'll just pretend I put some on one of these glass plates. Then we use a scalpel to cut slits in the patient's skin and insert a small amount of the cowpox virus." He demonstrated his technique with a roll of cloth. "Here, try practising." He handed us the fabric.

Dr. Carson went first, and then I took a turn.

"Don't make the cuts too deep," Reverend Crossman said. I felt an odd fluttering in my chest as he reached over and guided my hand. "We don't want the wound to fester."

I tried a few more times as he watched, then finally, he said, "You're a natural."

"Thank you," I replied, handing the cloth back. "Now, if you'll excuse me, I really should be getting back to my sister."

"Just wait a moment," Dr. Carson said, rummaging through his bag. "I'll walk you out."

I turned to John. "Good day."

"Good day, Miss Harding," he said. "I hope we meet again soon."

I felt myself flush furiously under his intense gaze. He was certainly charming, but I was not at all interested in idle flirtation. After my episode with George, I wanted a proper marriage to a very respectable gentleman. And I didn't want word to spread that I had been working with Dr. Carson. I would try my best to avoid John Crossman in the future.

Dr. Carson gestured to the door and outside he handed me a small vial of laudanum. He must have pocketed it when I was saying goodbye to John. "For tomorrow," he said.

I nodded, thankful for his discretion. "See you then."

Chapter Sixteen

Life on board the ship began to take on a sort of rhythm. The weather had calmed, and it was a relief to me that no one else in first class saw me working with Dr. Carson. I only saw Reverend Crossman at dinner or from a distance around the decks, but he hadn't said anything, as far as I could tell. My secret was safe, and I hoped it would stay that way.

Hari spent a good deal of her time in her room, exhausted and irritable as she slowly purged the drug from her system. But I was beginning to see an improvement in her health; her cheeks had a warmer colour to them, and the dark circles under her eyes had all but disappeared.

When she was feeling well, her time centred as much as possible on Lady Persephone, which meant long lingering lunches, slow promenades along the first-class deck, and, sometimes on particularly good days, cards in the tearoom in the afternoons. She still took most of her dinners in our cabin as evenings were the worst time. I called them her witching hours—though not to her face—as her moods swings were extreme and she would

often simply lie on her bed suffering chills and painful muscle spasms, sending me out of the room so not even I would
witness her lowest point. But she was persevering, and I was
deeply proud of her determination.

When I wasn't with Dr. Carson, I would take long walks on
all three decks. Hari insisted I spend lunch with her and Lady
Persephone, and each time, I tried my best to impress her by
asking polite questions about her own interests and listening
attentively as she talked of the important work the British were
doing in the colonies, a favourite subject. Slowly, she seemed
to warm to me.

At one such luncheon, I met the elusive Sir Richard, who
had finally gained his sea legs. He was around sixty, with a tall,
regal frame, though he had begun to stoop with age. He had
a beak of a nose and eyebrows so wild and overgrown that I
imagined they'd make a fine residence for some small bird.
Despite his reserved appearance, he was much more jovial than
his wife, and was at times almost irreverent, which I noticed
Lady Persephone frowned at, but said nothing. Conversations around the dinner table were quite lively. He took every
opportunity to play cards with the other first-class passengers
and had a charming devil-may-care twinkle in his eye whenever he did so.

Pretending to be fascinated by the conversation at these
lunches and dinners exhausted me to no end, and each day, I
looked forward to the solitude of my walks. On one such stroll,
I was delighted to find two animal pens on the second deck.
They were well-hidden, set in the lee of the large smoke funnel
that rose from the boiler room on the deck below. I couldn't

resist introducing myself to the fat rosy pigs, whose names were Hansel and Gretel, according to the sign on their cage. There were also several adorable piglets and a sleepy milk cow named Daisy. I looked into Daisy's large, trusting dark eyes, stroked her soft, wet nose, and promised her many more visits. She made me think longingly of Hari's dog, Belle—the only one who had escaped Charles's wrath—and I dearly hoped Cook was taking good care of her as promised.

I still had to push myself every morning to wake up and get out the door of our cabin. The suffering I witnessed on my daily rounds was heartbreaking. But more and more I found myself anxious to check in on the men, to see them progress towards recovery. I knew I was helping to make life easier for the crew—some even started to call me Florence, after the famous nurse Nightingale—but I was increasingly troubled by the inequity of the whole thing, how some men enjoyed the spoils of the empire while others toiled mightily in harsh environments to provide it.

Today, as I was looking for the right opportunity to slip unnoticed into Dr. Carson's surgery, my attention was drawn to a demonstration set up on the forward deck. There were often music recitals and presentations offered by fellow passengers and I took in as many as I could when I wasn't belowdecks tending to patients. I stopped at the back of a small crowd and rolled up on my tiptoes so that I could see what was going on.

Two gentlemen adventurers were offering a lesson on panning for gold, and they had set out their large flat tin pans, filled with loose sand and gravel, on a low table by a pail of water. I stifled a gasp when one of the gentlemen opened a tiny glass jar and tipped two nuggets of gold into a pan. With a great dramatic flourish, he asked the crowd, "Who would like to try their luck at panning for gold and recover my nuggets? Which one of you will be the next Cariboo Pete?"

I was curious myself, but didn't want to attract attention, so I stayed where I was as an older man volunteered. He was shown how to grasp the pan with both hands and to gently swirl it in a large circular motion, dipping it regularly into the water pail and letting the sand and gravel particles that collected on the top get washed away.

"That's the way to get the heavier gold to sink to the bottom," a deep voice next to me said.

I turned my head to see John Crossman smiling down at me.

"Oh, hello," I said, taking a step back in surprise. I accidently bumped into the woman behind me, flattening the front of her very large hat. She glared at me as she adjusted it. I flushed. "Sorry."

"I didn't mean to startle you," Reverend Crossman said, his eyes twinkling.

"No, you didn't," I said quickly.

"But I'm glad to run into you like this," he continued. "We really haven't had a chance to talk since that day with Dr. Carson. How's the first aid training coming along?"

"Oh, I gave that up a while ago," I lied.

"That's too bad." He studied my face. "I would have said you had a calling."

I looked at him, forgetting myself for a moment. I was not used to this kind of encouragement, but I caught myself before

I said the wrong thing. "It wasn't really appropriate work for me. It's frowned upon for a lady with my background."

"It's a shame that society puts such restrictions on women. I've never really understood it. It serves no one."

I had never heard such a thought expressed by a man, and it gave me pause. Was it possible we could be kindred spirits? *No, I told myself. Do not even think that.* I knew my duty, and John Crossman didn't figure into it. I changed the subject, nodding at the gold panning. "I recall that you have done this before."

"Nice to know you were listening. I usually bore everyone with endless stories of my adventures."

In front of us, the volunteer combed his fingers through the bottom sediment and produced the two gold nuggets, displaying them in his outstretched hand. The pea-size lumps sparkled in the light, as if winking at me. When the crowd cheered and applauded, I murmured an excuse to the reverend and slipped away to Dr. Carson's surgery. But the image of those glowing gold nuggets stayed with me for the rest of the morning. Was gold the reason the men belowdecks worked so hard in unspeakable conditions and why the emigrant women were willing to leave their loved ones and travel halfway around the world? Perhaps the goldfields of British Columbia offered them a real chance to leave a life of hardship and poverty behind.

When I pushed open the heavy oak door of the surgery, Dr. Carson was already busy with two patients. He looked relieved when he saw me and motioned me forward.

"I can't deal with these two at the same time," he said. "I'll stitch Jeff's bad gash here; you can set Ed's broken forearm."

I looked at the seaman sitting at the table. Ed was more of

a boy than a man, clearly fighting tears, his face flushed a deep red. "Me?"

"You've seen me do it enough times. You know the procedure; there's a sling on the table. I'll double-check it when you're done."

My knees felt a little like tomato jelly, but I didn't want to let the doctor down. It took a great deal of my strength to straighten Ed's muscles that had contracted in response to the break, but I managed it without too much discomfort for the poor boy. "I'll have you in a sling in a jiff," I told him, and he seemed relieved.

Dr. Carson inspected my work and pronounced it properly done, but I had no time to bask in glory. We went off on our rounds and spent an exhausting morning tending to the crew.

At the end of the day, Dr. Carson set himself heavily at his desk and sifted through his stores of laudanum. "And how is Harriet doing on the new dose?"

"Well, I think. Her withdrawal has been hard, but she's improved a great deal. Our plan is working, and we both can see the light at the end of the tunnel."

"Good," he said. "This is the smallest dose I have. She can take this for another week or two, and then we'll see about taking her off completely."

A weight I didn't know I had been carrying lifted off my shoulders. My sister would soon be free of this drug's hold and we could go back to our lives. "And your supply hasn't run out?"

"I'll have enough until we dock in Bermuda." He gave me a warm, rare smile. "You did well today. I realize that helping me to set that broken arm was hard, especially seeing that young lad in so much distress, but you didn't let that get in the way of doing your job. You are really making a difference here."

I felt a surge of pride ripple through me. I had lived up to the demands of a tough situation.

"Everyone seems to be in rather good health at the moment, so for the next few days, I could use your help counting and cataloging my supplies."

He reached across his desk and handed me two large iron skeleton keys. I raised my eyebrows in question.

"One key is to the surgery, and the other opens the medicine stores. Keep them safe. You can let yourself in and count our stock while I do the rounds tomorrow."

I nodded, looking forward to an easier few days ahead of me. I wondered how Dr. Carson did it every day.

"This is such hard work," I said. "I'm curious. What made you leave Wales to take this position?"

"My accent is as strong as that, is it?"

"Yes," I said, chuckling.

His expression grew serious. "As a young man my politics got me into trouble. I was inspired by the work of John Stuart Mill, a champion of the individual over the power of the state. Some thought my ideas were dangerous. I was charged with sedition. Trumped-up charges. Sedition is high treason, punishable with death. I had no choice but to flee."

I wasn't familiar with John Stuart Mill, but I recognized the similarities in mine and Dr. Carson's circumstances and murmured my condolences.

"That's why I'm here, a ship's surgeon, instead of in my little cottage in Wales doing the work I love, caring for the miners, and helping them with their unionizing. The irony is, I now strongly disagree with Mill's thinking."

"How so?"

"He's a great defender of British imperialism, sees Britain as a benevolent despot civilizing barbaric peoples. I've seen enough of the world to know that's not true. It's just a convenient argument for empire building."

It was a perspective I had not heard before, and it resonated with me, somehow. "Why don't you renounce Mill and return to Wales?" *If only it was that simple for me too*, I thought. I would do it, for Hari and me, and return home in a flash.

"Not now." Dr. Carson shook his head. "The men need me. I couldn't leave them."

∽⟁

Dr. Carson's comments left me pensive, and I took the long way back to my cabin to think them through. He was a man who had put the well-being of others ahead of his own needs. I had never truly encountered anyone like that. I thought of Charles, Lady Persephone, and Sir Richard, all people who saw others as useful tools, as pawns in the game of career building.

Down on the third deck, I passed the area roped off for the exclusive use of the future colonial brides. Even en route to a purportedly better life, they were cloistered without freedom of movement. I scanned their pale faces looking for Sarah, and I found her. I waved, and she came over to greet me.

"Miss Charlotte, 'tis fine to see you again." She moved slowly and I could see her eyes and neck were puffy, as they had been at her last checkup with Dr. Carson.

"How are you feeling?" I asked.

"I think this little one must be past due. If I could figure out how to move it along, I would."

"In the meantime, getting some air and sun is a good idea."

Sarah sighed deeply. "The air is full of soot here, but there's nothing else for us. The Burks never let us do anything. We never get to hear what's going on, and we are all so very, very bored." She gestured to a small group of women around her, who were looking at us curiously. "She's a proper nurse," Sarah told them loudly.

"No, no," I protested. "I'm just helping Dr. Carson during his rounds with the crew. He needs an extra set of hands, that's all."

"Nonsense. You're a regular Nurse Nightingale," Sarah said. "Let me introduce you to some of my friends. This is a not-so-famous Florence, Florence Wilson."

A dark-haired woman about my age and wearing a clean but worn day gown stepped up to the rope cordon and shook my hand.

"I'm Charlotte Harding," I said. "It's nice to meet you."

"A pleasure. Thank you for helping Sarah," Florence said. "We're all so excited about the baby, and we want the birth to be as smooth as possible."

Florence was clearly a gentlewoman like me, and I wondered at her circumstances but felt it improper to ask.

"And this is Emma Lazenby," Sarah said, turning to a particularly young woman. She was dressed in a plain grey cotton dress with a flared skirt that flowed to the tops of black ankle boots, the uniform of the working poor.

"Pleased to make your acquaintance, Emma," I said. "Where are you from?"

"Lancashire," she said with a strong accent. "I worked in the cotton mills, but I was a milkmaid afore that."

Around her neck was what I guessed was her prized possession, a small, white cameo necklace, held in place by a black velvet ribbon. I noticed Emma's unmarked skin, and I knew that milkmaids were renowned for their clear complexions. The thought reminded me of what John Crossman had said about cowpox preventing smallpox.

"How are you faring on the journey so far?" I asked her.

"Getting by. The Burks treat us like a bunch of little kiddies, they do. I can't wait to be rid of them."

"This whole Emigration Society is a joke," another woman nearby said. "'Good Christian lassies who'll settle down the wayward gold miners and raise wholesome families.' Ha!" She snorted with laughter, and the other women looked uneasy. "I can't wait to get out of this stinking hellhole and have some fun in the colonies."

"This is Alice Webb," Sarah said. "She's from London."

I guessed Alice was no more than eighteen or nineteen, but her demeanour was that of a woman who had seen much of the underside of life. In spite of the harsh conditions of the voyage, she was done up with plenty of gaudy jewellery, rouged lips, and even a dyed, limp feather in her upswept red hair. Her tight bodice showed off an ample bosom, only partly shrouded by a black lace shawl.

"What do you plan to do when we arrive, Alice?" I asked politely.

"Not sure, but I know whatever it is, it'll be my choice, and it'll be a relief that me dad won't be demanding me wages so's he can buy gin."

"Maybe you'll become an actress like Florence here," Sarah said.

Alice waved the suggestion away.

"I'm afraid actresses don't make a lot of money," Florence said. "I expect I'll have to take another position until I'm established."

"Not planning on marriage, then?" I asked.

"No. Several of us are hoping for something else," Florence said. "Of course no one mentioned that at the emigration interview back in London. It's just that this will be our first chance at freedom. Many of us want a taste of it, for a while at least. And you, Charlotte? What are your plans when we get to the colony?"

It was refreshing to hear women talk of a future that did not revolve around the man they hoped to marry. "Me? I expect I'll marry, if things go according to plan. What with family expectations and all."

Sarah nodded. "I used to be married myself. My man was in the army, killed in China, in the opium wars. He always told me that if anything happened to him, I was to go live with my father in the New World . . ." Her voice trailed off and she rubbed her belly, lost in a memory.

"Oh, Sarah. I'm so sorry," I said. I had wondered what had happened to force her to hide her pregnancy and come alone on this journey. She was brave, I realized, braver than I.

On the surface of it, I was in a better situation. I was a gentlewoman supported by my sister, not unmarried and pregnant. While most of these sixty women would marry, they had skills and the chance to work at any job. The choice was up to them. And if they chose marriage, they were free to follow their heart.

I had no option other than to make a respectable marriage, but the thought left me feeling cold. Perhaps with Lady Persephone's connections, I told myself, I would meet the right sort of gentleman with whom I genuinely felt a connection.

I wished Sarah well and said goodbye to the others just as Mrs. Burk appeared out from behind the ship's large funnel, a smug look on her face. How long had she been standing there? I wondered. I couldn't deny the uneasy feeling her presence always invoked in me.

Chapter Seventeen

"Charlotte, where have you been?" Harriet said, rushing over to me the minute I stepped into our cabin. She was edgier than usual, but I searched her eyes. It wasn't because of the laudanum.

"I was . . . out walking," I replied. "Why? Has something happened?"

"It's Lady Persephone. I was sitting with her in the card-room and she mentioned how impressed she was with you, how she would like to help you find a good husband when we get to Victoria. I didn't even have to ask her for the favour."

"That's wonderful news," I said without conviction. "But why are you so upset?"

Harriet began pacing the room. "Persephone went on to tell me that Sir Richard is extremely concerned about the threat of American annexation. Apparently, there has been a parade of politicians from the south, visiting the colony. They're trying to raise the expectation of American rule and they're speaking directly to the large number of gold seekers from California."

I didn't completely understand what she was saying. "But what does it have to do with us and my marriage prospects?"

"Everything. Sir Richard is writing to the prime minister, strongly advising him to send a contingent of senior members of the government to counter the American effort. He's gone so far as to make a suggested list of people to send. Charles is on that list."

"Isn't that good news? He'll be alone. It would give you a chance to reconcile with him."

"He's not the only one on the list." She stopped her pacing and turned to me. "So is George."

A wave of nausea threatened to overwhelm me as an image of George, standing over me, struggling to remove his trousers, flashed in my consciousness. I shuddered. "Can I never be quit of that man?"

She sat on her bed. "There's more."

"For heaven's sakes. What?"

"Lady Persephone knows George well, and she saw the two of you out on the boat together at my party. She thought you made a lovely couple and wondered why George had let you go without proposing."

I sank down on the bed next to her. "And you said?"

"That it seemed there simply was no spark between the two of you."

"She accepted that?"

Harriet shook her head. "She said that sparks have nothing to do with it, that George needs a wife and you would fit the bill nicely."

"At least she hasn't heard the rumours about me."

"Not yet. But if George does venture to the colony, she will sit him down and push him to make an offer for you. Of course, he'll no doubt tell her his dreadful story about how you tried to seduce him and blackmail him into marriage. And then, we are right back where we started."

I sat in silence for a few minutes, letting Harriet's news sink in. "No, not quite," I said. "Time is on our side. Sir Richard can't even mail the letter until we make it to Bermuda, and then it would be months until the dignitaries arrived. By then, I could be well and truly married to someone else. That would make everyone happy and help get you back in Charles's good graces."

"I suppose so. But Persephone will want you to wait for George, so she won't help with the matchmaking."

"And I have no dowry to entice anyone."

Harriet came to sit opposite me. "That's not exactly true," she said quietly.

"What do you mean? Papa didn't leave us a legacy."

"I know I should have told you this a long time ago, but the whole thing left me feeling so ashamed." She looked away. "It was early in my marriage. I was still nervous about getting my role as chatelaine just right. I came to the kitchen late one evening to leave Cook instructions about a special dinner we were having that week, and I overheard a conversation through the capsule pipeline. Charles was in his office, having a talk with his banker."

I thought of my own similar experience. It seemed a lifetime ago. "What did you hear?"

"Papa didn't forget about our dowry needs. He borrowed

against the estate. He took a loan from Cousin Edward's father, and in return, he promised to leave the estate to Edward. Charles was furious when he found out; he had agreed to marry me without a dowry thinking he would inherit the estate. *I* had even expected him to inherit. But Papa did leave a sum of money for both of us. I heard the banker say so. Charles insisted the funds be mingled with his own. When the banker protested, Charles assured him he would take care of your dowry when the time came, but he hasn't. You were his way of getting even with Papa."

I couldn't believe what I was hearing. All this time, I had felt obliged to Charles, ashamed of my father. "Papa left us a legacy, but we never knew? The solicitors didn't bother to advise us?" I clenched my hands into fists, my fingernails digging into my palms. "I can hear them now, 'Not a subject for a lady. Leave it to the menfolk to take care of.'"

"I'm so sorry, Char. If I told you it wouldn't have changed your circumstances; you still didn't have a dowry, but you had a right to know."

"It would have changed the way I remembered our father. I've harboured resentment that he didn't deserve." I felt tears prick at the corners of my eyes and blinked hard. "Was it so hard to just tell me?"

Hari hugged her elbows. "I felt caught up in my loyalty to Charles, as his wife. If I admitted that Charles was a thief and a liar, our marriage would be like a house of cards, everything would come tumbling down."

"But your marriage came apart months ago. You could have told me then."

Harriet met my gaze. "You might not agree, but in spite of

everything I would take Charles back if he would have me. I still have hope that I can reclaim my life and my place in society. That's why I didn't tell you."

I couldn't sit next to her a moment longer. I rose from the bed and began to pace the room, trying to tamp down my feelings of betrayal. "We have always trusted each other, but you've let me down."

"I haven't. I've always protected and looked out for you. That will never change. I found a way to make it up to you. Charles stole your future, so I stole it back."

I stopped and turned to face her. "How?"

"I oversaw the household accounts and submitted the invoices to Charles's bookkeeper to pay. When Charles told me he was sending us away, I sent the bookkeeper two very large demands for payment. I claimed amounts for several Persian carpets and new silver tableware. I plan to write him when we land in Victoria and tell him that if he agrees to bring us both home, I will give the money back, but he has to promise to give you a proper dowry."

"And if he doesn't?"

"We will use it as a dowry for you and to make our way in the New World." My sister looked at me, her expression open. "So you see, it's been sorted. Now, please say you forgive me. It's been eating me up inside keeping this from you for so long, but I did what I thought best for both of us."

"I forgive you," I said. I didn't want to upset her further. She seemed exhausted, spent by the events of the morning. I handed her the new vial from Dr. Carson. "For now, let's just focus on your health."

She took the medicine and lay down on her bed to rest, but I couldn't relax. I was like a boiling pot with the lid left on, full of unexpressed emotion. Knowing that Papa had thought of my welfare in his final months made me wish I could reach back in time for one last embrace. At the same time, I was full of anger at Charles and what he had done, and despite what I said to Harriet, I was still upset with her for keeping this a secret. Yes, she had my best interests at heart, but I didn't agree with what she'd done, not to me or to Charles. He was not the sort of man to take this lying down, but it was too late. Harriet had already taken the money. If Sir Richard succeeded in bringing him to Victoria, what would that mean for me and Harriet?

Chapter Eighteen

Hari spent so much time briefing me on what I was to say to Sir Richard and Lady Persephone that evening that I was almost late for the predinner drinks in the main dining room. I was told to encourage sympathy about Hari's continued poor health but not undue concern while making assurances that she would be right as rain in the coming days.

It was our usual crowd, the same as the first night in the captain's dining room, but now we were in the main dining room with the rest of the first- and second-class passengers, though a velvet rope divided the two classes. On the other side of the rope, the gentlemen adventurers who had put on such an intriguing display of the proper gold-panning technique were standing with a group of young swells who had earned a reputation as spoiled and frivolous young men. I avoided them at all costs.

Lady Persephone was speaking with Mrs. Burk and a few other women over in a corner, but I felt like I needed a bit more fortification before I approached them. I gladly accepted a glass of wine from the waiter and wandered over to the table where Sir Richard and the other men were playing cards.

When Sir Richard saw me, he called to the waiter for another chair—"Be quick about it, we can't leave this lovely lady standing"—and I sat down between him and John Crossman. I nodded at Captain Hellyer, and Reverend Burk sitting opposite. Dr. Carson arrived, Scotch in hand, and pulled up his own chair. He looked exhausted and said he was content just to watch the game.

"Nice to see you again, Miss Harding," Reverend Crossman said. He smelled of shaving soap and the earthy aromas of cigars and Scotch.

I smiled a greeting, and my hand trembled ever so slightly as I tipped my wineglass to my lips.

"Do you play, my dear?" Sir Richard asked.

"I do, but perhaps this is not the time or place."

"Nonsense, I know my wife thinks ladies shouldn't play with men . . ." He caught Lady Persephone's eye. She frowned almost imperceptibly but nodded. "We'll deal you in," he said with unforced glee.

One person tended to dominate in most marriages, usually the man, but not always, and it seemed that Sir Richard took his marching orders from Lady Persephone. I couldn't help but think it a shame that more marital unions weren't shared partnerships, but I supposed the chances of that were slim to none.

We settled into a game of whist, but there were too many distracting thoughts swirling in my head, and I made several blunders the first round. In spite of being my partner, Reverend Crossman gave me a sympathetic look. After making a few more silly errors, I offered to take over the role of dealer from Captain Hellyer, and I picked up the deck.

As a child I had spent many hours perfecting my shuffle, and it came back to me easily now. I fanned the cards first forward and then back with the skill of a professional.

"I'm impressed," Captain Hellyer commented. "Clearly you did not spend your youth in traditional female pastimes."

"My mother and her friends loved cards. I was often called upon to be their dealer. I made it a childish game to try to impress them with my skill."

"My wife tells me you are off to the colonies in search of a husband," Sir Richard said. "A good thing too. Men cooped up together with no women. It leads to, ah, unhealthy behaviour. Anyway, marriage shouldn't be a hard task for a girl like you." He looked wistful. "Ah, if only I were thirty years younger and unattached . . ."

I took his words as the innocent flirtation of an older man but stole a glance at Lady Persephone. She appeared not to have heard, or perhaps she chose to ignore it. I guessed she was used to this sort of behaviour from her husband. Was it his way of pushing back against her expectations? I dealt out the hand. Captain Hellyer chuckled as he looked at his cards while Sir Richard groaned. The two reverends appeared stone-faced, giving nothing away.

"There's need of English settlers, I'm told. I feel it is my duty to the empire to help to settle the colony of British Columbia." I recited Hari's words with as much enthusiasm as I could muster.

Reverend Burk gave me a condescending look over his

fanned cards. "The colony of British Columbia is not where we're going."

"I beg your pardon?"

"It's a common mistake," Captain Hellyer said. "You're headed to Victoria in the colony of Vancouver Island. The mainland and the island are separate colonies."

"I heard talk of a merger," Reverend Crossman said, tossing a card faceup into the centre of the table.

"You're right there, lad," Sir Richard said as he played a trump card to take the first trick. "I'm coming to broker the deal. And after that? Who knows? Looks like there may be a whole new federation in the works. They're thinking of calling it Canada, of all the daft names. It would be a great joining-together of all the British colonies in North America. We'll push the damn Yankees out of the north once and for all. Pardon my French, my dear."

"I don't think I've ever met an American," I said. "Are they so very different from us?"

"Oh, frightfully different. Nothing like us. They have the strangest notions."

"How so?" I asked.

"For one thing, they've done away with the class system. No more Sir *This* or Lady *That*; everyone's a commoner. One's station in life is not determined by the class one is born into. Can you credit it?"

Dr. Carson coughed. "It's an idea that has its merits," he said, before adding, "in my opinion."

I caught John nodding, but Sir Richard's brows knit together in annoyance.

"In America they're letting in hordes of penniless people from all over the world. Have you ever heard of anything so humbug? They think they're building a great country. Stuff and nonsense. We have to protect our values and the empire and keep the Americans and their ridiculous ideas south of the forty-ninth parallel." With that, Sir Richard triumphantly took another trick.

Dr. Carson was about to respond, but we were summoned to dinner, and I gathered up the cards before making my way to the table. Sir Richard insisted I sit next to him. Dr. Carson was to be on my right, but he went to have a word with the captain, briefly leaving Lady Persephone next to me on the other side of his vacant chair. She leaned towards me.

"How is poor, dear Harriet? It's such a shame that the ship's motion is taking such a toll on her."

I remembered my lines. "Yes, but she has been very brave and uncomplaining. She's improving every day and will soon be able to join you and Sir Richard for dinner."

"Wonderful." She daintily spread a linen napkin over her lap. "And you, Charlotte?"

"Me?"

She raised an eyebrow suggestively. "You mustn't worry excessively about making a good match in Victoria. One hears stories of colonists being a rather uncouth lot, but I'm confident I can help you find a civilized bachelor of superior breeding. In fact, I have someone in mind."

I took a large sip of wine. "You are too kind."

She was about to say something more, but thankfully, Dr. Carson took his seat and Captain Hellyer asked John to say grace.

Over the soup course, Sir Richard filled the others in on our earlier discussion of colonial politics and the need to keep the Americans at bay, then Reverend Burk spoke up.

"British rule backed up by the Church, that's what the colonies need. How else can we keep the Natives in line?"

"It's all well and good to encourage English settlers, but what opportunities are there once they arrive?" Dr. Carson asked. "If people uproot themselves and come all that way, they must find a better life. Those who stay won't be the gold seekers."

"That's where the gift of land comes in," Sir Richard said.

I looked up from my soup. "A land gift?"

Sir Richard turned to me. "Under the Proclamation of 1860, the colonial government, led by Governor Douglas, has promised one hundred and sixty acres of Crown land to qualified settlers. One need only promise to farm or ranch. It is excellent land, rich river delta and ideal grazing ranges. Some of the failed gold miners are taking advantage."

As I returned to my soup, I wondered if Sarah, Florence, Emma, Alice, and the other emigrant brides knew about this opportunity. I would make certain that they did. Perhaps my future husband and I might even take advantage of this generous offer. The idea of a ranch of my own appealed to me very much. I imagined myself on a beautiful mare, perhaps a spotted Appaloosa, riding the range, checking on the new calves in spring. Maybe I could even convince Harriet to stay with me.

Reverend Crossman cleared his throat. "All this land, Sir Richard, who did the government buy it from?"

"Buy? Nobody bought it from anyone. It was empty land. No one lived on it, so the government simply laid claim to it."

"But why would the Native peoples not work the land, if it's as good as you say?"

What was Reverend Crossman trying to say? That the British government had simply helped themselves to the land they wanted? If that were true, my dream of a ranch seemed less enticing. I knew what it was like to lose my home, and I didn't want to be a part of doing that to someone else.

Reverend Burk broke in. "I'm afraid not all peoples are as industrious as the English. We might well look askance at such indolence, but the Lord loves all his flock. That is why, in his great wisdom, he made some of us shepherds and the others sheep."

John flushed and opened his mouth to respond, but Lady Persephone spoke first.

"Enough talk of politics; I do get weary of it, while I know my husband never does." She scanned the table. "Tell us about yourself, Reverend Crossman, we know so little about you."

"There's not much to tell," he said. "My father was an only son and inherited land and a manor house in Yorkshire from my grandfather. I had an ordinary but happy childhood there. I am the older of two boys. I'm afraid we drove our poor mother to distraction with all the mischief we got up to as lads. Seems there was no tree we wouldn't climb or river we wouldn't swim. We fished a lot and practised with our bows and arrows while trying not to shoot each other. More than once Mother declared us the devil's spawn."

A look of amusement crossed Captain's Hellyer's face, but Mrs. Burk pursed her lips. I, for one, couldn't resist smiling at the reverend as he told us about his life. He had a habit of scrubbing his whiskers with his hands when he was think-ing, and he laughed easily whenever something struck him as funny, which was often.

"You are the oldest son and your family's estate will all go to you one day," Sir Richard said. "Why not stay home and enjoy the easy life you were born into? Why be a minister?"

"I have little interest in my father's way of life. He pro-vided me with the finest of educations, including Eton and Cambridge. I was meant to use it to further the family's busi-ness interests, but I resisted. In the end, my beleaguered father relented and gave me a choice of the clergy or teaching, though I had to agree to return home and manage the estate when it was time."

How wonderful it would be to have had the opportunity to do as one wished before family obligation asserted itself, I thought. Our lives were so different and yet in some ways similar. Our fathers' actions had set the course of our futures.

"Why did you choose the clergy?" I asked.

"It gave me a chance to see foreign lands, learn about other cultures, help some of the world's most needy," he replied. "I dread the day I'll have to return permanently to England. My father isn't getting any younger, and I know that time is not far off."

The conversation paused briefly as the main course of fresh-caught cod in butter sauce was served. Reverend Burk tried to steer the discussion to a Bible study he was planning for first-class passengers the next day, but Lady Persephone spoke over him, picking up the thread again.

"My own boys went to Eton. They loved their time there.

Of course, they excelled in both athletics and academics. Reverend Crossman, were you both an athlete and a scholar?"

"I'm afraid my attention was drawn elsewhere." There was a twinkle in the reverend's blue eyes. He went on to regale us with stories of youthful escapades and the severe punishments he had endured as a result. Both Dr. Carson and the captain laughed openly, while the Burks looked bored. I caught Lady Persephone giving Sir Richard a disapproving look when he chuckled, and he was quiet after that.

On one occasion, John recounted, he had been caught climbing out his third-floor window at Eton to spend an evening drinking at the local pub with a friend and fellow student, George Chalmers.

I almost choked on my scalloped potatoes. The man who had treated me with such cruelty and indifference was John's old school friend. I suddenly wanted to find a place to hide.

"George Chalmers, the government whip?" Sir Richard asked.

"The same," Reverend Crossman said. "I certainly would not have predicted his future."

"I should say," Lady Persephone said. "He's one of my cousin's closest friends, my cousin the prime minister, that is. We had dinner with him just before we sailed, such a charming man."

"He was a bit of an odd duck as a child, but he's turned out rather well in spite of his misspent youth."

"Well, I wouldn't know about any youthful indiscretions. I never knew him as a child, but he's one of my favourite people now." Lady Persephone tried to catch my eye, but I kept my face focused on my food. "So warm and clever. In fact,

Sir Richard is pressing him to come to the colony for a visit soon."

"Really? It would be great to see my old school friend again."

The shock of hearing George talked of in such warm, glowing terms was like a fresh slap to my cheek, but no one at the table seemed to notice my distress. I looked at Reverend Crossman with new eyes. Had he heard rumours about me? Did he think I had earned a reputation of ill repute? Would he look for favours that I was not prepared to give? I remembered my earlier misgivings about him, but I had been drawn in by his infectious charm. That wouldn't happen again. I had too much to lose, so even as I smiled outwardly at his latest story of schoolboy misadventure, I redoubled my resolve to keep my distance from Reverend Crossman from now on.

Chapter Nineteen

voiding someone on an oceangoing vessel of no more than a few hundred people was easier said than done. I couldn't risk bumping into the reverend on the decks, so when I wasn't with Dr. Carson, I stayed inside the cabin with Hari for hours on end.

"You needn't stay inside on my account," Hari said as we settled into our reading chairs for the fourth day in a row. "I'm feeling much better these days. I might even go to dinner tonight. You should see if you can find Lady Persephone, perhaps have tea with her."

"It's just that I'm so caught up in this novel I borrowed from the little library by the dining room." I waved the penny dreadful at her. "Can't wait to see how it turns out."

It was a lie. The book was deadly dull, so with nothing much to do to distract myself, my mind gave way to my worries. Out of everything that was weighing on me, the money Hari had taken from Charles was the most concerning. Could a wife be charged with theft from a husband? Possibly, I thought, but I doubted Charles would risk the scandal. He would demand the money back, taking it by force if he chose. If things didn't go as Hari thought, what recourse would we have? How could we appease Charles? We had no power in the equation. I thought of Lady Persephone and her position of superiority over Richard because of her familial relationship with the prime minister. That's when it struck me. Hari and I had another option, a back door to power over Charles.

"Hari," I said, looking up from the book in my lap. I hadn't turned a page in twenty minutes.

"Yes," she said absently, still reading herself.

"I had a thought."

Hari rubbed her eyes and set her book down. "What is it?"

"There's a flaw in Charles's plan to adopt Mary's children. He has to convince the Committee of Privileges to allow an adopted child to inherit the title. He may or may not be successful."

"We discussed this. It's an opportunity for him to try with me."

"Of course. And if you have a baby, that would be ideal. If, though, you continued to have difficulties, you . . . could look elsewhere for an heir." I said it as gently as I could, not wanting to remind her of her problems.

"Where else? His cousin has no children, and he and his wife must be middle-aged by now."

I took a deep breath before I spoke again. "Me. What if I were to have a son? Just as Charles is heir to his uncle's fortune and title, my child might play the same role for Charles. A nephew by marriage has a far superior claim over an adopted child. It could give us the upper hand. We would be a route to

Charles's success, as opposed to an obstacle. Right now, he has all the power. This could be our chance to gain some of it back."

When I met Harriet's gaze, I saw tears shining in her eyes. "And, it would mean you could come home someday. Char, you would really do that for me?"

"I'd be doing it for us. And you've cared for and protected me for so long. It's my turn."

Hari looked truly happy for the first time in a very long time. "You and your husband could settle on an estate nearby. We would have such fun together, just like the old days."

We basked for a few moments in the rosy glow of a perfectly planned future, full of optimism for a change. I imagined myself living close to Hari, sharing the joy of rearing my children. My husband would be a kind and loving father. I tried to conjure an image of him in my mind but he was a shadowy figure, beyond my imagination.

We were interrupted by a soft knock at the door, and I went to answer it. A cabin boy I recognized from belowdecks stood outside with a note, which he handed to me. I opened it.

Come at once. Sarah needs you.
    Carson.

She must be in labour. I felt my heart surge with adrenaline. "Who is it?" Harriet called.

I quickly crushed the paper and shoved it into my pocket, then turned to her. "Just a cabin boy letting us know that there's a knitting group starting up in the tearoom." I smiled. "I think I'll go."

Hari gave me an odd look. "You're interested in knitting?"

"Perhaps if I'm to be a mother one day I should learn."

"I can't imagine a more boring prospect, but be my guest."

I told Harriet I would see her later, then said goodbye. Outside, the boy was waiting for me, and I followed him to the lowest deck and through the dark, narrow hallway at the rear. I felt the roll of the ship much more keenly here, and I had to hold the rope handrail to keep my balance. There were no portholes or windows of any kind this low in the water. The air was humid and foul. We were deep in the bowels of the boat, and the sounds of a ship at sea were all around us. Like the old woman she was, the ship groaned and creaked with every gust of wind or ocean swell.

Florence, Emma, and Alice were standing outside Sarah's cabin.

"We wanted to give her some privacy," Florence said, pressing my arm. "She's in a lot of pain. Please, help her."

I nodded and entered the dim, hot cabin, which smelled musty, like tobacco and beeswax. Inside, there was barely enough space for one person to stand upright with the low ceiling and the four sets of wooden bunk beds. Dr. Carson was attending to Sarah, who was leaning back, knees bent, on the left lower bunk, naked except for a coverlet across her chest. Her wet hair was tied in a knot to the top of her head and perspiration dripped from every feature of her face.

I reached for her hand and leaned in close. "I'm here, Sarah. I'm going to help any way I can."

"Is that you, Miss Charlotte?" she whispered. "I'm so very grateful, truly I am. This little one is taking its time."

I turned to Dr. Carson. "How long has she been in labour?"

"Since last night." He frowned. "The Burks didn't tell me until this morning."

I suspected the Burks felt Sarah deserved to suffer for what they perceived as the sin of unwed motherhood. I took a cloth and patted Sarah's brow. "You must be exhausted."

She didn't reply, just squeezed my hand tightly and let out a slow moan that built in intensity. She curled her body forward as if wanting to bear down.

"Hold on," Dr. Carson said. "This contraction's almost done. They're coming faster now. It'll be time to push soon, but not yet. When you feel the urge to push, start panting until it passes."

Sarah fell back on the cot, breathless. "I don't know how much longer I can do this."

"You're doing so well, Sarah," I said. "You're almost there. Soon, you'll be holding your baby in your arms, won't she, Dr. Carson?"

But he was bent over her belly with his stethoscope and listening intently.

"What can you hear?"

He pulled the device from his ears and straightened up. "The baby's heartbeat."

"Did you hear that, Sarah? Your baby's heart is beating." But she had dozed off. I turned to Dr. Carson, who had a grim look on his face.

"She's been in hard labour for over five hours," he said, pulling out his pocket watch and taking Sarah's pulse. "She needs to deliver the baby soon."

Sarah began to moan again as another contraction swept

over her. I mopped her brow with a damp cloth and murmured encouragement. When it passed, she collapsed back on her pillows and drifted off again.

"She's ready to push, but the contractions are not forcing the baby into the birth canal," Dr. Carson said after an hour more had passed with no change. He scrubbed his unshaven jaw with both hands. "I know how to fix broken bones, but not this. She's very weak. The baby's heart rate is slowing as well. There's not much time."

I had heard those same words before, in another place and time. My mind flashed to an image of Dr. Boyd, the veterinary surgeon, as he struggled to help one of our mares give birth on our farm. The mother was ready, but the foal wouldn't come. But Dr. Boyd knew what to do and he had shown me. I didn't know if it would work for Sarah, but I had to ask.

"When that same thing happened to mares on our farm, the problem was the position of the foal, but our veterinary surgeon was able to change it. Would we be able to feel the baby through Sarah's stomach, to check its position?"

"We can try."

Dr. Carson started with Sarah's stomach, gently prodding, feeling for the outline of the baby, its limbs, back, head, and bottom. It looked like he was gently kneading dough, but as he worked I saw Sarah's muscles become rigid. Another contraction was coming. Sarah didn't fight the pain but let the contraction take hold of her, too weak now to cry out. It washed over her, producing nothing. The baby had not moved. Dr. Carson's face was grey, his mouth tight.

"I have to feel the baby's head," Dr. Carson said to Sarah,

but her eyes were closed. He gently pushed his hand up into the birth canal. "I think the position of the crown is wrong. It's facing the wrong way. The contractions must be thrusting the largest part of the head into the base of the spine instead of the birth canal."

"Can you turn it?" I asked.

"I'm going to try," Dr. Carson said. "She'll have to stay as still as possible. It will be very painful."

"Sarah, listen to me," I said, shaking her awake. "We know how to get the baby to come out. This is going to hurt, but you need to try not to move while we shift the baby's position." I spoke directly into her ear. "Do you understand me?"

Her eyes were blank, lost in a sea of pain, but she squeezed my hand and nodded faintly.

We didn't need the precautions. I knew how painful it must be for Sarah, but she had lost so much of her strength that she didn't fight us. Dr. Carson's fingers gripped as much of the baby as he could and applied pressure, rotating the head and shoulders. I caught Dr. Carson's eye and smiled. He had changed the position.

"Now, Sarah, get ready to push on the next contraction," he said.

But then, Sarah's stomach rippled again, and Dr. Carson shook his head at me. It wasn't a contraction. The baby had flipped back to its original position. I looked at Sarah. Her eyes fluttered in and out of consciousness, and her hands lay limp on the bed. I couldn't just sit there and watch this lovely young woman and her baby die. The only thing we could do was to try again. With precious time running out, I stepped forward.

"Let me try," I said. "My hands are smaller than yours, and I might get a better grip on the baby."

Dr. Carson shrugged, but pointed to the washbasin set on a small chair between two of the bunks in one corner of the room. As I washed my hands and forearms thoroughly as he had taught me, I tried to visualize Dr. Boyd's actions during the birth of the foal. It had been such an emotional experience for me; I had a very clear memory.

I moved towards the end of the bed and took a deep breath, then pushed my hands into the birth canal, feeling for the baby's head. With all ten fingers, I gripped it as strongly as I dared and rotated clockwise. Again, there was movement, but the timing was perfect. A strong contraction immediately followed, and Sarah's body took over, as if relieved to be able to do what it needed to.

"I see the head!" I cried. "Push, Sarah, push!"

Sarah was suddenly awake, her eyes wide and focused, pushing with all her might. Dr. Carson came to my side and within seconds, the baby emerged, slippery and wet, and we caught it in our hands. Its little lungs filled with air and it let out a life-claiming cry.

"It's a boy!" I said. "Sarah, you did it."

Dr. Carson worked furiously to cut the umbilical cord and clean out the baby's mouth and nose before presenting him to Sarah. "Well done! Here is your son."

Sarah held her baby to her bare chest and ran her hand over his limbs, counting his toes and fingers. "He's perfect."

"Of course he is," I said. "And look at that hair."

She smiled, smoothing his matted dark curls and kissing him on the forehead.

I went to the door and let in Florence, Emma, and Alice, who rushed to Sarah's side with water, towels, and a little food. They congratulated Sarah and admired the new baby, giggling at his angry, indignant cries. A new peace settled over the room. I stood watching the scene, stunned at what had just transpired.

Dr. Carson turned to me, tired relief in his eyes. "You saved a mother and baby today. You should be proud."

I wiped my eyes, which had grown wet again with fresh tears. "I am."

Chapter Twenty

When I returned to the cabin, I was beaming ear to ear.

"I didn't know you enjoyed knitting so much," Harriet commented and I instantly sobered.

"I think I'm just tired. Too much squinting at the yarn."

I was grateful when she suggested we both order a supper tray and stay in for the evening. If the Burks were at dinner, I was sure they would make disparaging comments about unwed emigrant mothers, and I was in no mood to suffer their nonsense.

The next morning, I woke early to the sounds of the ship springing to life, the drumbeat of many scurrying feet, the call and response of orders echoing throughout the vessel. The thick ropes whipped through cleats, and then came the hard snap of sails stretched tight by the wind. The ship was once again under full sail. But my first thought was for Sarah, and I rose, dressing quickly, and scurried out of my cabin, taking the servants' route to the lowest deck. As I passed through the kitchen, the clatter of large metal cooking pots accompanied the cook's cussing.

"Porridge will be ready when I say it's bloody ready," he shouted to the crew. "Leave me alone and stop pestering me, you nackle-ass buggers."

I kept moving towards Sarah's cabin. At my gentle knock, she beckoned me in. Sarah was sitting up with her baby and she smiled at me as I entered. Her face no longer was a mask of pain.

"Have you had anything to eat yet?" I asked.

She shook her head. "The others just left to cook breakfast. It'll take awhile." Her voice was a whisper croaked from a dry throat.

As a first-class passenger, I could take breakfast anytime. "How about some porridge with a little milk? I can run off to the galley."

"Yes, please, and tea too. I would love some tea."

"Of course." I headed for the kitchen.

Juggling a breakfast tray, I backed into Sarah's room, pushing open the door to the cabin with my derrière. I set the tray across her lap, then took the baby from her. I felt a surge of affection for the tiny being I held in my arms.

"Have you given this little one a name?" I asked, nuzzling him. He smelled of mother's milk and mild soap.

"Aye, Jacob, after his father. He was a fine, strong man. This little man will always remind me of him."

"It's a lovely name."

I watched with satisfaction as she took a long drink of the milk and sugar-sweetened tea before attacking her porridge with the dedication of someone who had not eaten in over a day.

When she was finished, I handed Jacob back, and she grasped

my hand. "You saved me, and now my son will get a chance at
life. He'll meet his grandpa in the New World."

"I'm just happy to have helped."

"I want to give you something as a thank-you."

"Oh, that's not necessary," I said. I was sure she could ill
afford any sort of gift, but hugging Jacob to her chest, Sarah
padded across the floor to her small trunk where she retrieved a
leather satchel. She pulled loose the ribbon that held the cover
closed, and sifted through a small stack of vanilla-coloured
parchment papers bearing official-looking stamps. She handed
me one, then settled back on the bed.

"What's this?"

She pointed to a flurry of signatures and imprint seals and I
read *Bearer Certificate, One Share, China Bar Claim, struck in accor-
dance with the laws of the Colony of British Columbia, July 1859.*

"My father buys this sort of thing all the time. They're shares
in a mining claim that looks promising. He pays a few coins
and then sells them when they hit pay dirt. Father's always been
so very clever. I want you to have one."

"I can't possibly take it, Sarah."

She rocked Jacob back and forth. "It's yours. Please. It's only
one share; Father sent me ten. Right now, it's not worth much.
But if they strike it rich, who knows?"

I could see her feelings would be hurt if I continued to
refuse, so I relented.

"Tell me about your father. How is it that he came to settle
in the colonies?"

"His name is Henry Roy. I'm very proud of him and so I
went back to my maiden name after Jacob died. He went to

British Columbia two years ago to try to find something better. He had a hard time of it in England, couldn't get work." She paused, studying me closely. "He's not white, you see. He was once a slave in Brazil. I don't tell that to everyone."

"Oh," I said, letting her words sink in. "I thought you were Spanish or from the north of France."

"Most people do." She looked at me. "It makes things easier for me."

"Why did you tell me? Do the other women know?"

She shrugged. "You saved Jacob's life, Charlotte, and mine. I want you to know who I truly am."

"You're not the only one with secrets," I said, then told her how I had come to be on the *Tynemouth*. Last night had forged a new bond between us, and I felt I could trust her, and finally being able to share my secret with someone other than Hari relieved some of the weight on my shoulders. I didn't relay all the details, but enough that she understood what had happened between me and George. "So you see," I said. "Your secret is safe with me."

"And yours with me," Sarah said. "I am sorry for what you've been through, Charlotte, but a small part of me is glad that it brought you into my life. Without you, I wouldn't have my son." She smoothed Jacob's hair. "And you won't have to keep my secret for long. Once I go to my father, my heritage will be quite obvious. But he says things have been better for him in the colony than in England. And, of course, in Brazil."

Charles used to talk of the trade advantage that the plantation owners with slaves enjoyed. But I realized now that he saw it strictly on economic terms with no thought to the human suffering. I hadn't ever contemplated their lives either, nor had I ever really thought about the freed slaves I saw in England, but if the past month had taught me anything, it was that the world was much bigger than what I saw in my daily life back home.

"Tell me more about your father," I said.

Sarah smiled, displaying her perfect white teeth. "He worked on a rubber plantation in Brazil, but when he was twenty, his old master brought him to England. New laws banned slavery while they were there, and his master was forced to set him free."

She told me how he had met her mother, Annie, on a farm when she was just sixteen. The farmers had taken her in as a servant years earlier when she was orphaned. They were happy together for a time, and then the farm was sold. The new owners said they would keep her mother, who was white, but not her dad.

"That's about the time Mum got sick and died. I was just two. My dad took odd jobs but was always the last hired and the first let go. When I got married, he left to find a new life in the colonies. He thought Jacob would take care of me, and he did, until he was killed in the army. I was so alone. I wrote to my father and he told me to come. I didn't have enough money for passage, so I signed up with the Emigration Society." I was deeply touched by her story. She had been through so much more than me.

"And you're going to see your father again soon and present him with his new grandchild."

"Yes," she said. "I just have to get to Barkerville. That's a town in the goldfields where my father is. He owns a restaurant there. He says there's lots of ways to make money. I'm not sure yet what I will do, but I know he'll take care of me and little Jacob."

How lovely, I thought, *to have a father waiting for you in the New World, someone to help guide you and provide loving support.* Perhaps my own father would have done that for me had he lived. Since Harriet had told me the truth, I found myself thinking of him differently now.

I stayed with Sarah until her cabinmates returned, then I gave the sleeping Jacob a little kiss on the forehead and said my goodbyes. As I turned to go, I almost walked right into John Crossman, who was in the process of knocking on the door.

"Sorry," we both said in unison. I tried to step past him, but he turned as well. "How are Sarah and her baby doing?"

"They're both doing very well," I said curtly. "Thank you for your interest. She needs her rest, best not to disturb her." I started down the hallway.

He gently touched my arm to stop me. "Have I done something to offend you, Miss Harding? I haven't seen you since dinner the other night. I confess, I had been hoping to spend some time getting to know you while we are on this journey together."

I found the directness of his speech strangely compelling. "It's not you, Reverend Crossman," I said, meeting his eye. "It's the company you keep, or should I say, your choice of friends."

"Choice of friends? The only friend I've spoken of is George Chalmers. Georgie Porgie, we used to call him. He was a mean little boy." He studied my face. "I suspect he's a mean adult, despite what Lady Persephone says. He just hides it better. How did he offend you?"

"You've not heard gossip about my entanglement with him?"

"I haven't heard any gossip, and if I had, I'd have ignored it. If George caused you pain or trouble in any way, then he's no friend of mine." His warm breath felt like the gentle brush of a feather on my neck. "I like you, Miss Harding. I want to get to know you a little better. Will you let me? Perhaps we could have tea tomorrow. At four o'clock?"

I knew Hari would never approve. Reverend Crossman had not been formally vetted and was not officially courting me. I knew I should not waste my time in a liaison that had no future, but I was drawn to him. It seemed we saw life through a similar lens. I should have demurred—offered a polite but firm refusal. I knew very well not to say yes, but I found myself nodding hesitantly.

Chapter Twenty-one

The tearoom was crowded, but we found a lovely table for two by the front window where we welcomed the cooling breeze. We were now sailing off the southern coast of North Carolina and the day was sunny and hot. I had dug deep into my trunk for a summer dress and had had to air it out. It was one of my favourites, a full-skirted cotton in yellow-and-white gingham with white lace around the neck and three-quarter sleeves. I had completed what I thought was a rather jaunty look with white lace gloves and a straw hat with matching ribbon.

I had debated whether or not to tell Hari I was having tea with Reverend Crossman but decided against it. What was there to discuss, really? We had simply agreed to get to know each other a little better, nothing more. Perhaps I was taking the easy way out. Hari might have angrily objected, but since I left her wrapped in a blanket, snoozing on a deck chair, I doubted she would ever know and there would be no harm done. So why was I thrilled at the closeness of him next to me now?

"Shall I pour, Reverend Crossman?" I asked when tea and a plate of cakes arrived.

"Yes, thank you, and call me John, please. May I call you Charlotte?"

"By all means." I managed to pour the tea without spilling a drop. "Cream and sugar, John?"

His mouth twitched up into a smile at the sound of his first name, and I had to admit that it was surprisingly comfortable to address him so informally.

"Yes, please," he answered, then held out the plate of cakes. Never one to turn down an offering of sweets, I chose a lovely ginger cake and took a bite.

"From what little I know of you, it's my guess that you ran a bit wild on your farm as a little girl. Am I right?" he said, struggling to grip the dainty handle of the teacup in his large hand.

I nodded. "Everyone called me a tomboy. Riding ponies, playing with the farm animals, that was my sort of pastime. My poor mother despaired, rather like your mother did, I gather. Hari was really my only playmate. We had a grand time inventing games and playing practical jokes on our parents and Wiggles, our governess."

"You had a governess named Wiggles? How very lucky for you."

I told John how I came to christen Miss Wiggins as Wiggles and he let out a booming laugh that I was starting to associate with him. I'd never been good at making ready small talk, but I found it easy to talk to John. He was a good listener, which encouraged me to open up about my life.

"Wiggles actually advised me to come on this journey," I said, and explained about the necklace. "I wasn't seriously considering coming, but of course, other events transpired . . ." I stopped, realizing what I was saying. Despite John's genuineness, I didn't know him well enough to share my scandal.

"The important thing is that now you're here, Charlotte," he said.

I was grateful he didn't pry. Best to stick to other topics, I thought. "Tell me, how did you become interested in smallpox? Why travel to British Columbia?"

His smile faltered and I worried that I had taken the conversation in a direction *he* did not want to go. "When I was little, I loved to read real-life adventure stories. For my twelfth birthday, my uncle gave me a copy of Captain George Vancouver's journals written in 1792, when he sailed and mapped much of the northwest coast of North America. I savoured every bit of the story. Both the good and the bad."

"The good and the bad?" I echoed, taking a sip of tea.

John stared off into the dazzling expanse of ocean for a moment. "There were descriptions of a beautiful land covered in massive forests that came right up to the shoreline, sandy coves replete with salmon, halibut, and shellfish. There were pods of whales and vast colonies of sea lions. On shore, there were huge numbers of game. It was a northern Garden of Eden, but with no people. It made no sense."

"How so?"

"There were small communities up and down the coast, but not what he would have expected. The land could have supported so many more. Vancouver couldn't figure it out until he started to find large abandoned town sites. There were canoes piled along the shores and evidence of once-thriving commerce. He sent a crew ashore to investigate. They found deserted villages full of skulls and bleached bones everywhere. People had simply died where they lay and there was no one to left to bury them. A large population had been wiped out by smallpox."

"That's awful. Rather like the black plague in Europe?"

"Considerably worse, I think. They started to rebuild their communities, but last March, a gold seeker from San Francisco arrived infected with smallpox. It quickly spread to the ship-yard workers who are largely Natives. The colonial govern-ment's method of dealing with it was to put all the sick into canoes and tow them back to their people up the coast. You can guess the result."

The cake I had been eating turned to dust in my mouth, and I swallowed the dry lump. I drew a rather shaky sip of tea, too shocked by the story to respond.

"Mining has already put poisonous chemicals into salmon-spawning streams and rivers, and fish are dying. Those Natives who survive smallpox are forced to take low-paying jobs in harsh conditions like the coal mines. Disease has spread like wildfire, and the women have no choice other than to sell themselves to white men. That's why I'm here," John said finally. "The epi-demic will be well established by the time I get to the col-ony, but there'll still be lots to do, what with trying to improve working conditions and stopping the worst of the exploitation, and who knows when the next wave of infection will hit."

I couldn't imagine the horror of watching all your loved ones, and every person you ever knew, become sick and die over the course of a few days and knowing you would die soon as well. And the few who did survive faced new horrors.

The empire had already bought misery to the most vulnerable. It was all so shocking. My own problems seemed so trivial in comparison.

"You are a good man, John. At least you are trying to do something." I reached my hand out to touch his arm, then remembered myself, and withdrew it, masking my gesture by taking another cake. "Your work is admirable. It'll save many."

"As is your work. I think what you're doing with Dr. Carson is admirable as well."

I caught my breath. "What I'm doing with Dr. Carson?" I asked.

"The emigrant ladies told me you are 'better than Florence Nightingale herself.' They said the crew are very thankful for your nursing and that you saved little Jacob's life."

"You're being kind, John, but I have a selfish motive. I'm only trying to help my sister."

"I guessed she had a problem. I've seen it before, the look of laudanum—some of the women in my mother's circle had it." I must have looked upset as he quickly added, "Don't worry, I won't mention it to anyone."

I felt somewhat reassured, but at the same time I was painfully aware that I didn't know him well enough to be sure I could trust him. I hadn't even told Sarah about Hari. The ship took on a slight roll and I moved the teapot to the middle of the table so it wouldn't tumble off.

"I'll be thankful when I'm on dry land again. I much prefer a horse to a ship," John said, a mischievous twinkle in his eyes. "I can usually get them to halt when I've been tossed around enough."

"You ride a lot in the colonies?" I asked, happy to be chatting about something else.

"My main mode of transport. It's how I hide from my enemies as well."

"You have enemies? What sort?"

"There are many who take a dim view of the work I do with the Natives. Mainly land-hungry miners and farmers, and big companies. It's easier to take land and not pay compensation when the rightful owners have died off or have been worked to death in overcrowded work camps."

I realized now what he was getting at during his conversation with Sir Richard at dinner. "That's terrible. Truly," I replied. "How does riding horses help you hide from these people?"

"Cattle drovers, or cowboys as the colonials call them, move cattle all over the open ranges, and no one bothers them. That's just part of life there. I simply join them and blend in. I can travel the whole territory, and no one is the wiser. I stop at all the remote villages along the routes and do my work. I show the people how to inoculate their own and explain where they can get supplies when they have used what I leave them."

We fell into an easy silence as we sipped our tea. I was pouring a second cup for John when I saw a quick movement on my right side. It was Mrs. Burk disappearing behind a pillar. She had been watching us. How much had she heard? In my agitation I sloshed tea over the side of the cup into the saucer.

"I'm sorry, Reverend Crossman. It's been lovely getting acquainted, but I should be checking on my sister."

"Charlotte, what's the matter?" he asked, but I was already standing, hurrying off, leaving him crestfallen behind me.

Chapter Twenty-two

That night I lay awake, plagued with guilt, and the prickly humidity didn't help. I kicked off my bedspread and lay on my back, my damp cotton nightdress sticking to my clammy body like the fuzzy skin of an overripe peach. I didn't even bother to wipe the endless sweat from my forehead.

I should have told Hari what I was up to, but it all seemed so innocent at the time. I hadn't expected to be quite so taken with John, to find him so commendable and, at the same time, charming and fun-loving. I was at a loss as to what to do, so I got up, lit a lamp, and wrote to Wiggles. It was a long, newsy letter full of my escapades to date. I knew she would cherish every word as she lived my adventures vicariously, but I ended it with a note about John, confiding my fledgling feelings for him. I planned to include the letter in the packet to be sent back to England. I returned to my bed, slightly relieved at having gotten my thoughts out on paper.

The next day, the ship was buzzing with excitement as Bermuda was clearly visible in the distance. Tomorrow, we would anchor in the Royal Naval Dockyard and, though no one was allowed ashore, the ship would be bringing fresh food and water on board along with the mail and some broadsheets from London. The promise of news from home had everyone in high spirits, and we received an invitation from Sir Richard and Lady Persephone to attend a dinner party to mark the occasion.

Anxious not to squander her opportunities with Lady Persephone, Hari was determined to go. She had just finished her last quarter dose of laudanum, and her health had blossomed. The dry, tight skin around her mouth and eyes had regained its plump, youthful suppleness. The lank, brittle hair she had struggled recently to tame lay coiled in a smooth, shiny knot atop her head. I was heartened to see her yellowing, cracked nails had become milky white once more. Her moods were more stable and predictable as well, and I did my part to not let anything upset her.

As we finished dressing, I took Wiggles's necklace from my jewellery box. It made the perfect accessory to my evening gown, and it felt right to mark this occasion by wearing it.

I was admiring it in the mirror when Hari came to my side. "I couldn't have done this without you, Char. You've helped me regain my health and my sanity." She put her arm around me. "Not to mention my hope. I have faith in the future once again, no easy task after what's happened, but we got through it together."

"You did the hard part, Harriet."

"Is Dr. Carson happy with the compensation? Was it enough money?"

I dropped my eyes to my jewellery box and fished around

for some earrings. "He's fine. No need of more money." I didn't like lying to her, but it had been the only way to get her to agree to stop taking the laudanum. And it wasn't as if she hadn't lied for my protection in the past. Of course, I now realized with some regret that my work with Dr. Carson was at an end. I had enjoyed ministering to the crew and I would miss many of them. I had grown rather attached to seeing their faces each day.

As we made our way to the dining room, I felt a flutter of nerves in my stomach at seeing John now that Harriet was with me. How could I pretend there was nothing between us? Would he mention our tea? Would Mrs. Burk?

A section of the main dining room had been roped off for the exclusive use of the private gathering and everyone was honouring the celebration in their best formal attire. We entered and joined our usual group, who all congratulated Hari on her return to good health.

After complimenting Hari, John lingered by me. "Lovely to see you again, Charlotte. That's a beautiful necklace. Is that the one Wiggles gave you?"

Hari raised an eyebrow but said nothing.

My hand went to the pendent, and I felt my cheeks grow warm. "Yes, yes, it is. Thank you."

Harriet pulled me towards the table. "Since when did he start calling you Charlotte? A little presumptuous, don't you think?" she whispered as we took our seats.

I shrugged, and then Captain Hellyer sat between us, putting an end on our conversation.

After Reverend Burk's signature long-winded grace, the

conversation flowed freely with speculation over the political happenings in England since we'd left. Near the end of the soup course, Mrs. Burk began to speak loudly and soon dominated the discussion with her complaints about the second-class passengers' poor attendance at their regular Bible study sessions. Then, she suddenly turned to John.

"My husband tells me that you marry the gold miners to the Native women. I thought he was making a joke. Is it true?"

"Surely everyone has the right to a church marriage if they choose?" John said.

"The women are heathens, and the men are only with them for convenience," Reverend Burk said. "Heathens can't be married in the High Church. Maybe you are better off in England, Reverend Crossman, where these ideas are popular with some of the bleeding hearts. Ideas like yours cause trouble in the colonies."

"I disagree," John said seriously. "It should be a decision left up to the individual, not the Church. Some of Victoria's most distinguished couples have chosen *not* to be married in a Christian ceremony. They are the Hudson's Bay fur traders and their Native wives, married 'after the custom of the country,' as they say, and are in long, loving relationships." John looked pointedly at Mrs. Burk and continued. "Governor and Mrs. Douglas are prime examples. Amelia is the Métis daughter of an Irish trader and a Cree woman whose own father was a chief. James served as a clerk to Amelia's father, who married them in a country ceremony. They chose to reaffirm their vows nine years later in a Christian service only because of public pressure."

Mrs. Burk scoffed, but John's argument intrigued me. I had

never met anyone so open to new ways of seeing the world, but my hands grew clammy at the tension now building in the room. If my conversation with Dr. Carson had taught me anything, it was that many would see John's views as blasphemous, even dangerous.

Lady Persephone coughed, clearly uncomfortable with the direction the conversation was taking. More than anything I guessed she was concerned with maintaining social decorum. Hari took her cue to move the discussion to a less controversial topic, the beautiful weather we were now enjoying, but Mrs. Burk was not one to back down.

"Tell me, Miss Harding, what is your opinion? You and Reverend Crossman both seem to have soft hearts. I see you working with Dr. Carson helping the sick crew, and I hear you assisted him with the birth. What do you think?" A slow smile spread across her face.

I felt the muscles in my chest tighten, and I glanced at John. I could tell by the look on his face that he hadn't said anything. Hari's eyes were boring into my skull, but I couldn't meet her gaze. I scanned the faces around the table. Dr. Carson was studying the bottom of his soup bowl and Lady Persephone had set down her cutlery, her attention focused on me expectantly.

"Administering to the crew?" Sir Richard said. "Helping with a birth? Dear heavens! Whatever made you want to do that?"

I searched my imagination for a plausible argument in my favour. "I've been so inspired by the work of the great Florence Nightingale, a—a beacon of hope for our poor soldiers and a woman above reproach, don't you agree, Sir Richard?"

"I suppose so," he replied, a bit subdued.

In the silence that followed, I snuck a peek at Hari's face. Her expression had evolved from shock to anger, and I dreaded the end of dinner and the return to our cabin. I began to rub the emerald between my thumb and forefinger as if the simple touch could conjure comfort and affection from Wiggles.

Chapter Twenty-three

"What the devil has been going on?" Harriet cried. "You were working with Dr. Carson as a *nurse*? I thought we talked about that. You promised you would be on your very best behaviour."

We had only just stepped back into our cabin after dinner, and she was demanding answers.

"I know, but he needed my help, and he didn't want our money. You were so ill, and I had to find a way to get you the laudanum. No one knew what I was doing until Mrs. Burk started putting her nose into it. It was harmless."

"Well, that's all over with now. You need to tell Dr. Carson tomorrow. Promise me."

"I promise. I will return the key to the surgery first thing and tell him I am quitting. I was going to anyway." I sat on Hari's bed and unlaced my dress shoes. They had been pinching my feet all evening. Hari went over to her small dressing table and began unpinning her hair.

"Fine, but what is going on between you and John Crossman? Don't think I didn't pick up on that."

"Hari, we've only had one tea together. He's not courting me. But if he were to declare his intensions," I paused, mustering up the courage to be honest, "I would be interested. I find him quite charming. We have much in common."

"We know nothing of his family, where they come from, and what sort of position they hold in society."

"He told me he's from Yorkshire. His father is a wealthy landowner, and he's to inherit . . ." I trailed off. "Not that that's what matters to me. He's kind, and a free thinker who deeply cares about others."

She came over to me. "But you have to admit, he's an odd sort. Is he even a properly ordained minister? It could all be lies. In truth, he reminds me of our father, and look how well that turned out for Mama." I could smell lavender and face powder as she leaned in. "Marriage is all women have. You know that full well, Charlotte. And to marry, you need to protect your virtue, not throw it away on some girlish romantic whim!"

"This is not a romantic whim! He's the first man I've ever truly felt a connection with. It's not just romance, there's something deeper."

"You haven't learned anything, have you?" Harriet said, her voice bitter. "Women don't get to choose their lives. We adapt our lives to the man we marry, the man who protects and supports us. The right sort of men."

"Men like Charles and George, you mean?"

"No. Men like Cousin Edward, for example."

"Edward? The man who cares more for his prize roses than his own children? Not to mention that he is our first cousin. How could he have possibly been right for me?"

"Marriage to first cousins happens in the aristocracy. We could have kept the estate if you married Edward. Mama told me it was a missed opportunity."

I felt my face go hot at the thought of my near miss, and at the two of them plotting my future without any regard for my wishes. In all honesty, I couldn't really fault them. Not once did I ever speak up for myself or challenge them. If I had married Edward, we probably wouldn't be in the predicament we were now. But there was still a part of me that resisted everything that Harriet was saying, a part that wanted my fate to be of my own making.

"Life is dealing us a whole new hand," I said, unclasping my necklace. "Let's play it and see where it takes us."

"And what if it takes us to another disaster?" she pressed. "You don't have the best track record, Char."

"Neither of us do."

It was such a rare thing for Hari and me to have strong words, and both our faces were flushed.

"It was just a cup of tea," I said, quietly but firmly. "But I'm going to take it further and see what comes of it."

Hari took a long look at me, as if seeing me anew.

Chapter Twenty-four

I had a fitful sleep, only dozing off in the early hours of the morning, and as a result, I overslept. Sunlight streamed through the window and outer door seams, filling the room with light. My first thought was for Harriet. I regretted some of what I had said last night to her and hoped we could make amends today. I swung my feet out of bed and padded towards the door to her room, but she wasn't in her bed. Had she already gone to breakfast?

I dressed quickly, cursing myself for not hanging up my gown the night before. I had left it lying across the top of my trunk and now it was in a heap on the floor. Outside, I squinted into the blinding light and was surprised to see us tied securely to a brightly painted blue dock. We were here. The island of Bermuda. Tall palm trees beckoned from a distance, and the intoxicating smell of tropical flowers infused the air. The ocean had lost the dark blue palette of the North Atlantic, replacing it with an exotic aquamarine.

Sir Richard would be sending off his letter to the prime minister, but mine would go to Wiggles as well. And of course, there would be news from home. I was sure the broadsheets would be in hot demand this morning.

The breakfast room was buzzing with excitement, and I could see several ladies absently nibbling at their breakfast as they pored over letters from home, while others, mostly the men, had broadsheets laid out on the table in front of them. A few patrons glanced up at me curiously as I scanned the room for Harriet. Where was she? Mrs. Burk appeared at my elbow. After last night, she was the last person I wanted to see.

"Charlotte, I didn't expect to see you out and about today."

I had no time for her nonsense. "Why is that?"

A wide grin spread across her face. "Why, the news from home! How is your poor dear sister? We all feel so sorry for her. Such a public humiliation!"

I stared uncomprehendingly at Mrs. Burk's large white teeth. Public humiliation? What was she talking about? Had news of George and me gotten out? I needed to find Harriet. I didn't even bother to excuse myself.

I searched the usual spots, the rows of deck chairs and the small library, everywhere encountering pointed looks and whispers. Eventually, I gave up and returned to our cabin. Hari lay on her bed with dishevelled hair, tear-streaked cheeks, and rumpled clothes.

"Hari, what on earth? I've been looking for you everywhere."

"You don't like my new look? This is what all the discarded, washed-up old women are wearing this season."

"What are you talking about?" I looked around the room. Strewn all over the floor were torn bits of paper. "What's all this?"

"Charles's solicitors have sent divorce papers." She made a sweeping gesture at the shredded papers. "You can see what I thought of them."

"Oh, my Lord!" I had expected the gossip to be about me. I knew Charles was ruthless, but never in a hundred years would I have predicated this. "Can he force the issue if you refuse?"

Hari's laugh was dry and hollow. "Too late. The divorce is duly executed. The papers don't require my signature. It's done. I'm a public laughingstock now."

"There must be some mistake. There has to be legal grounds for divorce."

"There is," Harriet said, picking at her fingernails. "Adultery."

"That's ridiculous! You were trying to have a baby with him. Surely we can fight this."

"It doesn't matter. No one would believe me."

"But what would make Charles think you've been unfaithful?"

"Dr. Randolph."

My mind flashed back to a cold rainy day and the image of a darkly handsome man solicitously helping Hari into her coach. "What's your doctor got to do with this?"

"He has a certain . . . reputation," Hari said, not meeting my eyes. "I lied before. I did wonder if the reason I wasn't getting pregnant was due to some problem with Charles, but of course, I couldn't say that to him. I needed to produce an heir at any cost. On some level, it made perfect sense. But . . ."

"But?" I held my breath, waiting for her next words, not sure if I wanted to hear them.

"I couldn't bring myself to do it. I wanted to save our marriage, not destroy it. And this is my reward. Charles convinced a judge to dissolve our marriage without any input from me. He even didn't give me a chance to explain."

I had been fearing retribution, though I couldn't have anticipated it would look like this. I sat next to Harriet. "Perhaps he didn't want to know the truth. His ambition blinded him. He saw a convenient opportunity and seized it. I'm sorry, Harriet. I know it can't be easy."

"I wasn't under any illusions that Charles and I were deeply in love, but I thought he held notions of honour and loyalty. The worst part is the broadsheets. The divorce is front-page news." Hari took a shaky breath. "That and a sketch of the new presumptive Lord Ainsley. Included in the picture are his three adorable adopted sons. The oldest, James, is named as his heir."

A dull anger churned inside me. I wished I lived in a world where I could give Charles a good telling off, make him right his wrongs, but I knew I would never get the chance. He was the winner of this high-stakes game. "We will weather this storm just as we have all the others. We'll build a new life in the colonies where no one has ever heard of us."

Even as I said it, I knew there would be no avoiding this scandal. This news would surely reach Victoria and everywhere else in the empire. There was no escape for Hari. I just prayed it wouldn't destroy her. I put my arm around her, but she grew rigid and pushed me away.

"Leave me now, Char," she said. Her eyes glazed over and she had an oddly detached look on her face. "All I want to do is sleep."

Chapter Twenty-five

Life on the ship changed drastically. While Captain Hellyer still occasionally asked us to dine with him, Sir Richard, Lady Persephone, and most of the other first-class passengers shunned us. Whenever we entered the dining room, there were stares and whispers. Other than Dr. Carson and John, no one invited us to join them. Dr. Carson expressed his sympathy for what Harriet was going through, as did John.

"It doesn't seem right," he said. "But these things are seldom fair to women."

He was so understanding and easy to talk to—part of me wanted to confide the whole story, but I couldn't betray Harriet's confidence. She was polite but cool to the two men and withdrew from shipboard society once again. I followed suit, and we took most of our meals in the cabin. Now, more than ever, I needed to make a good marriage. I was determined to make a home for Hari, just as she had for me when Papa died. As much as I liked him, John wasn't that man, but I was still drawn to him.

On the other hand, Hari no longer minded my working

with Dr. Carson, and I continued to do so. The work gave me the opportunity to see Sarah and little Jacob, and Florence, whom I had become quite close to. I appreciated that they didn't judge me the way the other passengers did. I didn't have much time to socialize with them though. Dr. Carson needed my help. The number of accidents belowdecks had spiked because of a change in weather.

Ever since we left Bermuda, it had become horribly hot and humid. With the winds nonexistent, the sails were tied off and the ship's steady progress came from the coal-fed screw engine alone. No trade winds provided relief from the hourly hauling of coal and stoking of engines. I was thankful we had replenished stores of laudanum, which we were handing out to treat burns and crushed fingers and toes with surprising regularity even for Dr. Carson.

As the weeks went by, Hari remained confined to our cabin, though once or twice in the night I woke to find her gone. I never asked her where she went, but assumed she was walking the deck when she could be alone and free of judging stares. When she wasn't sleeping, she lay listlessly on her bed looking off into space, saying little. The bloom that had flowered in her cheeks in recent weeks was on the wane. She was beginning to have the same hollow-eyed, white-faced look of before. I was deeply worried about her, but I had no idea how to help her this time.

I tried to draw her out with various things, a game of cards, or sweets I regularly bought from the small canteen. Wiggles had sent me a letter, and I even read it out loud in an attempt to buoy her spirits. It was full of news and a funny anecdote about how Edward had made a pompous fool of himself at the village flower show when his roses didn't win first place. It made me laugh. As much as our prospects were dire, I was thankful that my destiny was no longer caught up with him and his children.

∽

I was standing at the rail, looking forlornly out at the horizon, lost in my worries, when I felt the wind begin to pick up for the first time in weeks. I turned back to the deck, now a blur of activity as the crew scrambled to unfurl some of the sails. For so long, it had felt as if we were almost sitting still, but now, finally we were really moving. All I wanted to do was to get off the ship and be back on dry land.

Many of the first- and second-class passengers came out on top deck to admire the impressive clouds forming in the sky. I saw Sir Richard, Lady Persephone, and the Burks all taking in the sight. A group of young swells gathered at the railing, dressed as though they were heading out for a Sunday afternoon stroll in Hyde Park. They laughed and poked each other with their elbows, pointing at the clouds as they called out names like Thor's hammer, Odin's anvil, and Zeus's chariot with jocularity.

The names that the young men had given the formations were apt. I could imagine what the ancient Greeks would have thought of such a scene. There was Zeus himself, in a mighty chariot, drawn across the sky by four gold-winged chargers. His left hand was drawn back, preparing to release a deluge of lightning bolts. And behind him rode the lesser gods, coming to amuse themselves by wreaking havoc on the wretched mortals below. I had once had the good fortune to visit Covent Garden to attend a performance of Wagner's *Die Walküre* and hear "Ride of the Valkyries." Its bold percussions filled my head as I gazed skyward.

Sun caught the very highest snow-white plumes, giving them the inviting appearance of spun sugar, but below them, the clouds darkened ominously until the sky overhead turned from whitewashed blue to dark, angry grey, then black. A storm was coming.

I felt a nudge at my elbow. It was Hari. She looked pale and tired in spite of spending much of her time sleeping. Her hand sought mine and I gave it a squeeze, happy that she was up and out of our cabin.

"Ladies and gentlemen," Captain Hellyer called, coming out into the centre of the upper deck. "As you can no doubt see for yourselves, we are heading into a gale. The barometric pressure is extremely low, which means this will be a storm force we seldom see. But there's no need to panic. The *Tynemouth* is an extremely sturdy ship. She's withstood major gales in the Black and Mediterranean Seas when she was on duty with the Royal Navy. But for safety's sake, no one will be allowed on the decks for any reason during the storm, so I'd kindly ask you all to return to your cabins."

As people quickly began to disperse, Reverend Burk waved his arms in the air to capture Captain Hellyer's attention. "Please, Captain, a moment for the Lord. Let us pray for deliverance."

Without waiting for Captain Hellyer's permission, he and

Mrs. Burk clutched hands and bowed their heads. The captain sighed deeply, dropped his chin slightly, and closed his eyes.

"Let's go," I said to Harriet, a prickle of anxiety taking root in my brain. But our pace was slow because there were too many people in front of us blocking the deck, all trying to make it through the main door that led directly into the dining room.

"Dear Lord, look down upon these poor, wretched souls and save us from this devil-sent apocalypse," Reverend Burk began. "Smite the devil, dear Lord, so that we, with your grace, may survive this journey through the fringes of hell and live to glory in your bright light another day."

I smelled the tropical dampness—a mixture of palm, cocoa, and sugar cane—before I saw the rogue wave bearing down on us. It was still some distance away but moving at incredible speed. We had to go.

"And, Lord, for those of us wretched sinners who are not destined to survive this cataclysmic catastrophe, take us unto your bosom, Lord. Forgive us our sins and make room in the kingdom of heaven. Let us sit at the feet of Jesus for all eternity."

"Wave!" a woman in the crowd screamed.

Captain Hellyer looked up and saw the curtain of white headed towards us. "Everyone inside!"

There was a moment of eerie calm when the muggy air seemed to stand still, and then the crowd surged forward. Beside me, Harriet tripped, and as I stooped to reach for her, I felt a hand pulling me up.

"John," I said. He didn't say anything, only kept a tight grip on Harriet and me, pulling us through the crowd.

"Bring her about, Mr. Fulbright," Captain Hellyer yelled shrilly at the pilot. The wind snatched at his words, but I could just make out, "Head into the wind or we'll be swamped!"

The boat lurched to one side and we struggled to remain upright as a sheet of blinding, stinging water pummeled the ship, surging over the deck and soaking our bodies. We worked our way along the deck, past several cabins until we reached our door. John didn't let go until we were safely inside.

The three of us stood there wet and shivering until I rummaged through our things and found towels to wrap up in. "Thank you for your help out there," I said to John. It was only then that I noticed he had a thick rope tied around his waist and crisscrossed across his chest and back.

"What's this for?"

"It's a harness so I can't be washed overboard."

"Why? You're not going back out there?"

"Yes, I'm moving the animal pens. The cow and pigs aren't safe where they are, so we're moving them up to this deck." He couldn't suppress a grin. "They'll be travelling first-class from now on."

"And so they should." I smiled back. "But be careful."

"Yes, please do take good care, Reverend Crossman," Hari said, and her voice was sincere. "You've been very kind to help us today. Thank you."

John nodded, then headed out of our cabin directly onto the storm-tossed deck. Hari and I set about changing out of our wet things and then we vowed to remain safely where we were for the storm's duration. But I couldn't help but worry about John.

Chapter Twenty-six

Ipoured myself a glass of sherry to steady my nerves and sat up with my book even though the gyrations of the ship made it hard to read. I was surprised Hari could sleep. I thought back to the first storm, when I discovered Hari's addiction. She had slept through that gale as well, I recalled. And then it struck me, her listlessness, declining health, and endless sleeping—Hari was taking drugs again.

"No, no, no, no," I muttered, getting up and going into her room. "Harriet," I said, but she didn't stir. Her breathing was very shallow and her pulse was hard to find. I opened the drawer in the bedside table. Several spent vials rattled in the bottom of the space. I had no idea how much she had taken today, but it must have been more than the two she took to get her through the first storm. I tried to shake her, but with no luck.

"How could you do this again?" I yelled, but I knew the answer. And I knew that she would die if I didn't get help soon. I had to find Dr. Carson.

As I opened the front door of our cabin, the storm, in all its fury, took my breath away. The sound struck me first. The wind had turned the sail spars on all three masts into high-pitched tuning forks, screeching a cacophony of vibrating flat notes, and my ears ached at the noise.

All I could see in any direction was a vast cauldron of boiling, churning seas. There was no rhythm or organization, as if the gods were fighting, each one throwing a different set of currents, winds, and wave directions into the pot, each one trying to claim superiority over the others as they toyed with the mortals below. A few waves were splashing over the railing, sending a skim of foamy seawater scuttling across the deck, like dozens of scurrying crabs trying to find purchase before being sucked back over the side into the boiling ocean once more.

I decided I could make a run for it. Just fifty feet on the outside deck, I figured. Once I was through the door to the dining room I could take the inside stairs down a deck to Dr. Carson's surgery. The whole trip would only take a few minutes. As I stood there, still-larger waves began breaking and some washed up against the door to our cabin. I turned to have one last look at Hari, then stepped outside. I slammed the door behind me and ran.

I gripped the handrail with all my might just as a giant wave hit me with shocking force. Fear numbed my limbs and kept me frozen there for a moment. A series of waves washed over me, threatening to whip my feet out from under me and send me skidding across the deck, but I held on to the railing for dear life, advancing forwards hand over hand.

After what seemed like an age, I finally reached the dining room door, but with the wind billowing against me, I couldn't open the heavy oak door with my one free hand. Taking a breath, I let go of the handrail completely and pulled with all my might on the door. When a breaker hit with what felt like the strength of the entire ocean, I lost my grip. I screamed for help as I fell through the air and the cold black water.

Trapped in the churning wave I tumbled head over feet and flailed with both arms, trying desperately to find something, anything to stop me from being washed over the side. A sharp, intense pain rippled through my back as I struck something hard. My lungs demanded air as the wave began its retreat over the side of the ship, pulling me with it.

Another huge wave hit. The urgent protest from my lungs became a silent scream. I tried to swim through the swirling water, kicking with my feet in the direction I thought was up. I snagged on something, or at least something powerful had me in a grip, and then I was being dragged. Gasping, I broke through the surface and opened my eyes to the angry face of John Crossman.

"What the hell do you think you're doing? You were to stay in your cabin," he bellowed at me.

"My sister needs help!"

Between coughing and crying, I said no more. My strength was gone. I could barely stand as he tethered us to the safety line. Then he threw me over his shoulder and, gripping the inside handrail, slowly inched his way along the row of cabins. He opened the door of one and unceremoniously dumped me on the floor of the darkened chamber, all the time cursing my idiocy in one long string of blasphemy.

I cut him off. "My sister has taken an overdose of her medicine. She needs Dr. Carson now."

He stopped his berating and turned back to the door. "I'll fetch him. Do not go anywhere."

Exhausted from my fight with the sea and from the fear of losing Harriet, I remained in a damp heap on the floor, whispering desperate prayers for all of us. The minutes dragged by. Where was John? Had he been lost? Finally, the door creaked open and I jumped to my feet and rushed over to him.

"How is she?"

"Carson's with her now," he said, running his hands through his dripping hair. He had a weary look in his eyes. "He's given her something. She's awake and breathing normally. He'll stay with her until it's safe for you to go back to your cabin."

"Thank God," I said, my teeth chattering. "And thank you, John."

He threw me a fur-lined robe. "Get yourself out of those wet things and wrap up in this."

He pointed to the adjoining servant's room, and I retreated there without another word. It felt wonderful to shed my sodden, seaweed-smelling clothes and wrap the plush fur robe around me. My red-chafed skin responded to its warm caress with instant pleasure, and my shivering ceased as warmth found its way to my extremities.

Bracing myself against an extreme roll of the ship, I opened the door to the main room a crack. I peered out and found John wrapped in a blanket sitting on the edge of his bed. He had poured two whiskies. He took a sip of one and held out the other for me. Stepping with some hesitancy from the privacy of the servant's nook, I moved into the room, accepted the glass of golden liquid, and took a sip. The alcohol sent warmth spreading through my chest, but it didn't erase the shock I still felt at how close I had come to death. If John hadn't found me . . .

"How did you know I was there?"

He shrugged. "I was checking on the animals and heard a scream."

Neither of us spoke for several minutes until John broke the ice. "All I can say is you're the strangest-looking mermaid I've ever plucked from the sea."

He pointed to the wall-mounted mirror. I gasped, then began to giggle at the sight. My hair had dried into an odd cone shape, sweeping across my forehead and spiralling up into a knot at the top of my head with a crown of broken coral protruding at the apex. My attempts to fix it only made it worse. The coral crumbled into tiny bits, and my hair remained hopelessly knotted.

My giggle turned into loud guffaws from the depths of my belly, and I didn't even try to collect myself. I just let go. It felt wonderful, a great purging of weeks of stress. John stared at me and then began to laugh himself until we were both lost in help-less mirth. When we regained our composure, the mood in the cabin had shifted. There was a hum of something new, some-thing amorphous. We were suddenly very aware of the closeness of our bodies. John leaned forward and touched his lips to mine. They were soft and gentle, and I lost myself for a moment until I remembered how inappropriate it all was—us sitting alone together, drinking, in a state of undress. My mind flashed back to the night of Hari's party, and panic prickled my skin.

"I'm sorry," I said, pulling away.

"No, I am," John said, getting up and walking over to the servant's room. "You have my bed, I'll bunk in here." He shut the door firmly between us.

I lay awake listening to the howling storm and thinking of John just on the other side of the door. An hour or so before a dim grey dawn, the wind diminished, and I finally nodded off. When I awoke, I could tell by the roll of the ship that the storm had subsided. John was still sound asleep. In spite of feeling sore from head to toe, I hurriedly dressed and slipped from his room.

When I got back to our cabin, Hari was sitting up in bed, a sheepish look on her face, and Dr. Carson was packing up his medical bag. A worried look passed between us. I knew what he was thinking. Where had Hari gotten the drugs and how could we prevent another overdose? I had no answers but resolved to get some, and soon.

Chapter Twenty-seven

By the time the seas were completely calm again, Harriet had regained most of her strength and I made a point of confiscating her vials of laudanum, but not before demanding she tell me where she got them.

"You are guileless, aren't you, Char?" Harriet said wearily. "So trusting. Once I found out you were working with Carson, I knew he would have given you keys to the surgery. It was easy enough to find it in your trunk, the trunk you rarely remember to lock."

My face reddened in shame. It was my lack of forethought that had caused this. I went to my trunk and rummaged for the keys, which I then tucked into my pocket. I wouldn't make that mistake again. There was still something that was bothering me about Harriet's actions.

I stood in the doorway of the main room and studied her lying on the bed. "After all you did to overcome your dependency, why slip back?"

"I've needed help to cope with the divorce."

"I know it's been hard, but burying your pain in drugs is not coping."

"I had no other way. I'm not like you. I have nothing else in my life. Being Charles's wife was everything. It was who I was, my identity. You have your books, your love of animals, and your interest in medicine. You could be perfectly happy as an unmarried woman."

I detected a note of jealousy in her voice, and I sat down on the edge of the bed. "Hari, you once told me that women define themselves through marriage. That's not true. The emigrant women taught me that. They are single and have endured hardship we'll never know, and yet they have made lives for themselves. They'll arrive in the New World with nothing but the spirit and resolve to start fresh and make the most of the opportunity."

Hari's eyes welled up with tears, but I wasn't through.

"You have more than most. It's time to forget Charles and your old life. You have me, and together we can create a good future for ourselves." I held up the keys for her to see. "These are going back to Dr. Carson today. You won't be getting any more laudanum from me or Dr. Carson."

Harriet sniffed and wiped at her eyes. "I don't even want it anymore. It doesn't comfort me like it used to."

It was a relief to hear her say that, and I wanted to believe that she was coming out of her depression, but I would have to wait and see.

In the following days, I didn't have much time to spend with Harriet as the storm had wreaked havoc on the rest of the crew and passengers, and Dr. Carson needed my help with injuries and unsettled stomachs. I ignored my own aching limbs and soldiered on while my bruises healed. I was relieved that Sarah and little Jacob had made it through all right. But there was no denying that everyone was desperate to be on land once again. Fortunately, we didn't have too long to wait. Within the week, we would be in Port Stanley in the Falkland Islands and its coaling station, the first of two more scheduled stops on our journey, and then we would finally be allowed to leave the ship.

We smelled the land before we saw it. It was mid-July, so winter in the southern hemisphere. It was cool but sunny, and after a month and a half at sea, the intoxicating smell of earth, grass, and newly overturned fallow fields rejuvenated our tired bodies like a tonic.

When someone cried out that they had spotted the light-house at Cape Pembroke, I ran to my cabin for my opera glasses.

"Harriet, we're nearly there," I cried. "Shall we go ashore together? I've written Wiggles, and I should like to post the letter." I also was eager to see if there was any news from her. She would have heard about Charles and Harriet by now, and I longed for her advice.

Harriet nodded, but she took her time dressing properly before joining me on deck. That didn't bother me. The fact that she was taking pains with her appearance once more was a good sign.

Excited chatter and anticipation reverberated through the crowd as the ship rounded a jut of land and we beheld the vast, busy harbour of Port Stanley. Under engine power alone, we glided past the many anchored vessels in the outer harbour and made for our mooring buoy closer to shore. I trained my opera glasses on the long dock running along the shoreline ahead of us. It was alive with all manner of commerce and trade, as crews from the many oceangoing vessels purchased goods from the locals. With arms waving wildly, they bartered for baskets of fruits, nuts, fresh and dried meats, water, and what looked to be luxuries, like alcohol and tobacco. I could only guess at how they made their purchases, likely an odd mixture of languages and gestures.

As Hari and I stood in line to go ashore, I searched the crowd for Sarah and the other emigrant women, and saw Lady Persephone and Sir Richard preparing to board the tender, but the women were nowhere in sight.

"You and your sister are going to town unescorted?" Mrs. Burk asked, appearing at our sides.

"Yes," I replied curtly. "And where are the emigrant women?"

"Oh, my husband won't allow them to go. So many cor-rupting influences on shore. But perhaps you and the former Mrs. Baldwin are not troubled by these things." She watched our faces for signs of distress, and when we showed none, she huffed and shuffled away.

In truth, I cared little for her pointed comments about us, but my heart was pained for Sarah and the women. They had suffered more than most, confined to windowless rooms on the lower deck and with only a small outside area to catch a few breaths of air, and I knew they were looking forward to getting off the ship, just like the rest of us, and I said so to Hari.

"Why don't you ask them if you can purchase anything on their behalf?" she suggested. "From everything you've told me, they deserve a bit of kindness."

"That's a lovely idea," I said, delighted that she had thought of it herself. I told her I would be right back and ran to the steerage deck.

Sarah was trying to take the news as stoically as possible, but she couldn't stop a few tears from escaping. Alice was quick to point out that the Burks themselves were happily going ashore. She declared the women should stand up for their rights and not be pushed around by the likes of "a two-faced blowhard preacher and his fat, stupid wife."

I commiserated with them, then offered to make purchases on their behalf and quickly put together a list of their needs and headed back to the debarkation point. Just as I reached the first-class queue, I bumped into John, who was carrying a large black bag with one hand and a well-worn leather satchel with the other. The sudden closeness made my lips tingle at the memory of our kiss.

He didn't seem to be suffering from any such memories. His eyes were alive with a new excitement. "Charlotte, I've received permission to visit the prison and vaccinate the inmates," he said. "Finally, I get to put my medical supplies to good use."

"That's wonderful, John. Good luck with it."

He smiled, and a small part of me wished I could accompany him and finally test my vaccination skills on more than just a piece of cloth, but I had promised the emigrant women, and besides, Hari was with me and I excused myself to find her now.

Once ashore, I could see the place was alive with people in all manner of dress and clothing style, representing the four corners of this vast world. A group of men who appeared to be of Eastern European descent wore billowy shirts trimmed with embroidered sashes, brightly coloured knee breeches, and high black boots. Kilted Scots and elegant English gentlemen mixed easily with swaggering voyageurs with their jaunty neck scarves and wide sashes tied around their middles. There were naval uniforms of every fashion and colour representing most of the seafaring nations of the world.

And there were women everywhere. Spanish ladies in vivid red and gold gowns, their hair shrouded by black lace, sat together off to one side of the open-air market, sheltered from the sun by their parasols while maids brought them samples of the merchants' wares. On the opposite side of the market were the women of East India. The sun danced off their gold headdresses and jewellery every time they moved.

Harriet and I sought out the Royal Mail office and I mailed my latest letter to Wiggles. Harriet asked if there was anything for her, to which the clerk shook his head. But there was a letter from Wiggles waiting for me. Feeling bad for Harriet, I tried to suppress my excitement and quickly tucked it away in my pocket, and we dutifully went about buying what the emi-grant women had requested. My shopping basket quickly filled with all sorts of everyday things that had become unimag-inable indulgences during the voyage. Sweet-smelling bars of lavender soap, beeswax hand cream, hair wash made with goat's milk. And then there were the teas and sweets.

Hari seemed content to trundle along after me, occasionally making a purchase for herself, but her heart wasn't in it, and when I suggested we stop at a quiet little spot for tea, she readily agreed.

Over tea I opened Wiggles's letter and began to read it out loud, thinking it might lift Harriet's spirits, but I stopped short when I saw Charles's name.

"What is it?" Harriet asked, studying me over her teacup. "Something about Charles?"

"Yes," I replied. "We don't have to do this now." I began folding away the letter, which was when I noticed there was a separate sheet of paper. It was the monthly bulletin from our church. Wiggles had circled a small announcement at the bottom of the page. I looked closer. It was a notice of the upcoming marriage of the Honourable Charles Baldwin to the widow Mrs. Mary Sledge. Charles had clearly lost no time moving forward. I looked up to see Hari holding out her hand.

"Show me," she said. "It's all right. I can take it."

Reluctantly I passed the notice to her.

"No doubt his title will follow soon," she said calmly after she had read it.

"He may be sorry if the Committee of Privileges rejects his appeal to let the oldest boy be next in line for the title."

"No, he won't." Hari took a sip of her tea. "He's counting on Mary to provide a legitimate heir. She's produced three healthy boys already."

She was right. Of course. I just hoped she realized that despite what she'd lost, she'd gained so much freedom. "Good riddance to Charles. He's well out of our lives. You have no one's expectations you have to live up to anymore."

"It's a curious feeling and strangely liberating to hear this." She raised her chin and met my gaze. "For so long, I've felt trapped in a life that was not of my own making. I married for wealth and position, certainly not love. In some ways, having Charles divorce me feels like I've sloughed off a huge burden. For the first time I've started to think about what would make *me* happy."

I reached across the table and put my hand on hers. She smiled and did not try to pull away, and then began to talk about what she might do in Victoria, open a fashionable dress shop or, maybe hats and gloves were more the thing in the colonies.

"It's a new beginning and this time it'll be on my terms. Perhaps I'll marry again, but if I do, it'll be for all the right reasons."

"Hari, you don't know how happy it makes me to hear you say that."

She squeezed my hand. "Well, this brings me to the subject of you and John."

"Yes?"

"If you want to pursue that relationship and see where it takes you, you have my blessing."

For a moment, I didn't know what to say. I was drawn to John and had played with the idea of marriage to him. I was still trying to decide what I would say if he asked, but I never expected Hari to be so open to the possibility. After all the secrets between us, it felt like we were truly starting over. Gratitude and love for my sister swept over me, bringing tears.

Over the next few days, Hari's health and spirits improved dramatically, and we made the best of our island stopover, packing each day with splendid outings and wondrous sight-seeing. We both abandoned our corsets—a first for Hari—and donned loose-fitting walking dresses and boots. The weather stayed cool but sunny, and we tramped for miles along the coast and over the hills, stopping often to marvel at the unparalleled sights, including the exotic array of birds and sea life. The highlight was the penguin colony, where we stayed for hours, laughing at the antics of these most unusual flightless birds.

That week, it felt as if the past years had disappeared, and Hari and I were children once more, free to roam and discover at will. We were just two sisters, sharing old jokes and retelling the stories of our girlhood. We answered to no one. They were priceless days that I would treasure in the weeks to come.

And then, before we knew it, it was our last night in Port Stanley. We were due to weigh anchor that evening, as soon as the captain had finished loading the fresh food for the final leg of the journey, and Hari and I decided that we would no longer hide in our cabin at dinner.

"Everyone will have heard of Charles's marriage by now. Let the gossips have their day," she said. "I no longer care."

I couldn't have agreed more. After we dressed in our finest gowns, we entered the dining room. Lady Persephone watched our progress through the room, but she made no offer to have us join her, Sir Richard, and the Burks. A few others looked up, surprised to see us in their midst after so long, but for the most part, they were engrossed in their own company.

A waiter beckoned us to a table for two. "Good evening, ladies. The captain asked me to invite all first- and second-class passengers to a dance party on the main deck after dinner. A post-storm celebration. In the meantime, please enjoy the special supper he brought on board for tonight—Falkland Island game hens in butter cream sauce."

"Shall we go to the dance?" I asked Harriet. "It's been so long since we've been to a party." The last one we had attended was Hari's infamous soirée that she had christened "A Fairy's Garden Party." That night had changed our lives forever, but tonight we had so much to celebrate.

"I've never seen you so excited about a party," Harriet said, a small smile on her lips. "You usually hate polite conversation."

"I guess I've changed," I replied. I was buzzing with excitement and for once, I pushed my dinner away, anxious for the fun to start. I waited for Hari to finish, heartened at her new robust appetite, but underneath the table my toes were tapping.

When we made our way to the main deck, it was already filled with an assortment of chairs and stools set in a semicircle. In the middle an odd group of musicians was preparing to strike up the first tune. I recognized their faces as fellow passengers and my heart quickened at the thought of them coming together to put on a dance. A few large, wooden chairs stood empty in the back row, and we claimed them as the volunteer band started a fiery jig.

I was so engrossed in the music that I didn't notice John

approach and extend his hand. "May I have this dance, Charlotte?" he asked, his blue eyes twinkling.

I felt a stir of excitement, but I hesitated, looking at Hari. She just nodded and smiled. This was the new Hari, I realized. She was seeing life through a different lens.

"I would love to," I said, placing my hand in John's large one.

He gently pulled me to my feet and carved a path to the dance floor, where couples were beginning to gather. He began a frenzied step dance punctuated by wrapping his great arm around my waist and twirling me through the air. I was a poor, uncoordinated dancer, but that mattered little as my feet rarely touched the ground. At first, I tried to find my footing, but eventually I gave myself over to John's lead and trusted him not to let go of me, as I was sure I might fly overboard.

By the third dance, my hair had broken free of the pins that held it and my carefully constricted chignon slid from the top of my head to one side. At a break in the music, I made a rather inept attempt to fix it.

"Don't," John said, leaning in close. "I rather prefer the mermaid look."

I laughed and, once more, felt the energy between us change. And at the moment, the music slowed. I went to return to my seat, but John took my hand.

"You can't leave just when I finally get a chance to put my arms around you," he whispered in my ear.

His warm hand pressed the small of my back, and I put my right hand in his and the other on his shoulder. For a man of his size, he was surprisingly graceful, and I felt equally elegant as we covered the floor with great swirling steps.

"You're a wonderful dancer," I said, looking up at him. My curiosity got the better of me. "It seems you've had plenty of dancing partners before me."

"Yes, many," he said. "But none like you. I certainly didn't expect to find someone so charming and intelligent on the voyage."

We continued to dance our slow waltz, and I had nowhere to look but into his cobalt-blue eyes. The rest of the world fell away. There was no boat under our feet, no people around us.

At the end of the evening, I scanned the seats for Harriet, but she must have already gone back to the cabin. John walked me to my door. Other passengers lingered on deck, so he politely kissed my hand before heading off to his own room. As I watched him go, I thought about what had transpired between us in the last weeks. I felt such a strong attraction to him, but a sliver of doubt lingered in my heart—not in John, but in myself. It was my own words that came back to me, what I had told Hari about the emigrant women being on the verge of real freedom.

As I stood on the threshold, I heard the metallic rumble of the ship's anchor followed by a gentle roll of the deck beneath my feet. We had set sail for the dreaded Cape Horn and the bottom of the earth.

Chapter Twenty-eight

I woke at first light to the sounds of someone being sick.

"Harriet?" I croaked, rubbing my eyes. "Is that you?"

I stumbled out into the main room, where Hari was pooled in a heap on the floor, vomiting into the blue basin. She looked up at me, face pale.

"I don't feel well, Char," she said hoarsely.

I went to her side and pulled her hair out of her face. Slowly, she told me that she had been vomiting for a couple of hours, and the pain in her stomach was getting worse. I helped her back into bed, then ran to get Dr. Carson.

"Others have this as well," he told me. He had examined Harriet and given her something to calm her stomach, and she was now asleep. "It came on so quickly that I think it must be some sort of food poisoning."

"But I'm not sick," I said, then I remembered the dinner of game hens I had pushed away. "Do you think she'll be okay?"

"At this point I don't know."

I detected a note of urgency in his voice that I had come to know. "Tell me honestly, Dr. Carson."

He sighed. "I wish she hadn't relapsed with the drug taking. She'll need all her strength to recover from this. The key is getting her to hold down fluids. I'll leave her with you. If she wakes up, have her suck on a cloth dipped in water."

After touching my arm lightly in sympathy, he closed the door behind him softly, but the hollow thud was enough to wake Hari from her fitful sleep. I sat gingerly on the edge of her bed.

"How do I look?" Harriet asked with a faint smile.

"As beautiful as always," I said, mustering a grin of my own. "More important, how are you feeling?"

"Better now. Just weak."

"Rest. I'm here to take care of you." I handed Hari the damp cloth, and her stomach seemed to tolerate the tiny bit of fluid.

There was a soft knock at the cabin door, and I went to answer it. John stood at the threshold, concern on his face. "I just ran into Dr. Carson. How is she?"

"We hope she's on the mend," I said. "Just a matter of rest now."

"Glad to hear it. Sarah sends her best," he said, taking my hand and squeezing it gently. "I don't want to pull you away. I just wanted to see you. I'll check again later."

"Thank you, John."

He went to leave, then turned back and offered a small smile. When he'd gone, I came back into the room. "That was John, Hari, wishing you a speedy recovery."

At the mention of his name, Hari's brow creased. "Charlotte, there's something I need to tell you. I've heard something about John. Reverend Burk saw the two of you dancing and bombarded me on my way back to my cabin."

Nothing the Burks had to say was ever good, and my stomach knotted. "What did he say?"

"I'm sorry to tell you this. Truly I am, but he's not the man you think he is." Hari's hand reached for mine. It was as cold as ice. "He has a fiancée waiting for him back in England. The banns haven't been read in church yet, but there's some sort of understanding between him and a young woman named Agnes."

For a moment, I couldn't breathe, as if the wind had been knocked out of me. I gripped the edge of the bed to steady myself. So he had not been sincere, I realized. He had a fiancée. I was a dalliance, someone to while away the time with on a long, boring voyage. How could I have been so trusting? Would I never learn?

"Charlotte?"

"I'm fine," I said, swallowing the lump that had come to my throat. "I'm angry at myself. You tried to caution me that we didn't really know him. I wouldn't listen."

"I am sor—" She was cut off by a coughing fit.

I got another damp cloth for her to suck on and the bit of moisture in her mouth eased her parched throat. When her cough settled down, she began to speak. She had things she needed to tell me, about money, she said, but my mind had shut down with the knowledge of Agnes's existence. She was probably the daughter of someone wealthy, someone connected. How could I think John would be interested in me, a poor woman from a disgraced family?

"Char," she said, bringing me back. I roused myself from my daze. Hari seemed to have gone limp, her face turning the colour of alabaster. I ran the cloth over her forehead and cheeks, trying to bring a healthy tint back to them.

Her hand went to her bosom. "My chest feels so tight, and there's pain."

I studied her face. There was swelling around her eyes and throat. "I'll fetch Dr. Carson."

"No! Stay with me. I don't want to be alone. I feel so tired. I just need to sleep."

"Just for a little while," I said, relenting. I tried to make her more comfortable by smoothing the sheet over her and tucking it in, then I lowered the lantern light and stroked her forehead, urging her to sleep, and she finally drifted off for a couple of hours.

⋙⋘

"Char, are you there?" She woke with a start. Her eyes looked feverish, but her hand was cold when it sought mine.

I leaned over her so she could see me. "I'm right here. I won't leave you." The swelling I had noticed earlier was worse, and now her colour had a distinct green tinge to it. "Should I fetch Dr. Carson now?"

She ignored the question. "Do you remember the day Papa came home with our jewellery boxes? Birthday presents for each of us. We were over the moon with excitement. Remember?"

I smiled, my eyes growing moist at the memory. "How could I forget? You let me choose mine first. I loved the red one."

"And we played such games with them, pretending we were fine ladies dressing in our jewels for the ball."

"Do you recall the play jewellery we made out of string and beads? Yours were always the best."

She smiled weakly. "Always keep my box safe, Char. Keep it for me."

"Of course," I said, wiping her forehead once more. "I promise to look after it until you're better, then you can care for it yourself."

Hari dropped off again, and then her breathing changed. Her chest rose and fell with long slow inhales followed by short puffy exhales. I tried to rouse her to take more fluids, but I couldn't wake her. I needed Dr. Carson. I ran to get him, and he came immediately, but by the time we got back to the cabin, Harriet's breathing had slowed even more. After a quick check, Dr. Carson looked at me and shook his head. My heart dropped to my stomach like a stone. My sister was dying.

I went to her and held her in my arms. "I love you, Hari," I whispered. "You've always been there for me, caring for me, looking out for me. More of a mother than a sister. I'm so sorry for the pain I caused you."

Her eyelids flickered open for a moment. There was one last breath and then no more. I sat with her a long time, holding her head against my chest and weeping as I felt my heart shatter into a million pieces.

Chapter Twenty-nine

What happened next was a blur. I know that John appeared and enveloped me in his arms. I couldn't stop myself. I buried myself in his massive chest, letting his presence comfort me while Dr. Carson administered to Harriet's body.

When my sobs had finally ceased, I realised that I had to focus if I was going to get through the next few hours and give Hari a proper burial at sea. I pulled back from John.

"I need you to say a few words," I stammered. "I don't want Reverend Burk to do it. I want this to be dignified."

"Of course, but is that all?" He searched my face. "I can be of more support for you if you'll only let me."

I didn't know how to respond. Harriet's final words still echoed in my head, so I said nothing, and he left me. As soon as he was gone, I turned to face the cabin. Harriet's presence was everywhere. Her clothes, her shoes, and even her hairbrushes. I couldn't stand to see her things scattered about. Fighting fresh tears, I hurried through into my room and quickly changed into a sombre gown and found my hat and gloves.

I made my way through first class and then to the lower stern deck, accepting the sympathetic nods of the passengers I met along the way. Captain Hellyer. Dr. Carson. Sir Richard stepped forward and patted my arm as I passed, but there was no sign of Lady Persephone or the Burks. Perhaps they were ill, but I vaguely recalled Dr. Carson saying everyone else was on the mend.

The ship's carpenter had already managed to hammer together a casket out of rough wooden planks and square-headed nails. I stared at it, unable to connect my beautiful, living, breathing sister with the inert body in the box before me. *Wasn't it just yesterday that we had a glorious time on the island together? How could I know they would be our last happy moments?*

I felt my chest heave just as a small, delicate arm slipped into mine. I looked over and was surprised to see that Sarah had found a way to sneak out. She reached out her other arm and held me close, her head on my shoulder, and then Captain Hellyer cleared his throat, signalling to John.

As John spoke about life and loss, I turned my head to the sea and the setting sun that coloured the sparkling ocean a bloodred. And finally my gaze rested on the frothing wake that would soon accept the body of my beloved Hari.

When John was done, two crewmen stepped forward, and I recognized Sam from the boiler room. He touched his cap to me, then moved forward with his partner to close the coffin lid. They hoisted it on their shoulders and moved towards the rail.

"Goodbye, Harriet," I whispered.

Then they let the coffin slide off their shoulders and into the sea, and my broken heart went with it.

Chapter Thirty

After Harriet's death, time seemed to lurch from excruciatingly slow moments of deep grief to whole days that slipped by unnoticed. I knew I had to write to Wiggles, but when I sat down to do it, I didn't know where to begin. How could I tell her that our Hari was dead? In the end, I found the words, however inadequate. I asked her to tell both Charles and Cousin Edward and to post a notice of Hari's death at our church. And finally, I gave her the address of Hari's bank and asked her to inform them of her death. Since I was Hari's sole heir, all her funds should be forwarded to the Royal Mail office in Victoria, to my attention. I included the death certificate that Dr. Carson provided, then sealed the envelope. I would post it at our next stop, San Francisco Bay.

Sarah got special permission to visit me, and she helped me deal with Hari's things. I would never wear any of her clothes and decided to give them to Sarah, Florence, Emma, Alice, and the other emigrant women. Several of them told me that they planned to throw their stained and filthy clothes overboard and don one of Hari's fine dresses for their arrival. It brought a little sunshine to my days to see their gratitude.

I packed the rest of Hari's things in my own trunk, though I broke down again when I came across her jewellery box. I tucked it away with my belongings. Our twin boxes would stay with me forever.

For the next two weeks, I took meals in my room. Once, when I forced myself out the door to have tea, Sir Richard approached me.

"Deepest sympathies, my dear," he said as he doffed his silk hat. "I'd just like to say that I'm dashed sorry you won't be joining us at Governor Douglas's residence as originally planned. I did so enjoy our talks together and hoped for more in Victoria, but Lady Persephone overruled me. She says it's quite out of the question, what with everything that's happened. I did try to get her to change her mind but, well, you know."

I thanked him. When Charles divorced Harriet, we knew the Douglases would not welcome us. Despite the unknowns, I simply didn't have the energy to even contemplate my future in Victoria.

But others did. Mrs. Burk came to see me in my cabin with a clear message. "You have made many friends with the emigrant women. They seem to be a better fit for you than the first-class passengers."

I was in no mood for her snide comments. "What do you want, Mrs. Burk?" I said coldly.

"I won't waste your time. Do you have any money?"

"A little."

"I will take what you have. You can stay with the women in Victoria until you get a job."

I had no choice. I said yes.

∽

The blast of the ship's horn signalled our arrival in San Francisco Bay, and I stepped out on deck and dropped my letter for Wiggles into the bag that the mail jitney would soon pick up. In the distance I knew was the great gold rush town of San Francisco, of which I had heard so much about during our journey, but I couldn't see it. A fog hung low over the water, and the city was shrouded in a misty veil of white, though in moments of shifting breeze I thought I could make out the ghostlike images of some of the buildings in the town. All I could hear in the eerie quiet around me were the mournful cries of foghorns and the gentle lapping of waves against the ship. As the mail jitney came alongside, I blinked back tears, knowing the little rowboat would soon carry my sad news to a clipper ship destined for England.

After a long turn around the deck, I returned to my room and dug out my jewellery box. I wound the crank on the bottom, then lifted the lid. Tinkling musical notes filled the small room, and I closed my eyes, allowing myself to be soothed by the lilting notes of "Greensleeves."

I was still feeling low when John knocked on my door later. I had been avoiding him in the last weeks, not yet ready to have the painful conversation I knew we must. I let him in now and invited him to sit down. He slowly lowered his large frame into one of the chairs, crossed and uncrossed his legs a few times, and then began to pace the floor of the small cabin, his usual jovial expression sombre.

He held a letter in his hands. "It's from my brother," he said. "My father's had a stroke and can't manage the estate anymore. Andrew has taken over for the time being, but . . . it's my duty to return. Today. In a few minutes."

Despite my anger towards him, I knew what it was like to have a sick parent. At the same time, I couldn't help but suspect he was going back to Agnes.

"I'm very sorry, John. I know how much you were looking forward to your work in the colony, but maybe this is for the best."

He looked up at me suddenly. "What do you mean?"

I took a deep breath. "John, we can't be close. You're betrothed to Agnes. I know all about it. Reverend Burk told Hari."

John flushed. "Burk is an idiot. He thinks he knows everything, but he understands little of the real story." He swallowed hard. "I'm sorry, Charlotte. That man gets under my skin. What I'm trying to say is that Agnes is the daughter of my father's best friend. The two men betrothed us when we were just five years old. It was partly a joke at the time. I have never taken it seriously, and I don't feel any obligation towards her."

It seemed like such an easy response, and I didn't trust it. After all, what was Agnes's side of the story?

"Does Agnes know you have no intention of marrying her? There must be some reason why Reverend Burk thinks you are betrothed. What is Agnes telling people?"

"Up until now I haven't given it much thought. Perhaps she and her father are trying to pressure me, but I would never marry her. I want to marry you." He reached forward and took my hand. "Since that dinner the first night of our journey, I was attracted to you. And later when we talked over tea, I felt a connection like never before. Come with me now; we'll have the captain marry us." He smiled. "You'll be the first of the brideship women to become a wife. We'll return to England together."

I could hardly comprehend what I was hearing. I knew I should feel happy, ecstatic. Wasn't a proposal everything that I was working for? But all I felt was numb. I wished Harriet were here to advise me. Would she tell me to follow my heart? But where was it leading me now?

"Charlotte?" John said. "Will you marry me?"

I tried to picture my life with John if I said yes. Upper-class English society was a small world. Gossip traveled like wild-fire. John's friends and family would hear stories about me if I returned as his bride. And then there was the stigma of my sister's divorce on the grounds of adultery. It was in all the papers. The thought brought with it a wave of sadness and anxiety.

While my future in Victoria was murky and unclear, the picture, however dim, didn't frighten me as it once did. If anything, it was an opportunity to start over. I remembered the foreboding I felt when Charles had pronounced what had felt like a life sentence in the colony. But instead of a punishment, I now saw it as an opportunity, a chance at freedom. I didn't want to give up on it. As much as I cared for John, I knew it wouldn't work.

"No," I said, pulling my hand from his. "I can't marry you."

His eyes widened. "I seem to be buggering this whole proposal up rather badly. Look, come with me now—there's little time, the jitney is leaving soon. We'll sort everything out in due course." He gestured to the door. I remained where I was.

"John, I can't. I can never return to England. I plan to start a new life in the colonies."

"I care deeply for you and no one else. However poorly I presented it, my proposal is sincere and heartfelt. I think we could be happy together, if you would just give it a chance."

I didn't respond to his final plea, letting the silence hang in the air. His eyes reddened and grew wet, then he turned his face from me and left the cabin. I stood there on the threshold, uncertain for a moment, before slowly latching the door behind him. He was gone. Back to England. I tucked my jewellery box away next to Hari's. Tomorrow, we would set sail for Victoria, in the colony of Vancouver Island.

PART THREE

The New World

Chapter Thirty-one

There was a hint of autumn in the air as the tender from the *Tynemouth* slowly approached the city of Victoria's inner harbour, and I pulled my shawl tight around me as if to steel myself against what was to come. But nothing could have prepared me for my first glimpse of my new home.

All manner of men, well-scrubbed and in their Sunday best, stood thick like lemmings on the edge of a seaside cliff, ten or twelve deep in some cases, jostling and pushing each other for a better vantage point. Some men hung off lampposts, while others sat dangling their legs from rooftops, and still others took turns hoisting each other in the air for a better look.

It seemed as though every red-blooded, single man, and some I guessed who were not so single, was here. I heard later that hundreds of prospective bridegrooms had come from as far north as the Cariboo goldfields and as far south as Washington Territory.

As the men caught sight of us, a great roar went up. Next to me in Sarah's arms, Jacob startled at the sound and began to cry.

"What on earth?" Sarah breathed.

Just before we reached shore, Florence Wilson leaned in close to me. "One of us needs to speak up for the rest, and we don't trust Mrs. Burk to do it. The ladies want you."

"Me?" I said. "But I'm not even officially one of you."

"That's the point. No one pays us the slightest mind. We all want food, shelter, and hot water for washing right away," she said. "But there's more. We need to know about jobs, not just husbands, and now that we're off the boat, we all want to be free to move about at will."

"I'll see what I can do," I replied, but I wasn't sure anyone would listen to me.

The vast crowd of men had grown restless waiting for us, and some had clearly brought out strong drink. By the time we were all ashore, we faced a near riot of unruly, besotted men who seemed convinced they were in love with each and every one of us. After the navy band, looking festive in their dress blues on a floating barge tied to the dock, struck up "Rule Britannia," the crowd of several hundred erupted into their own ribald version of this most patriotic of songs, the lyrics slurred and off tune.

We blushed deeply and kept our eyes glued to the ground, but Mrs. Burk clucked like a mother hen, prevailing upon each of us to stand tall in rows of two and to walk off the dock with calm dignity. "Come, girls," she squawked, "show them how true Christian daughters of the empire conduct themselves."

"Once I get my hands on some of that whisky, I plan on showing them a thing or two about how daughters of the empire really behave," Alice murmured next to me.

I had come to accept Alice and her ways. In fact, I had grown fond of her. Under her brash exterior was a heart of gold. Still, I was somewhat dismayed at her chosen gown, which I thought gave these men the wrong impression. It was black muslin with a low-cut, close-fitting bodice, only partially shrouded by a red lace shawl. Dangling earrings made of red feathers, a red velvet choker necklace, and black gloves that sported fur trim at the wrists accented her entire ensemble. She had rouged her face and rimmed her eyes with kohl, and there was even a rather saucy black beauty mark pasted to one corner of her mouth. But I knew that Alice could take care of herself. The question was, could I?

As I gathered my skirts to step off the dock, I called upon all my inner resources to quiet my fluttering stomach. There was a surprising moment of calm, as if shyness had gotten the best of these lonely bachelors, but it didn't last long. Then someone from the back shouted, "I love you, marry me!" and the crowd erupted into raucous laughter. More cries were taken up, and pandemonium broke loose. The few members of the navy there presumably to keep order had their hands full as men pushed from behind to get a better look, threatening to send some of those at the front spilling forward at our feet.

A small delegation of men, in starched white shirts and freshly pressed suits, stood at the front of the crowd and introduced themselves as the welcoming committee. One of them, a tall man who seemed to be the leader, doffed his hat and read slowly from a script.

"'On behalf of Governor Douglas we would like to welcome you to the colony of Vancouver Island. May you prosper in this wonderful place and live long, fruitful lives here.'"

I couldn't help but notice the sly sidelong glances as the dignitaries openly appraised us. I overheard one tell the man next to him that some of us were a bit long in the tooth and had seen better days. *I may have left England far behind*, I thought, *but not the base attitudes of some of the men.*

Florence nudged me, and I stepped forward. "These women have had a long, exhausting journey," I said, "and now all they want is a place to rest, some warm water for bathing, and food, of course. They'd also like—"

"The welcoming committee has it all well in hand," the spokesperson interrupted.

I tried once more to press our requests upon them. They continued to dismiss me, but I persevered, and they finally agreed to meet with me in the morning to address my other concerns.

A fair-haired man burst through the crowd and came to a stop in front of Alice.

"You are the most beautiful woman I ever seen. Will you marry me?" he asked, bending his knee. He pulled a large wad of bills from his breast pocket. "You can use this to buy the best wedding clothes you ever imagined. And we'll have a wedding feast to top all, no expenses spared."

A hush fell over the scene as everyone waited for Alice's answer, but she looked dumbfounded and turned to me. "What should I do?"

I could see the young man was earnest and had a touch of youthful innocence in his wide, blue eyes. And while I couldn't imagine saying yes to someone I had just met, I knew Alice didn't have the luxury of waiting.

"Come what may, he doesn't look the sort to treat you ill," I replied. "But only you can decide."

She said nothing for another moment or two and then, in a calm, clear voice, declared, "I will!"

With both hands, she took the money from her new fiancé's hand and tucked it down the front of her dress. The groom jumped to his feet and twirled her around in the air as the crowd cheered.

The welcoming committee impatiently beckoned us forward, and Alice broke away to keep up with us, beaming with delight.

"Your friend has made an excellent match," a slim, dark-haired man said, falling into step beside me as we continued along the edge of the harbour. "That's Mr. Pioneer. He's just struck a very rich vein of gold in the Cariboo."

"I'm sure they'll be very happy," I said, taking hold of Sarah's elbow and briskly moving forward. I hoped this man wasn't trying to propose to me. If he was, he'd be disappointed.

"Amor De Cosmos," he said, holding out his card. He was the editor of the *Daily British Colonist*. "How are you and the other sixty marriageable lasses feeling right now?" He pulled out a notepad and pen.

"We're all feeling a little overwhelmed."

I picked up my pace, but he matched it.

"And what led you to leave England and come here? In need of a husband, I presume?"

"I—we are hoping for a better life than we could have had back home."

"My readers will want to know what sort of man will attract

the ladies' interest? They are all vying for your favour. The strong woodsman? The intellectual businessman? The sensitive poet?"

Would he not stop? "I . . . can't say."

"That's a shame," he said, and turned to Sarah, ready to interview her, but seeing the baby in her arms, thought better of it and hustled after Florence.

The quivering, undulating crowd of expectant bridegrooms reluctantly parted as we made our way two by two, like captured prisoners of war, through the harbour and into the town. At one point, we had to stop and step around the luggage cart that had lost a wheel and overturned, spilling trunks and cases out onto the street. Some of the women stopped, seeing to their belongings, but the welcome committee urged us on. We marched up a wide dirt street lined on one side with several two-story brick and stone buildings. On the other side, on the edge of the harbour, were wooden warehouses and fisher's shacks. On several of these, I saw a poster proclaiming our arrival.

THE *TYNEMOUTH'S* INVOICE OF YOUNG LADIES

A general holiday should be proclaimed; all the bunting waved from flagstaffs; salutes fired from Beacon Hill; clean shirts and suits of good cloths brought into requisition, and every preparation made to give this precious "invoice" a warm welcome.

How fitting that I should see the notice of the Tynemouth's *arrival today*, I thought. It was a bookend to the one that Charles had handed me only a few short months ago at the beginning of this journey. As much as I still grieved Harriet, and always would, I took it as a sign that I needed to put the tragedy behind me.

We continued on to our new home, a narrow one-story building of grey wood and few windows on a large fenced property. Stepping inside, we discovered a low-ceilinged room with two long rows of tightly packed cots arranged military style.

"We're ladies, not soldiers," Florence said in disgust.

I had to agree. The accommodations were sparse. My private maid's room on board the ship seemed like luxury in comparison.

Through the main window, we had a view of the backyard, where an open fire served as a kitchen and a line of washbasins and tubs as a laundry room. Given the barrels of rainwater, there was likely no running water. At the back of the property sat one decrepit latrine with only a half door for privacy. My spirits fell at the sight. This was a far cry from how I imagined Sir Richard and Lady Persephone were being welcomed at Governor Douglas's.

Behind us, Reverend Burk cleared his throat and called for our attention. I cringed at the thought of another long prayer, but it was Mrs. Burk who held up her hand.

"Ladies, Reverend Burk and I must leave you now. We are under the employ of the Columbia Emigration Society and they are sending another shipment of brides. We are going back to England and will chaperone them just as we did you."

"Poor buggers," Alice mumbled.

As we waved our goodbyes at the front door, I was shocked to see men standing behind the fence just fifty feet away, watching our every move.

"Sarah, look," I said, pointing.

"Don't worry," she replied, patting Jacob's back. "This is only temporary. Ignore them and come inside and unpack your things."

Sarah's small trunk rested neatly on her bed, and my larger one was at the foot of mine. As soon as I saw it, I knew something was wrong. At first, I thought it was just the new scuffs and scrapes, but my stomach turned when I realized the lock was broken too. I threw back the trunk lid and dug deep. My fingers easily found the jewellery boxes on the bottom and I let out a short laugh of relief. But when I flipped open my red-lacquered box, I couldn't believe what I saw. It was empty. Wiggles's necklace was gone.

I flopped down on the bed, my head in my hands. How could I have let this happen? I should have worn the jewel, not packed it. How would I ever tell Wiggles her precious gift was gone? How would I start a new life with no way to raise money? It could be months, maybe years, before I received Hari's money, if I ever did.

Sarah tried to soothe me, telling me everything would work out all right. I knew she meant to comfort me, but she would be leaving soon, heading north to her father. In that moment, I envied that she had family here and desperately wished Harriet was still by my side. My grief hung on me like a stone. How would I find a way forward without Hari? During those last weeks on the boat, the one thing that had brought me solace was a new, fragile dream of buying my own house and maybe some land. That dream had disappeared with my empty jewellery box.

Chapter Thirty-two

The welcoming committee arrived just after breakfast the next morning. They were clearly in a hurry to say what they needed to and get on with their day, but the women were all anxious to hear about employment opportunities and wages—myself included, now that Wiggles's precious necklace had been taken.

Sarah and Alice didn't join us. Sarah had set off to the BC Express Company to buy her ticket for the next coach to Barkerville while I watched Jacob. Alice, having found a fiancé and set a wedding date, refused to come to the meeting and slept late.

The spokesman introduced himself as Mr. Simms and gestured towards a matronly woman standing next to him. "Ladies, this is Mrs. Graham. She has arranged for all the girls younger than fifteen to be taken in as servants into good homes, and to remain there until they are old enough for marriage. For older women seeking such positions, we have a list of households who are in need. I suggest you make yourselves presentable and begin making calls."

Florence nudged me, and I handed a snoozing Jacob to her and got to my feet. "What is the compensation, please?"

My apparent audacity at speaking was met with frowns from the men. Mrs. Graham answered, "Room and board, Sunday afternoons off, and a small monthly sum for spending money, to be determined by the employer."

The women around me began to mutter. Many hoped the robust economy in the New World would mean higher wages for all, but it seemed the servant class did not share in the new wealth.

"For ladies with education," Mrs. Graham continued, "we have several governess positions available from some of the best families in town. They pay room and board and one pound per month."

That wasn't much better, I thought ruefully. "What about those seeking other employment?" I asked.

Mrs. Graham turned to Mr. Simms, perplexed.

"I have information on one or two other positions," he said, referring to his notes. "Please see me after the meeting. I believe that's it; thank you, ladies, and good luck."

Emma raised a timid hand. "Are we free to go into town? I want to shop and go to church."

It was a question that burned in all the women's minds after months of being cooped up on the ship.

Mr. Simms faced the crowd once more. "You must sign in and out of a logbook when you leave here to seek employment. Church is allowed but no other outings will be permitted. Gentlemen callers may only be received in the afternoon under the awning in the backyard. And in the interests of safety and propriety, we will be placing guards around the property."

The women groaned, and I heard a few angry comments, but the welcoming committee was gathering their things, ready to leave us behind in our near prison. Leaving Jacob with Florence, I managed to catch Mr. Simms, and he handed me a scrap of paper. It was a notice placed by the Royal Victoria Tea Society, an organization apparently devoted to "the preservation of the proper and decorous taking of afternoon tea," according to the paper. They were seeking to hire "a genteel lady of quality" to greet and serve tea to the ladies of the highest echelons of Victoria society. The advertisement also mentioned that the position might be suitable for one of the newly landed, single emigrant women of middle or upper class.

It was not at all what I hoped or imagined for myself, but it was that or a governess position. My body felt heavy as I took Jacob from Florence and shuffled back to my trunk to search for a suitable gown for an interview. After settling him in the wooden box we had made into his bed, I dug my dreaded corset out of my trunk and began airing out one of my best day gowns, a wide-skirted, red-and-white-striped cotton dress with puffed sleeves and a ruffled neckline. Before long, Sarah returned, a defeated look on her face.

"What happened?" I asked as she sunk onto her cot. She peered over at her son, then turned back to me.

"All the tickets for the last coaches of the season were snatched up before I even got to the counter. The men all pushed in ahead of me. No more stages will go north till spring." She blinked back tears. "What am I to do? I have no employment. And if I did, who would watch Jacob? I'll have to live on my travel money for the winter."

"Oh, Sarah, I'm so sorry." I went to her and gave her a hug. Would nothing go our way? "Do you think your father can send another fare?"

"I hate to ask him, but I'm sure he'll find a way. Seeing me again—meeting little Jacob—it's what he lives for, he told me so in his letters."

Her words made me think wistfully of my own father. If he had had his way, Harriet and I would have been provided for and life would have turned out much differently. Now, I had no one. But not Sarah. She had family and she needed to be with them.

"We will find a way to get you to Barkerville, don't fret. Come spring, I will go with you to the office and demand the first ticket be sold to you."

She wiped a tear away. "Thank you. I don't know what I'd do without you."

"We'll have each other for a time yet."

I filled her in on the meeting and my potential teahouse job. I tried to be optimistic, but so far the colony was not what either of us had expected.

Chapter Thirty-three

The next morning, Sarah wished me luck as I signed out and left for the teahouse. Without the crowds, I could really see the town and was buoyed at the sight of a library. I needn't starve for reading materials in the coming winter. Outside the library door, a schoolteacher shepherded a group of rosy-cheeked, uniformed children. There seemed to be a lot of young families here, and I smiled at the thought of the emigrant women's children being among them in the future.

But my smile left me as I rounded the corner and saw a small group of forlorn Native children dressed in ragged shirts and trousers. They were thin, and some of their little faces bore scars. Smallpox, I realized. One poor boy looked blinded in one eye. I guessed they were survivors of the recent epidemic John had spoken of, and I wondered what had happened to their parents and relations. My thoughts turned to John and his unfinished work here, and his vaccination materials packed in my trunk.

When he had rushed to leave the ship, he had left them with Dr. Carson, who passed them on to me. "John thought you could find a use for these in the colony," he had said. "He didn't want them to go to waste."

Guilt tugged at my heart at the sight of these children. How different their lives were from the happy brood I saw at the library. I wanted to help, but I just didn't know how. I didn't even have enough money to buy the cowpox serum that I needed for the vaccinations. Nor did I know where or how to find those who needed the medicine the most so I could pass it on to them. But more than that, I knew that I was part of the greater problem, that I and those of my kind had forever changed this land so that the Native peoples struggled for a decent life, even to survive.

I hurried on towards the teahouse, a Tudor-style building that would not have been out of place in the centre of London. Inside, I met with Miss Hardcastle, a humourless, greying, middle-aged woman, and told her I was interested in the job posting.

She nodded. "As the *volunteer* director of the society, I *never* set foot in the kitchen or serve patrons, thus the need to hire."

She guided me to a sitting room with a commanding view of the ocean. In the distance, I could see vague outlines of islands.

"Which islands are those?" I asked.

"The San Juan Islands," she replied, taking a seat.

The name rang a bell. They were the source of an angry dispute with the Americans over sovereignty that had culminated in the Pig War just three years earlier. I remembered reading about it in a book back home in England. It all seemed so long ago. I felt a lump in my throat at my first twinge of homesickness.

"Now, why don't you tell me about yourself?" Miss Hard-castle asked, tucking her ankles under her.

I took a breath and explained my situation, leaving out the scandals, of course.

"How very shocking for you, my dear, that you are forced to take paid employment," she said when I had finished. "I count myself blessed by the Almighty that I was born into a family of substance. Such a shame it is not the same for you."

I was beginning to see the sort of person Miss Hardcastle was, and while I wasn't impressed, I needed this position, so I kept a polite smile on my face.

Oblivious to any offense she may have caused, she carried on. "The mission of the society is to preserve the traditions and lifestyle that made Britain and her empire the greatest in the world. We are of the view that the fine etiquette and class distinctions of England need to be maintained here in the colonies, and what better way to do that than through a proper English tea? You are new to this part of the world. But once you have become acquainted with its customs, you will no doubt be quite shocked at the lack of the locals' understanding and concern for the relative positions of class."

I thought of the poor children I had seen outside. What class did they belong to? Were the glories of the great British empire only for the privileged few? *Perhaps there are far more important things to be concerned about than class distinction*, I wanted to say, but I swallowed my words.

Miss Hardcastle accepted my silence as agreement and got down to business, explaining my duties and terms of employment. I was to greet the patrons appropriately as to their station in society, to engage in polite chat, and of course to serve food and pour the tea. For this, I would be paid the grand sum of two pounds per month. It wasn't much, but it was more than governess work, and for that, I was grateful.

Without further ado, she handed me a white apron and told me that lunch would start in one hour. As she requested, I began setting the tables with a full lunch service—three forks, two spoons, butter knife, one side plate, one large plate, teacup and saucer, water glass, and sherry glass.

"One more thing," she said. "This table by the window is for Mrs. Douglas's tea. I wouldn't normally seat her at the best table, but she is the governor's wife and etiquette requires it."

I was puzzled. "Why not?"

Miss Hardcastle leaned forward and whispered in my ear, "Those women think they're special because their husbands are rich Hudson's Bay fur traders, but I'll never accept them as equals. They're Métis." When I didn't respond, she clarified, "Amelia Douglas is half French, half . . . you know."

I kept my face open and unruffled in an effort to show her that the information didn't affect me. "I've only heard lovely things about her," I said. It was a lie, but I didn't care. I remembered what John had said about the governor and his wife's marriage. It had been a union of two powerful families where each had much to gain. Amelia, the granddaughter of a Cree chief and daughter of a successful fur trader, and James Douglas, an up-and-comer in the Hudson's Bay Company, had been clearly destined for great things together.

Miss Hardcastle let out a guffaw, and as she bustled away, I vowed to make Mrs. Douglas feel very welcome when she arrived.

As the ladies began gathering, it quickly became apparent that there was little for upper-class women to do in the colony other than to take luncheon or, I presumed, afternoon tea. The tables began to fill at twelve o'clock and I was hard-pressed to keep up with the basic demands of the patrons and soon gave up on engaging any of them in polite talk. Each table had a small hand-rung bell to summon me when a need arose, and it was not long before the tearoom began to sound like Chichester Cathedral on a Sunday morning.

I ran from table to table, refilling teapots, serving food and beverages, clearing and resetting tables, and bouncing in and out of the kitchen at an exhausting pace. Numerous times I spilled tea into the saucer as I poured, but I found it almost impossible to avoid it. My face flamed relentlessly, but after a couple of hours, I was too tired to care anymore about shaming myself. Miss Hardcastle checked in on me regularly, but all she did was frown severely, then leave me to muddle through on my own.

When the lunch crowd drifted away, I wearily settled at a table and helped myself to a generous portion of cucumber sandwiches. I had just taken a bite when Miss Hardcastle accosted me. "The tea crowd will be here shortly, and you've not cleared and reset all the tables."

I wolfed down the rest of my sandwich, and, dragging myself to my feet, I began restoring the dining room to its former order. By four o'clock, another onslaught of women filled the room. The end of the day could not arrive soon enough. I was dog-tired, and all I wanted to do was head back to my little cot and rest until dinner. Near the end of the tea hour, two women walked in and sat at the reserved table by the window. Mrs. Douglas, I deduced. And a friend.

I pasted a fresh smile on my face and approached the table.

"Mrs. Douglas?" I asked.

She nodded. She was a small, plump woman with determined dark eyes and a practised smile. At my greeting, her guest, a tall woman wearing a large white hat with a veil, turned her face to me.

"Miss Harding? Is that you?" The woman removed her veil.

"Lady Persephone!" I wanted to sink into the floor.

"I never expected to find you here," she said. "At least not as part of the staff."

"I have little choice . . ." I glanced at Mrs. Douglas.

"We had looked forward to hosting you at the residence," she said. "But I'm sure you'll do very well here." There was something in her eyes. I sensed that she understood what I was going through, how hard it was to fit into a strict society, trying to hold on and not let go.

"You and your sister. What a pair you turned out to be," Lady Persephone scoffed. "To think I once thought you the perfect bride for dear George Chalmers—that I was set on promoting the marriage."

"Perhaps George is the one you have misjudged," I said lightly.

"I hardly think so. He *is* Pam's handpicked successor."

I felt a burn in the back of my throat. I'd put up with so much, taking everything with a smile and a brave face. Something in me snapped.

"George is a man with no moral compass," I said in a low,

hard voice. "He is lascivious and cunning, certainly not fit to hold high office. Nothing could have induced me to marry him, no matter what you said or did."

A sliver of recognition passed over Lady Persephone's face. She'd heard this kind of talk about George before.

"How dare you slander him in this way. You're not fit to scrape the mud off his boots, let alone marry him." She turned to Mrs. Douglas, who was looking with distaste at her guest, and then resettled her features into her usual porcelain mask. "I believe I've lost my appetite. Do you mind if we have tea another day?"

Mrs. Douglas cast a glance at me, then turned back to Lady Persephone. "Certainly," she said. As she gathered up her things, part of me thought she seemed relieved to have a reason to cut short the outing, and I wondered what she thought of Lady Persephone or even me.

After the two women left, the anger in me evaporated and my exhaustion returned in full force. I slumped down into Mrs. Douglas's vacated chair. What had I just done? Would I never be rid of my past? The few remaining ladies in the tea shop gave me curious looks and talked behind their hands. *Hari would have known how to handle that*, I thought. And then I was flooded with the reminder that she was gone, that I was on my own, and that maybe I had just made a huge misstep.

Chapter Thirty-four

I had expected an early winter with snow and ice in the northern colony, but the seasons here were not as harsh as I predicted. Autumn deepened, the air cooled, and the leaves changed colour and began to drop. A dusting of frost made them crunch under my feet when I went to work each morning, but I was warm enough in my wool cape. Once inside, I didn't have much time to think of the weather, and as the branches of the evergreens hung low with dew, as if wrapping their arms around themselves for comfort, each day became a mindless routine of waking, working, and sleeping, with a few snatched moments of enjoyment with Sarah and Jacob each night.

After Miss Hardcastle was satisfied that I was getting by, I made some small adjustments to ease my work. I set fewer dishes for each place—less to clear and clean—and one night, I took a pair of shears and decommissioned the handheld bells the patrons used to summon me. Fortunately for me, Miss Hardcastle's role as director meant she rarely ventured into the tearoom. Mrs. Douglas came in a few times, nodding pleasantly to me, and I kept an eye out for Lady Persephone, but so far she hadn't returned, and I was relieved.

The barracks were cold with nothing other than a potbellied stove at one end for heat. As women went to live with their employers or got married, our group dwindled, and by mid-October there were only twenty of us left. Alice's wedding had been as her groom had promised; a lavish affair that we were all invited to. Later she had confided in me that marrying Timothy—Mr. Pioneer's real name—was the best decision of her life, as she had quite fallen for him, and he for her. He worshipped the ground she walked on, and in her eyes, he could do no wrong. Sarah continued to look for work, but she struggled.

"It's as I feared. Everyone's working, and I can't find anyone to watch Jacob, so I have to bring him with me. No one wants a mum with a babe in her arms," she told me with a heavy sigh one evening while we sat playing cribbage. I had taught her a few card games, and it helped pass the time as the days grew longer and night came on sooner. "But there's more to it. One lady told me she'd hire me to do the laundry, but I couldn't expect to be paid the same as the others."

"Why's that?"

Sarah kept her eyes on her cards. "Because I'm black. She saw Jacob's curls and she guessed. She said my people had been slaves not long ago and shouldn't expect the same pay as others."

"Oh, Sarah, I'm so sorry. She's an ignorant fool. Miss Hardcastle told me the other day that Governor Douglas's heritage is part black. I hoped there would be more tolerance here. Have you heard back from your father about sending money for another ticket to Barkerville?"

"He's promised to send it soon. I just hope it comes in time for the first spring coaches."

We both sat in silence. Above us, Jacob's laundered nappies hung on a clothesline to dry, looking rather like neat rows of white surrender flags.

∽◌∽

A cool dampness descended over the town as winter arrived. Day after day went by with no hint of sun, as low clouds clung to the landscape, trapping moisture near the ground. Looking out the windows in the tearoom, one would not guess that a string of islands lay in the distance, as the mist rarely left them. My wool clothing acted like a wick, drawing in the wetness and holding it next to my body. Everything felt soggy, and my skin was chronically chafed. By mid-November, the rain was a constant, just as it had been in England. A small part of me had hoped to somehow escape that weather.

One particularly soggy day, I stopped at the Royal Mail office on my way home in hopes of a letter from Wiggles. The mail clipper ship had just come in, and to my delight, the postmaster handed me two envelopes. I practically snatched them from his hand and raced home to read them.

Throwing myself on my cot, I ripped the seal on first letter. I knew the script instantly. Wiggles.

October 30, 1862
Dear Charlotte,

No words can express my sadness over the passing of Harriet.
My concern now is for you. I am consoled in my knowledge
of your character. I know you to be stalwart and robust. As a
child, you were not easily pushed off any task or course you
had set for yourself. I remember you as a twelve-year-old, when
you were determined to read five novels over Christmas break.
I'm sure you must have stayed up very late every night, but
you did it.

I encourage you not to lose sight of your future. You have
the opportunity to choose your own path and to live a full and
complete life, something that so few women have the opportunity
to do. Try not to be disheartened. Press on through this dark time.

I paused, relishing her words. They were like a gift, a loving
embrace from afar.

Charles came to see me last week. At first I wasn't entirely
sure why. He told me of his wedding to Mary Sledge, which
was apparently a grand affair at St. Paul's. When he asked after
you, the real purpose for his visit became clear. He requested
your address and mentioned that he needed you to return any
monies that Harriet had at the time of her death. I thought of
ignoring his request, but he wouldn't take no for an answer. At
least you have the necklace to help you as you make a way for
yourself.

Write me soon with your news. I cherish letters from you.

Hortense Wiggins

P.S. I went around to Harriet's bank as you asked. See the enclosed letter.

I hugged Wiggles's letter to my chest just as I would have her, if she were with me now, and digested all that she had written. I felt guilt about the necklace, but I didn't have the heart to tell her that it had been stolen. As for Charles, he would be disappointed. There was no money to send. What little was left of Harriet's money from the voyage had been spent long ago on accommodation. I had searched her things for the money she had taken from Charles but hadn't found it. I had thought that maybe she had deposited it in her bank in England. If she had socked money away for my dowry, there was no way I would give it to Charles. I truly felt it was mine to keep, my father's legacy. Charles, no doubt, would feel otherwise.

Tucked into Wiggles's envelope was another sheet of paper, a one-page formal letter from Hari's bank. The funds in Mrs. Baldwin's account, it said, were insufficient to cover the cost of sending a bank draft from England to Victoria. I was to send further instructions. They recommended I donate the small sum to a favourite charity in my late sister's name.

I crumpled the paper in my hand. It seemed nothing would go my way. Had Charles found out about the bank account and beaten me to it? As Hari's former husband he might have persuaded the bank manager that the funds were his. I would likely never know the answer. I sagged under the weight of this new information.

My earnings at the tea shop were slowly accumulating, but

I could never save enough to buy a house and some land. In truth, after the loss of the necklace, I hadn't had the energy to think of a new plan. Harriet had always been the one with the ideas, and I missed hearing her guidance now. Wiggles was right, though. I had to press on and not squander my opportunities.

I turned to the last letter. *Probably from Charles gloating over the money*, I thought, not recognizing the writing. But when I tore the seal and scanned the bottom for the sender's name, I was surprised to see that it was from John.

October 27, 1862
Dear Charlotte,

Words cannot express how sorry I am for the way we parted last. I've just arrived in England, and I haven't thought of anything else the entire trip back. I see now how foolish I was to think you could rush into a marriage. I regret that I didn't listen to you. I was afraid to lose you, and I did anyway.

I trust that Dr. Carson gave you the vaccination tools. Since I had no use for them, I wanted to leave them in good hands. Your compassion for others and your medical skills impressed me, and I hoped you might find a way to put them to good use in the colony.

I hope our goodbye was not our last. And that we might remain friends.

Deepest affection,
John

I traced over his salutation with my fingertips, remembering the happier moments we shared, our dance, our kiss. I folded the letter. It seemed like another life in another world. I was happy to hear from him and would write back to assure him that we were still friends and that I would find a way to use the vaccination equipment, but I knew I would never see him again. His life was in England and mine was here. Beyond that, other circumstances and obligation separated us. I had to pick up the pieces of my life and move on.

Chapter Thirty-five

"You won't believe what I have just found out, you just won't believe it!" Sarah gasped as she burst in the barracks in a whirlwind of snow.

"You've found work?" I asked hopefully. Christmas had come and gone and we were now the only women left in the barracks. We had twice asked the welcoming committee for a little more time to find other lodgings but we knew we had to make other arrangements soon.

"Better than that." She put little Jacob down in his bed and took my hands in hers and squeezed.

"Ouch," I said, "this news better be worth a couple of broken fingers."

She let go, then twirled around the room.

"All right, then. I'm all ears. What's your news?"

"It's *your* great news as well." With a flurry, she opened her satchel and took out some papers with official seals. They were the stock certificates she had shown me on the boat the day of Jacob's birth.

"My father sent me a letter telling me to sell the shares, so I went to the assay office and asked about them. They've gone up in value and are worth much more than the pennies my father paid for them." She giggled. "We can sell 'em tomorrow for five pounds each! I have nine shares and don't forget you have one."

I stared at her, disbelieving for a minute. "Five pounds?" I echoed. That was almost three months' salary at the tea shop. With it I could rent a decent place to live, maybe even a house.

We both danced about this time, silently mouthing shouts of joy and waving our hands in the air, so not to awaken Jacob.

Sarah grew serious and once again took my hands in her own cold ones. "Come with me."

"Come with you where?"

"To Barkerville. There are far more opportunities there than here, and five pounds is more than enough for the stagecoach. My father said he'll help us get on. I told him all about you, and he said he has a job for you, if you want it."

"Yes," I said, without a second thought. Sarah was my best friend, and the thought of her leaving had been gnawing at me the past months. I had nothing holding me here, and according to the audacious De Cosmos of the *Colonist*, Barkerville was a place where "opportunity waited around every corner, where gold nuggets lay scattered in riverbeds, free for the taking." Perhaps there I would be able to truly make a fresh start.

Sarah and I began counting down the days until the stagecoach line opened again in the spring and we were determined to be first in line to purchase our tickets. Sarah fretted about her previous experience and was nervous we'd get turned away again.

"Why don't we ask some of our friends, Florence, Emma, and Alice, to come with us?" I suggested. "We'll tell them about how you were treated last time. There's strength in numbers."

When the ticket office did reopen, Sarah and I arrived two hours before and were surprised to see our friends and twelve other emigrant women already waiting. There were so many of us that when the doors opened, we trooped inside and filled the entire small space. Not a single man made it in off the street. The bald-headed clerk at the counter looked up at us with narrow eyes.

"Two tickets on the first Barkerville stage, please," I said, placing the funds on the counter.

He didn't move a muscle. "It's gentlemen first, then ladies. Them's the rules."

"Whose rules?"

"My rules."

"I don't see any gentlemen in this room, do you? And I believe the usual procedure is first come, first served."

The clerk flushed. "What game are you ladies playing at? The tickets are reserved for men with serious business in Bark-erville, not ladies out sightseeing. Now you girls clear out of here and stop wasting my time."

Alice pushed in next to me and leaned across the counter. She grabbed the clerk's shirt collar in her fist. "Listen up, bucko, we ain't leaving here till you sell these ladies their tickets. So get off your scrawny flee-bitten arse and get on with it!"

His eyes widened. "All right. Have it your way."

"Glad we have an understanding," Alice said, releasing her grip. The clerk swept our money off the counter and placed two tickets to Barkerville in front of us. "Now, that wasn't so hard, was it?" she said.

I gave her an appreciative look and scooped up the tickets. They were for the first of April. We were leaving in just two days' time.

Back out on the street, we took turns hugging each other and promising to write. Alice insisted we come for a visit in the fall.

"Timothy's building me a fine house, and you're all welcome to come and stay," she said.

She was very happy in her marriage, and I was glad the risk had worked out and that she and her husband were so well-suited for each other.

Florence hugged me and gave me a copy of Dickens's *A Christmas Carol* to keep as a memento of her. She couldn't disguise her envy. "I'm not going to stay a governess forever," she said. "I'll find a way to get into the theatre somehow."

Emma gave us each a Bible for the journey. "My friend David Spencer got these for me," she said shyly. "I met him at church. We're sweet on each other. He's asked me to marry him, and I said yes."

We all congratulated Emma and, with a final round of hugs, then said our final goodbyes.

That night, I wrote letters to both Wiggles and John telling them of my plans to travel to Barkerville and to advise them that letters could be sent to my attention at the Royal Mail office there. I felt a heady mixture of sadness and excitement, but overall I was happy to be leaving Victoria behind and taking a new path. Where it would lead and if it would prove to be what I wanted, I had no way of knowing.

Chapter Thirty-six

Once we had sailed from Vancouver Island to New Westminster on the mainland of British Columbia, the first part of the journey would be by an ignominious horse-drawn wagon on a narrow path as far as the town of Yale and the start of the Cariboo Wagon Road. The second part would be a stagecoach up the Fraser Canyon, through the Cariboo range lands, and finally to Barkerville. I was reluctant to board a ship again, but the distance across the water was short, and we were in the wagon in a matter of hours.

I recalled the conversation on the *Tynemouth* about the colony of Vancouver Island and the colony of British Columbia being separate, but when we arrived on the mainland, I could see that it made good sense to merge the two colonies into one, as they were very similar. Vast tracts of logged land, sawmills, and fishing boats dominated the landscape. What I didn't like was the idea of consolidating British rule. Since my journey and my arrival in Victoria, I had begun to realize that the empire only benefited the privileged few. Perhaps if a new independent country was formed—Canada, as Sir Richard had called it—

there would be more equity, but who knew when that would happen or whether it would bring freedom for everyone.

Sarah, Jacob, and myself jostled inside the old, wooden wagon as it creaked and bumped along the deeply rutted roads. We were squeezed in next to three other male passengers—presumably the highly regarded businessmen the stagecoach clerk had mentioned. They eyed us curiously, but didn't engage in conversation.

Our progress was slow, and I took in the sights before me. All I knew of Yale was that it was a teeming gold rush town. There were only a small number of actual buildings, but tents and lean-to huts stretched along the river as far as I could see. The whole place was one seething mass of agitated, grim-faced men. They were everywhere—spilling out of overstuffed rude accommodations, loafing three and four deep on the wooden boardwalks, squatting around large campfires drinking coffee. The feeling of impatience and frustration was palpable.

Our driver, Louis Jandin, a boyishly handsome young man with black curls, explained that they were waiting for the Fraser River spring runoff to subside once the snow in the surrounding mountains had melted. Then they had a chance of tackling the notorious, death-defying rapids with some hope of success. The prospectors would either work the sandy bars along the river or travel north to the Cariboo. Some gold seekers had come from as far away as the coal pits of Wales and battlefields of the American Civil War, he said.

These were desperate men, I realized. They had risked all that was dear to them for a chance to escape lives of poverty and misery. As time wore on, they must have found it harder and harder to believe that they would strike it rich.

Louis stopped the coach in front of a small, dubious-looking wooden hut with a badly constructed sign out front proclaiming it to be an American-style restaurant. Sarah and I exchanged a doubtful look.

When we prepared to climb from the wagon, there was a great commotion as a group of strangers rushed forward to assist us. I murmured a thank-you and reached for the grimy hand of the closest man, but just at that moment, he was shoved out of the way.

"What in God's name do you think you're doing, Jeremy? I was here first! Get ye yellow scurvy face out of here," the first man shouted at the man behind him.

I began to pitch forward into the street and had to grasp the wooden side of the wagon to keep my balance. A general shoving match ensued, and a brawl seemed likely, but Louis rescued Sarah and me by helping us down on the opposite side of the wagon. The three businessmen had made it out of the wagon unscathed.

Louis cleared his throat. "This is where you can get a bite to eat," he informed us. "After that, you have rooms set aside for you in the hotel across the street." He pointed to a two-storey, rough-hewn wood building with an elaborate sign in white scrolling letters declaring *The Ritz Hotel and Saloon.*

"I'll have the stagecoach ready for you tomorrow morning. One more thing," he said, turning to Sarah and me, his eyes resting on Sarah for a moment longer. "You two should not leave your rooms till the stage is here. It's a rough town, no place for ladies."

We had not even made it to the door of the restaurant before the sudden boom of a firearm caused us all to jump nervously and instinctively huddle together. The door to the Ritz burst open, and one man backed onto the street, his revolver drawn, while a second, taller man followed with his pistol pointed squarely at the first. A fellow traveller from our group spread his arms wide and pushed us backwards, through the door of the restaurant, where we huddled, peering through the windows to see what would happen next.

"Where are the constables?" I asked the stout proprietor.

"New Westminster," he replied.

"But how can they police the town from there?"

He shrugged. "They can't. There is no law here. Men get away with all kinds of bad things—no punishment. The cemetery's the fastest-filling hotel in town."

The men in the street were clearly both extremely inebriated, and they were having trouble holding their firearms steady as they waved them in each other's faces.

"I did not try to steal your goddamned business, you ignorant dim-witted hornswoggler," the first man shouted up at his fair-haired nemesis.

"You tried to, but I put a stop to it, you two-faced lying Yankee," the other man rejoined.

As he said this, the first man seemed to tip forward, losing his balance. In an attempt to steady himself, he desperately shuffled his feet and tripped, waving his hands in the air for balance, and the gun he was holding went off. Sarah gripped my arm, and we watched in horrified silence as both men peered at each other, obviously unsure what had happened, until a dark, seeping stain appeared on the left shoulder of the

Yankee. He slowly curled forward, falling into a pile at the feet of his hapless assailant.

I turned to the restaurant owner. "We must do something. Is there a doctor in town we can send for?"

He gestured to the duellers, seemingly unruffled by the scene. "Them two be the only doctors in this town, ma'am." Sarah and I looked at each other with wide eyes, and I silently prayed that Barkerville would not turn out to be lawless and violent like Yale.

❧

Though the stagecoach offered more comfort than the wagon, the second leg of our journey was not for the faint of heart, but Louis promised us he was an experienced driver. The route through Fraser Canyon was a narrow roadway cut into the granite cliffs of a steep-walled canyon. Sarah and I settled in together and took turns holding Jacob. The three quiet businessmen sat stone-faced across from us. I was pleased to have an empty seat beside me, but at the last minute a new traveller joined us.

He ignored the men and offered Sarah and me his hand. "Jack Harris, ladies," he said with a slow, flat drawl. "Out of California. And you are?"

We politely introduced ourselves. He was handsome in a severe way, with tight skin over sharp cheekbones and a square jaw.

"Where are you from and what brings you two lovely ladies to Barkerville?" he asked, his broad shoulders knocking against mine as the coach set off.

"We're from England and have offers of employment in

Barkerville," I said dismissively, glancing at Sarah. The truth was we had no idea what jobs Sarah's father had in mind for us. We knew that options were pretty limited in a restaurant, none of them terribly interesting, but we were thankful for the opportunity to start somewhere new.

"Don't take my question the wrong way," he said, his dark eyes holding mine in a cool, level gaze. Then he winked. "I didn't take you for Hurdy-Gurdy dancers."

I had no idea who these dancers might be, but they didn't sound respectable, and I tried to ignore Mr. Harris by focusing on the sights outside the window. After all I had witnessed, I planned on being cautious.

The coach started its slow climb from the river valley up the canyon walls, and Sarah and I were forced to look away many times, as the sheer drop to the raging waters below got higher and higher. At one point, one of the horses stumbled, and the coach lurched. I let out an involuntary gasp. Beside me, Mr. Harris chuckled.

"First time on this road?" he asked.

Not wanting to be rude, I nodded. This was going to be a long journey.

"I've come this way many times for business," he said. "Don't fuss. This road is an engineering marvel thanks to the Royal Engineers. Wait till we pass over the part built out on stilts."

"Stilts?" Sarah and I echoed in unison.

"When they couldn't find a way to blast a road surface into the granite, they built sections on wooden stilts."

When we passed over the wood-surfaced section an hour later, my stomach began a series of somersaults, and Sarah tightened her arms around Jacob. He sensed our tension and began to fuss. Turning away from Mr. Harris, I closed my eyes for a long while until we entered a long, dark tunnel.

"Sometimes the engineers used dynamite to make these tunnels," Mr. Harris said, continuing his commentary unfazed by the sheer blackness around us.

The horses whinnied, fearful of what beast or reptile might lurk in the dark, dank shadows. Finally, we emerged into daylight once more, but the roar of water was so loud Mr. Harris had to shout.

"Hell's Gate," he yelled, pointing down.

Below were dizzying rapids. By some freak of nature, the deep canyon narrowed to a width of one hundred feet or so, forcing the white water through a tight channel, where, as if set to high heat upon a giant stove, it boiled and frothed furiously.

At this first look, I bolted back into my seat and stared straight ahead. Sarah hugged Jacob, who had quieted, to her chest, refusing even to peer out the window, but Mr. Harris leaned forward, enjoying the view, and began telling us about the explorer Simon Fraser, the namesake of the river and its canyon.

"He's noted for saying that he and his men 'had to travel where no human being should venture, for surely we have encountered the gates of hell.'"

Sarah and I both shivered. I could not imagine men in canoes trying to navigate the rapids safely, but I knew it was often attempted, and many died.

Jack Harris was clearly enjoying his role as a guide through the wilderness, and in spite of my resolve to keep my distance, I was drawn in by his storytelling.

"What do you know of the gold rush, Mr. Harris?" I asked when the roar of the water began to subside.

"Lots," he said with a shrug. "It was in the sandy bars that skirt this shoreline where the first gold was discovered."

"When was that?" Sarah asked, obviously as interested as I was.

"Only a few years ago. Those miners who chose not to go north to the Cariboo are still here, working their claims by panning the sand." He pointed out signs along the roadway that marked the claims and spoke of the men who laid them: YANKEE DOODLE BAR, LAST-CHANCE FLAT, KANAKA BAR. "*Kanaka* is slang for 'Hawaiian,'" he explained.

I felt my heart beat faster, not from the sheer drop below us, but at the dangerous beauty of the scenery. Never before had I seen such a captivating landscape. England was gentle and rolling, but here, the countryside was both stunning and treacherous. The many sad-looking, white wooden crosses along the road were a testament to the perils the gold seekers faced.

I thought about Simon Fraser, George Vancouver, and the men who had been determined to make a path through this great land. This was truly a land of new beginnings, and I began to feel the trauma and grief of the past year ebb away. Here was a place where my past and the shames of my family would not follow, a place where I could listen to my heart and live the life I chose.

Chapter Thirty-seven

As we neared Barkerville, the stagecoach hummed with anticipation. Sarah in particular was brimming with excitement, and understandably so—she was about to be reunited with her father, whom she had not seen in five years, and she busied herself by changing little Jacob into his best clothes, a darling little sailor suit, for his first meeting with his grandpa.

The stage came to an abrupt halt, and we were forced to wait for an endless hour while a group of men on horseback drove a large herd of cattle across the road and into the valley beyond. I fidgeted in my seat and strained out the window, recalling John's talk of riding with the cowboys.

"The Cariboo's other big moneymaker," Mr. Harris said, pointing to the cattle.

"A profitable business?" I asked.

"All these prospectors have to be fed, and many have the money to eat well. Cattle ranchers are as rich as the successful miners."

"Who controls the ranges?"

"No one. The cattle are free to roam unless a landowner puts up fences. There's more and more fences now that land is being given away to settlers."

Given away, I thought ruefully. *Not quite.* "But people can buy land as well?"

"I guess, but why would they? The land is free to couples willing to settle and work it. All you have to do is be lawfully wedded to get the land." He held my gaze. If he was flirting, I wasn't interested.

Outside the coach, the landscape began to change as evidence of prospecting was everywhere. I couldn't help but think that it resembled a battlefield. Wooden flumes, giant waterwheels, and sluice gates crisscrossed bleak hillsides denuded of trees, and the smell of fresh-cut logs hung thick in the air, the fine particulates of sawdust tickling my throat. Heavy rains had caused washouts at various places, as rainwater rampaged down hillsides unchecked, carrying away with it precious topsoil. Caught up in a feverish quest for gold, these prospectors didn't seem to care how they left the land.

I remembered John telling me how the gold miners used chemicals like mercury that destroyed salmon spawning grounds, depriving the Natives of food. The decimation had taken just six short months.

We passed a sign carved rather crudely into the shape of a man's head. Underneath, in white paint, it read, WELCOME TO BARKERVILLE, POPULATION 5,000, THE BIGGEST TOWN NORTH OF SAN FRANCISCO AND WEST OF CHICAGO.

"Who's the head supposed to be?" I asked Mr. Harris, sure he would know.

"Billy Barker, the town's namesake. He's a Brit, like you, and he discovered a rich vein of gold here only a year and a half ago. This whole town has sprung up since then. They say old Billy is spending his gold faster than he's making it."

Evening was starting to set in, but there was still enough light to get a view of the town as we entered the main street, and Sarah and I hung out the window, curious to see all we could. Many men and some women were out walking in spite of the chill. They seemed friendly, with several small groups engaged in cheerful chatter.

Along the main street, there were twenty or so commercial buildings, many of which boasted elaborate, two-storey false fronts nailed onto rough shacks, and they were all several feet above road level and connected by wooden boardwalks. The reason for this was soon obvious: Main Street was a mud-filled bog.

There was a creek in the distance, and running along it we could see rough wooden shacks and shanties stretching out willy-nilly in every direction, and behind them were white, single-pole canvas tents and a row of ten or so latrines.

"Oh, look!" Sarah pointed. There was the Wake Up Jake Restaurant, one of the more solid and well-kept premises. She bounced Jacob on her knee. "You're going to meet Grandpa very soon."

Farther down the street were Martha's Sweet Shoppe, the colonial assay office, Blanc Photo Studio, the imposing Billy Barker Saloon, and the Theatre Royal.

At the far end, the signs began to change, and I realized they were a mixture of English and Chinese and offered all manner of things. The banner outside Kwong Lee and Co. proclaimed, ALL KINDS OF CHINESE MERCHANDISE INCLUDING OPIUM AND DRY GOODS. I wondered what had brought these people to this remote spot all the way from China.

Our horses picked up their pace as we approached our final destination, the BC Express office, a crude affair across from a gravel pit, where a small crowd had gathered. Once the coach came to a bobbing stop, the door was flung open and we emerged from its confines. I saw Sarah's father right away. He was slighter than I had imagined, no doubt due to the poor treatment he received as a child slave. His thick black hair was interwoven with strands of grey, but I recognized his smile as Sarah's. In a flash, Sarah and Jacob were in his arms, and her father clung to them both as if, having found each other again, he never wanted to ever let go.

My heart ached at the sight before me at the realization that I would never share in an embrace like this one.

"There's someone I'd like you to meet," Sarah said finally, pulling back from her father and gesturing for me to step close. "This is Charlotte. Charlotte, this is my father, Henry Roy."

Mr. Roy's eyes were gentle and moist, and his firm handshake belied the grey streaks in his hair. "You are the dear woman who saved my daughter's life and gave me my grandson. I'm in your debt. I can't thank you enough," he said. "Please—you will come and stay in my home with us. It's the very least I can do."

"Are you quite sure? I wouldn't want to be an imposition."

"An awful lickpenny you would think me if I pointed you in the direction of the hotel," he said. "Consider it settled. You'll stay with us."

In truth, it was a relief. After all this time, I didn't want to be parted from Sarah, and the gift of accommodation would surely help me make a better start here.

Louis handed down the luggage and placed ours in a small pushcart for the walk home. He whipped off his cap as he brought it to us. We thanked him, and Mr. Roy tried to offer a tip, but he waved it away.

"Miss Roy?" he said, hustling after us. "I—ah, ah—was wondering if, I mean." A red flush coloured his neck. "I'd like to come calling next Sunday afternoon. Perhaps we could take a walk together?"

Sarah smiled and looked over at her father for a moment, who seemed delighted by the young dimpled lad in front of him. "I'd like that," she answered politely.

Louis's face broke out into a wide grin, then he nodded and headed back to the stage. He looked back one more time, and I waved, but my hand hung in the air as Jack Harris, who stood waiting for his satchel, tipped his wide-brimmed hat to me. I quickly turned back to Sarah.

As we shuffled along the boardwalk towards the Wake Up Jake, most of the locals we passed nodded pleasantly to us. Mr. Roy was clearly well-known and a respected part of the community here, a far cry from Victoria, where I had witnessed Sarah being treated differently because of the colour of her skin.

The restaurant itself was a clean and wholesome place with ten wooden tables set with red-and-white-checked cloths and glowing coal oil lanterns. White gathered curtains accented the paned-glass windows, and a warm potbelly stove gave the room a welcoming warmth.

"You have a lovely spot here, Mr. Roy," I said. "How did the restaurant get its name?"

"I bought the place from old Jake Franklin. He built it and ran it all by himself for years. He was always so exhausted by his long hours and hard work that the patrons had to yell, 'Wake up, Jake,' whenever they entered, and the name stuck."

I wondered if it was a tall story, and Sarah and I laughed and shook our heads.

"The living quarters are back through here," Mr. Roy said. "Follow me."

We passed through the kitchen, which was quite modern with a large, woodburning cooking stove and porcelain sinks, and then down a hallway to the living quarters. I noticed another, separate room off to the side. Glancing in, I realized it was a cardroom with five round poker tables, each covered in green felt and boasting a Tiffany lamp as a centrepiece on the table. It must have been a challenge bringing those delicate lamps with their coloured glass shades and stylish green fringes all the way here by wagon.

The sitting room was sparsely furnished, but there was a comfortable-looking settee, two standing lamps, and a highly polished wood table crafted from what had to have been a massive cedar tree. My heart leapt at the sight of a handmade bookcase full of leather-bound books.

As we entered the dining room, Sarah let out a gasp. "Father, this is beautiful."

A pine dining room table was set for tea with robin's-egg blue Wedgwood china on a brilliant gold damask cloth. My mouth watered at the sight of plates of raisin scones and raspberry-jam tarts. I had come halfway around the world to end up in a place that truly felt like home.

"This is too much," I said to Mr. Roy.

"I wanted to go to a little trouble for you, after your long journey," he replied. "Now, let's sit and enjoy what the cook's prepared."

Over tea, I tentatively broached the subject of my future employment.

"I hear from Sarah that you've experience in a tearoom," Mr. Roy said.

"Yes, I do." I forced a smile. I expected as much, but I hoped for a job that offered a little more challenge and remuneration.

"I've got plenty of work for both of you. Miss Charlotte, you can serve in the restaurant." He turned to Sarah. "And you, my dear, can serve drinks in the cardroom after you put Jacob to bed in the evenings."

"Perfect," Sarah said.

"Cardroom?" I repeated, raising an eyebrow.

Mr. Roy sipped his tea. "I run a high-stakes five-card-stud game in the room just off the restaurant most evenings. It is by invitation only. I tolerate no bad manners or cursing. The house takes five percent of the pot. It's where I make my real money, not in the restaurant.

I could see that Mr. Roy was a very astute businessman, and I knew I would never get ahead working as a server, so I took a chance. "Do you need a dealer?"

Mr. Roy looked taken aback.

"My mother loved cards and played games of chance with her friends. She taught me how to be a dealer. I'm confident

I can deal cards at a professional level." It was a lie—I had no such confidence, but I desperately wanted to try.

He rubbed his chin thoughtfully. "I could use someone with an understanding of the game, and I won't lie to you, a pretty young woman will give me an edge over the tables at the Billy Barker."

He was just being kind, I knew, but I smiled at his back-handed compliment. "I guess I could try you out for a bit, but if it doesn't work out, it'll have to be the serving job in the restaurant."

I nodded, crossing my fingers under the table. "I understand. Thank you very much. You won't be disappointed."

Mr. Roy explained that the winner of each game tipped the dealer. I would have to work evenings, but my days would be free to do whatever I wanted. With the promise of tips, I expected I'd make more in an evening than in two weeks at my old job. Mr. Roy suggested I practise my dealing skills in the morning, as the men would expect only the best and would be impatient with any delays.

"I like your gumption," he said. "A person needs it in this world. My whole life, people have talked in front of me like I'm not there. But I kept my ears open, and over the years I've heard a lot of things I shouldn't. It's because of who I am."

I wasn't sure where he was taking this conversation, but I felt certain there was a lesson in it somewhere for me. He looked over at Sarah.

"Sarah already knows this, but from my earliest days in Barkerville, people ignored me while I cooked and waited tables here. They figured I didn't have the smarts or the wherewithal to act on what I heard, so they openly discussed business secrets. I used the information I overheard to invest, and after a while I bought the Wake Up Jake with my investment returns."

He's a clever man, I thought.

"Well done," I said, my mind turning over all he'd just said. "I think I'd like to do something similar."

"What is that?"

I hesitated. Was it too soon to give voice to my plan? Were there too many obstacles, and it would evaporate in a puff of smoke like all the others? "An idea has come to me in bits and pieces," I said slowly.

Sarah was helping Jacob hold a piece of a scone that he was trying to chew but was mostly spitting out. "Well, tell us!"

"I want a life with animals, in the outdoors. I want to build a house and buy a cattle ranch. I'll hire cowboys, and when we drive the cattle from one range to another, I'll visit every village and offer training and vaccinations supplies to anyone who wants it." I turned to Sarah. "Reverend Crossman gave me his equipment. And someday, perhaps I can open a clinic." I thought of the duelling doctors in Yale. "So there is always help for anyone who needs it."

"A worthy goal," Mr. Roy said. "I've heard some awful stories about smallpox from prospectors coming in from the north." He paused. "But why would you buy land when all you have to do is find a husband and get it for free from the Crown?"

"I don't believe that land is the Crown's to give away," I said, feeling my conviction harden inside me like cement. I was going to make a home for myself. "I know it'll take me a long time to save enough, but I'm going to start tomorrow."

Chapter Thirty-eight

"You look lovely," Sarah said, clasping her paste-glass necklace around my neck.

It was my first night of card dealing, and every muscle in my body felt tight with nerves. Mr. Roy said he was impressed with my dealing earlier that day, but he was an easy audience. Even the games on the ship where I had dealt paled in comparison to this. That was polite society, and these men were serious players. I fidgeted with my dress, an emerald-green paduasoy gown, and tugged at my white gloves. Sarah had piled my reddish-blond locks high on my head and held them in place with three jewelled combs and a green velvet ribbon. *At least I look the part.*

"Good luck," Sarah said as we parted ways in the hallway, she to the kitchen and I to the cardroom.

I took a deep breath and forced myself forward. Some men had arrived and were bent low over their tables. Two of the other dealers were already in place, shuffling cards to warm up. Pungent cigar smoke hung suspended in the air, mingling with the biting aromas of strong drink and just a hint of human sweat. The Tiffany lamps cast a dark green hue over everything.

As I sat on a velvet chair in the corner waiting for Mr. Roy to direct me to a table, two new gamblers walked in as if they owned the place. They preened like a pair of peacocks, dressed in the most outlandish garb. Small, wiry men, they both sported large handlebar moustaches and wide muttonchop sideburns. Their tight-fitting suits were made of the most bizarre fabrics I had ever seen. I tried not to stare.

One man's suit was made of a yellow-and-blue wool plaid, accented with a robin's-egg-blue waistcoat and a white shirt with collar points so high that I marvelled at his ability to turn his head from side to side. His trouser legs flared and were hemmed inches above the ankles, in part, I guessed, to display a fine pair of high-heeled kid-leather shoes. Remembering the muddy streets, I couldn't imagine more impractical footwear for these parts. Not to be outdone, the other man was dressed in a white raw silk suit, and he had accented his outfit with a white cowboy hat, a string necktie, and a pair of hand-tooled, black leather boots. I scanned the room, realizing that no one else seemed surprised by their appearance.

They ambled over to the dealer next to me, and I tried to listen to their conversation but couldn't make head or tail of it.

"I don't know if you heard tell of us," the first man said. "But we're the fellas who took out a hundred pounds of gold in just eight hours. We've been piling the agonies down in the mines till we're all caved in. Took a trip down to New Westminster to spend a little of our blunt and now we want a good betting game."

He opened a cloth bag and poured a handful of shimmering, mesmerizing gold nuggets on the table. Never had I seen such beauty that represented such wealth, and I gaped in wonder. The dealer didn't react, and I could only surmise that this was not an uncommon sight. I thought about the prospectors I met on the ship who all dreamt of gold. If they found it, did that dream become surreal? Did it cause them to lose all sense and squander their riches? It seemed these men couldn't spend their newfound wealth fast enough.

Mr. Roy waved me towards a table and pulled out a chair for me. "Gentlemen, let me introduce our newest addition, Miss Harding."

There was a great flurry of scraping chairs, as the five men leapt to their feet and doffed their hats. One man was slower than the others.

"I believe I've already had the pleasure of your acquaintance," he said. Standing in front of me was Jack Harris.

"Mr. Harris," I said quickly, sitting down. "You didn't mention that you liked a betting game." I placed my purse on the table, removed my gloves, and tried to hide my trembling hands as the men took their seats.

"Let's just say I'm a man who enjoys risk-taking." He was dressed in formal clothes, all black, and they set off his looks very well.

Mr. Roy beamed. "For those of you who haven't had the pleasure of Miss Harding's company, she is a recent arrival from England along with my daughter, Sarah, who will be serving drinks any moment now."

He introduced each man in turn, starting on my right. Albert Poole, a dentist, was a small man who looked up at me from under a bowed head with squinty-eyed distrust. Next to him was Josh Hurley, a successful gold miner who was flushing deeply, clearly having trouble recovering from the shock of having a young woman act as dealer.

As Mr. Roy was speaking, Sarah arrived with a crystal tray of golden Scotch whiskies, and I took the opportunity to try and settle my shaky hands by shuffling and reshuffling the deck. The motions came easily to me, and some of my nerves dissipated.

Once Sarah retreated, Mr. Roy continued the introductions. Dr. Nickolas Jones—"Call him Sawbones Jones," Mr. Roy said—seemed more interested in the whiskies than anything. His pale, thin hand curled tightly around his shot glass as he bobbed his head in my general direction. And then there was Mr. Harris. Throughout the introductions, his eyes rarely left my face and the slightest of smiles played on his thin lips.

The last player at the table was Dick Canning from the colonial assay office. He was a tall man with a high forehead and a pale, bony face, and he stared at the cards as I shuffled them, clearly anxious to get the game underway. I knew it as a sign of a recent big loser expecting to make back his losses. With quick, staccato motions, I began to deal. The men's attention moved from me to the game at hand, which soon took on a life of its own.

The feverish light of redemption shone in Mr. Canning's eyes when he won the first two hands, one with no less than three kings. He did not begrudge my tips and made a show of the generous sum he tucked into my purse. With the next hand, he upped the ante dramatically, and I suspected he was bluffing, hoping to convince the others to fold. Mr. Harris called his bluff, and Mr. Canning was forced to display his meagre pair of twos for all to see.

Mr. Harris's tight smile widened, and he couldn't suppress a small laugh as he spread his winning cards on the table. Instead of tucking his tip into my open purse as I expected, he reached across the table and folded some notes into my hand, closing his hand over mine as he did so. I felt an urge to pull my hand away. Was he merely being friendly, or was he interested in something more? If it was flirtation, I wished he'd stop.

As the evening wore on, I felt more at ease. Mr. Roy moved silently from table to table, and his patrons tended to ignore his presence as they talked animatedly to one another. I thought about what he had said last night.

Is it the same for me? As a woman, men naturally assumed I would have no head for the business of investing.

By midnight, Sawbones Jones called for their third round of whiskies, urging the others to join him, and Mr. Roy suggested we take a break so that I could have some refreshment. While I sipped my tea, the men relit their cigars and pipes.

"What's the news at the assay office, Dick?" Sawbones asked.

"Man came in the other day from the Horsefly Creek claim," he replied, releasing a puff of smoke. "He dropped a big bag of nuggets the size of peas on the scales and wanted cash for them right away—had no grub, needed money so's he could eat. We didn't have enough cash on hand to buy the whole bag, so I gave him what money I had and sent for more on the next stage. He just grabbed what I gave him and ran off to the saloon."

"Horsefly Creek?" Mr. Poole, the dentist, echoed. "I haven't heard of any big strikes up on the river since '59. Didn't know anyone was digging there."

"Group of Welshmen have moved on up there, couldn't make a go of it here," Mr. Canning said. "Poor bugger looked half-starved, like he barely made it through the winter. Don't know if the sack of gold was a whole winter's work or just what they got since the snow's come off. Be interesting to know, though."

Mr. Hurley, the miner, took a long pull of his cigar. "Sure would."

When our break was over, I dealt out a new round. Now quite comfortable in my role, I tried to parse what the men were saying, but they seemed to be talking cryptically—bids and offers, last trades, escrow shares.

By one o'clock, Mr. Roy closed down the tables, and the men bid their goodbyes. The mood was jovial, as it seemed there were no big losers. Some were not ready to call it a night and talked of heading over to the Billy Barker for a night-cap. Jack Harris lingered and was the last to leave. Perhaps he wanted a last word with me, but I ignored him.

Once everyone was gone, I dumped the contents of my purse on the table and counted my tips. Ten American dollars! The men had been generous. I hoped the trend would continue. It was a good start, but I needed much more. I resolved to find out all I could about the market in gold-mining shares. If Henry Roy could buy a restaurant, then maybe I could buy ranchland.

Chapter Thirty-nine

Two weeks later, when Sarah and I had settled in more, I worked up the nerve to tell Mr. Roy about the conversations I had overheard while dealing cards and asked him how the whole investment game worked. It was Sunday, the restaurant was closed, and we were having a quiet cup of tea together by the warm, crackling fire after church. Sarah bathed little Jacob in a tin bucket next to us. The child splashed and giggled as she blew soap bubbles at him.

"They're talking about what goes on at the share exchange in the back of the colonial assay office," Mr. Roy explained to me. "In a nutshell, the exchange was set up to let men buy and sell share ownership in the different mining claims. Once the miners stake a claim, the only way they can finance big operations is by selling shares to investors. Josh Hurley is a perfect example. He sold interests in his China Bar claim and that's how I came to buy the ten shares that I sent to Sarah. Some of the richest men in Barkerville have never panned a single nugget of gold. They speculate on mining shares—and around here rumours run fast and furious."

Mr. Roy had carved a toy boat out of a piece of wood and tossed it into the tub for Jacob, who squealed with delight. He tried clumsily to pick the toy out of the water with his plump little hand.

"Are you thinking of investing, Charlotte?" Sarah asked.

"Yes, I am. I'm just not quite sure where to begin with it all."

"Let me take you to the share exchange next week when it opens for the season," Mr. Roy said. "You'll get a better idea how it all works when you see it in action."

A knock at the door interrupted our conversation, and he left to answer it. He returned a few moments later and told me there was a gentleman wishing to speak with me in the parlor.

"Me?"

He nodded. What gentleman would be paying me a visit? I wondered for a moment if it was Mr. Harris but was too embarrassed to ask, so I smoothed my skirts and stepped into the front hall, where I was met by a young man dressed in a brown tweed three-piece suit and a matching brown derby hat. Judging by his clean, polished shoes, he was new to Barkerville.

"Miss Harding?" he asked.

I bobbed an uncertain curtsey.

"Cecil Swinton, of Swinton, Smithers, and Carlyle," he said, removing his hat. "We are a law firm in Victoria. My client has asked me to find you, and fortunately you've not been hard to locate."

"Your client?" My heart gave a dip. Was this about George?

"I've been retained by Mr. Charles Baldwin, Lord Ainsley," he said with emphasis. I guessed that not many lawyers in Victoria could claim an English lord as a client.

I relaxed a little. Of course, this was about the money. I didn't ask him to be seated, nor did I offer refreshment. He didn't seem to take offense.

"I understand he was your brother-in-law before *the divorce*." Mr. Swinton's mouth twitched. Was that a sneer?

"That's correct," I said, straightening. "And why are you here?"

"Under the divorce agreement with your late sister, my client is entitled to the return of all gifts and money he generously bestowed on his then-wife. Your sister forfeited all her rights due to the judge's finding of *adultery*." This time I was sure it was a sneer.

My body flared with heat as I found my voice. "My sister had no money of her own, and she left her jewels with Charles, at his insistence. She died penniless. Charles can't get blood from a stone."

"Yes, quite." Mr. Swinton coughed as if to clear his throat. "I understand your late sister, ah, stole money from Lord Ainsley's household accounts. A substantial sum, I believe."

"If that's true, I have no idea where the money is." I thought of the letter I received from Hari's bank. "Perhaps you should check back with your client, in case he has located the funds by now."

"I will. And her wedding and engagement rings?"

Blood pulsed in my ears. "She was buried at sea with them."

Mr. Swinton had the decency to lower his eyes. "I have only your word. Lord Ainsley will want proof."

I clenched my jaw so tightly it started to ache. "What proof could I possibly have?"

"A bank statement, perhaps?"

"I don't have enough money to have need of a bank."

Mr. Swinton glanced at his pocket watch. "I'm not sure Lord Ainsley will be satisfied with your claim; however, I do see you live modestly, not as one would who recently had a windfall of a substantial sum of money."

He replaced his hat on his head and took his leave. No doubt he would claim a hefty fee even if he hadn't retrieved anything for his client, and hopefully this would be the last I ever heard from Charles.

I returned to the sitting room, and Sarah met me with a questioning look. "That was my former brother-in-law's lawyer demanding money that my sister didn't have. At least, if she did, I've never found it," I said with a sigh. "Thank goodness I can close that chapter of my life now. I'm ready to make my own money, and I can't wait to get started."

∽

True to his word, the following week, Mr. Roy took me around to the exchange hut out back of the assay office. A small but intense crowd had already gathered by the time we arrived and were closely peering at two large chalkboards set up on stilts in the alley. Men jostled for position in front of the boards, squinting to read the chalk scribbles. Some called out bids to buy shares or offers to sell while a clerk scurried to record the transactions.

It was a free-for-all, but as Mr. Roy explained what was going on, I began to make some sense of it. Speculation was the driving force for many investors who were buying shares in companies that were rumoured to have found gold in the hopes of a quick profit. Others appeared to have the confidence of inside knowledge and were buying and holding for the long term. Others still were selling their "losers" for whatever they could get for them. The excitement was contagious, and swept up by it all, I decided to get my feet wet.

Recalling the story of the half-starved miner with the big bag of nuggets, I purchased ten shares of the Horsefly Creek claim. It cost me all my savings, but as I tucked the share certificate into my purse, I felt butterflies inside, and happy daydreams of my future filled my head as we slowly made our way back home.

The next night, my table of gamblers, Mr. Harris, Mr. Canning, Mr. Hurley, Mr. Poole, and Sawbones Jones, was abuzz with news about Horsefly Creek. It was Mr. Canning who once again had the latest scoop.

"I'm telling you, boys, I never seen the like! Nuggets as big as pebbles—a hundred pounds a day. We had to send for a special coach with armed guards so we can ship it all south. If you want part of the action, you better be quick."

The rest of the men looked interested but remained cool, calmly reading the cards I had just dealt them, but I was not fooled by their poker faces. I worked hard to keep from beaming and to focus on my dealing. This was very exciting news indeed, and I was quite certain each one of them would be at the share exchange hut first thing in the morning. I would check daily, and as soon as the news broke of the big strike, I would offer my shares to the highest bidder.

Chapter Forty

"He's lovely, so funny and clever," Sarah said. In the reflection of her mirror, I could see her eyes dancing. I'd asked her about Louis. He and Sarah had gone on a few walks, and he was stopping by again this afternoon. "He's bringing me some red ribbon for the new bonnet I made. It's hard to get it here."

"That's very sweet," I replied.

"His French family were Acadians from New Brunswick till they moved to Upper Canada and became English speakers," Sarah was saying as she checked her hair. "But they kept their old ways. He told me such stories of what they call their kitchen parties—can you believe they made music with spoons! He's promised to show me."

"And do you fancy him?" I asked.

She turned to face me. "I think I do," she said seriously. "After my husband died, I didn't think I could ever feel that way about another man. And when little Jacob was born, I felt he was all I wanted or needed."

"But?"

"But Louis . . . has made me realize that I was wrong. The love for a child is a different sort of love, and perhaps I needed more. Of course, I want to take my time getting to know him better before anything changes." She smiled. "But I do feel excited when he's around. Like a young girl again."

I was happy for Sarah. Of anyone, she deserved to find happiness again, but I had to tamp down the sprig of envy that sprouted inside me. When was the last time I felt that way about a man, the only time, really? A flash of John's handsome smiling face filled my vision, and then it was gone.

It was not long before Mr. Roy called us downstairs. Louis was standing in the doorway next to a tall, dark-haired woman.

"Florence Wilson, can it really be you?" I said.

"Charlotte and Sarah!"

Sarah and I flung our arms around our old friend, laughing with delight. Neither of us expected to see her so soon.

"She came in on the coach, and when she asked after you, I thought I'd bring her right over," Louis explained.

"How lovely! But tell us how and why you've come to the goldfields," I demanded. "Have you married a prospector?"

She chuckled. "No, I've done something even more outlandish than that. Shortly after you left, I received a small inheritance from my great-uncle back in England. When I heard the Theatre Royal was for sale, I came north. It was my love of the stage that made me leave England, and so to be sure I land some good roles, I want to buy a theatre. I have an appointment with the owner today."

"Marvelous," Sarah breathed, and wrapped an arm around her friend. "If only the Burks could see you now."

We chatted for a few more minutes, and then Florence told us she needed to be off. Louis offered to show her the way, but before he left, he handed Sarah the promised ribbon and she blushed her thanks. As we shut the door behind them, Sarah and I both murmured our hopes that Florence was here to stay.

Our wish came true. The next day, Florence was back waving her keys. "I bought it!" she said.

We congratulated her on her good fortune and begged for a tour. We were curious to see it for the first time, and she was only too happy to oblige. Mr. Roy offered to watch Jacob, and so we grabbed our hats, then, linking arms, set out for the theatre. Striding along in the company of my two dear friends, I was reminded that the greatest pleasure in life was to be with those you care for.

The Theatre Royal was a formidable two-storey structure housing a fire hall beneath it, and as we approached, we could see a bright-red fire wagon poking out of the building's lower level. The volunteer firefighters, a group of six or seven burly young men, were cleaning and polishing the leather horse bridles and reins, but doffed their hats and smiled at us as we passed by.

"Fire is a constant threat for most theatres," Florence said, pointing up at the fire bell that hung from the rafters, "what with the lighting, paint, props, and all. After the last theatre burnt down, the previous owners saw fit to rebuild over the fire hall."

Over dinner not that long ago, Mr. Roy had told Sarah and me how dangerous fire was for a hardscrabble town like Barkerville, where the buildings touch each other and everything was made of wood. He explained that he had put a ladder on the side of the restaurant that led from the second storey to the ground for our safety. Now, I looked at the wagon with its water barrels and buckets. It didn't seem like it would be much use in the face of an out-of-control fire.

"Come on," Florence said. "Let me show you the stage."

We followed Florence into the theatre and up a long staircase to the main stage, then entered the stuffy, dark, wood foyer. Frenzied sounds of an upright piano filled the dimmed room.

"What's that?" Sarah asked.

"I'm afraid it's the Hurdy-Gurdy girls rehearsing."

We moved through the double doors into the theatre, where lanterns in wire cages rimmed the stage, illuminating four young women in wide-skirted, bell-shaped dresses with tightly cinched waists. Male dancers stood in a group behind the women, and a piano was on the floor below the stage.

Florence wrinkled her nose. "This is called the bell ringer dance."

The men stepped forward and held the young women by the waist as they jumped and swung their legs sideways to the right, then jumped and swung to the left like the swinging pendulum on a grandfather clock. They swung higher and higher with each swing until they finally had enough momentum to twirl around 360 degrees. Sarah and I gasped as the ample folds of their billowing skirts fell away, revealing the girls' crinoline undergarments, white satin garters, and black stockings. I could imagine the catcalls and lewd comments that dance would elicit from a crowd of rowdy miners.

Florence turned back to us. "Needless to say, I plan to phase

out the Hurdy-Gurdy girls and bring in more refined offer-
ings. I already have my first production selected—*The Irish
Lass*. You'll both have to come and see it debut in a few weeks."

"We certainly will," I promised.

"Good." She smiled. "Well, now that I've shown you my
new venture, will you show me around the rest of Barkerville?"

Linking arms again, we made our way along the boardwalk, stopping every so often to peer into a shop window or
to purchase some little knickknack. First stop was Martha's
Sweet Shoppe, where we treated ourselves to several confec-
tions, including soft toffees, caramels, and nougat. Martha, we
explained to Florence, was really a fiftyish former miner from
Cornwall who had learned candy-making at his mother's knee.
He had told us he was too old for mining and found the con-
fectionary much more fun.

Outside Blanc Photo Studio, Florence suggested we stop
and have our picture taken to celebrate our first day in Barkerville together. After checking our purses to make certain
we had the requisite funds, we went in, trying to contain our
excitement.

Monsieur Blanc welcomed us in an enthusiastic flurry.
"Wait till you see the very latest glass-plate technique, ladies,"
he said. "You don't have to sit perfectly still holding a rather
grim expression. The picture's taken quite literally in a flash.
You can even smile if you want."

He studied us each in turn, then centred Sarah on a red-
velvet-covered stool and gestured for Florence and me to stand
behind. We each placed one hand on Sarah's shoulder and
grinned broadly. When all was ready, Monsieur Blanc took a

lit candle and touched it to a tray of loose powder. There was a sharp hissing sound, and then a brilliant flash of white light that left me seeing spots as I stumbled about the studio. In the end, I was thrilled with our picture, or *photograph*, as Monsieur Blanc called it. I bought an extra copy to send to Wiggles, a testament to my new independent life in the colonies.

Sarah and I bid Florence farewell, then made our way home to get ready for our shifts, stopping by the mail office. We almost collided with Mr. Harris on his way out as he'd been focused on the letters in his hand. He seemed discomfited to see us and stammered out an apology.

"Lucky you, look at all those letters," I said. My spirits were high from a day spent with friends, and I thought I'd try to put him at ease. "From your family, Mr. Harris?"

He flushed. "Just business, I'm afraid, Miss Harding. Nothing that would interest you. Ladies," he said, touching his hat and turning to go.

There were a few letters for Mr. Roy, which Sarah collected along with a copy of the *Colonist*, and there was one small envelope for me. I felt a small thrill when I saw it was post-marked Yorkshire.

When we got home, I hurried to my room to change for my shift, and then sat down to read John's letter.

April 7, 1863
Dear Charlotte,

I trust that by now you and Sarah have made it safely to Barkerville. The gold rush town is somewhat familiar to me as I stopped there for a few days on my last trip. I remember fondly the sweet shop, Martha's, I think it's called.

I'm writing with some exciting news of my own. The Royal Geographical Society has asked me to present a series of lectures on my work in the colonies. News of the continuing smallpox epidemic in the New World appears regularly in the papers here and many are asking questions about what Britain is doing to help. I plan to talk about the plight of the Native peoples in the colony of British Columbia and their ill treatment at the hands of the colonial government, settlers, and many of the lawless gold seekers. Some well-known abolitionists are joining forces with me. It's a highly controversial and emotionally charged subject, but it is one I cannot, and will not, in good conscience, shy away from. As you can see, even in Yorkshire, my thoughts continually return to British Columbia.

My father passed away two days after I got home. He never let on in his letters, but his health had been poor before his stroke, and my brother, Andrew, had been doing the real work of managing the estate and doing a splendid job, really. His wife, Roberta, and their two daughters are quite the mistresses of the house. They happily fulfill the social obligations of our family and see to our traditional charitable endeavours. There's no real need for me to be here. I am the fifth wheel in the family and an unhappy one at that.

For the past six years, I have roamed far and wide as a clergyman, bringing medical knowledge and care to people in the farthest corners of British Columbia. That's the life for me, not the life of a country lord. I'm in the process of gathering fresh medical supplies and plan to set sail for Victoria once my lectures are over in three weeks' time.

*It's not just my mind that draws me back to British
Columbia, but my heart as well. I confess my feelings for you
have not abated since I have been home, and know that I have
made it clear to Agnes (and her father) that we are not engaged.
Agnes seemed more relieved than anything. She gave me her
blessing and confessed that, while she had been prepared to do
her duty to her father and marry me, she was not comfortable
with the controversy that swirled about me and my work. She
preferred a quiet life.*

*I don't expect you to feel the same about me after all that has
transpired between us, but I hope you will allow me to call on
you when I return to Barkerville soon.*

Love,
John

I set the letter on my bed and looked out at the maple
tree outside my window. Its new tender green leaves were just
beginning to reach their maturity. They would sustain this tree
for the summer to come, allowing it to strengthen and deepen
the roots needed to withstand the storms of winter. *Perhaps
that's what loving relationships do for people.* Would I deny myself
the chance to mature and grow if I didn't explore this relationship with John? My heart was pulling me towards him, I
realized, and unlike before, I felt compelled to follow.

I found a piece of paper and scribbled a brief calculation.
John's letter took about two months to get to me on one of the
clipper ships, or perhaps it took the new faster route through
Panama by train. Depending on the ship and the route, I could

expect John to arrive in Barkerville as early as midsummer. Of course, there were so many variables and he could be much later. I told myself not to get excited, but my heart wouldn't listen.

Just then, Sarah came into my room, holding out the *Colonist*. "I thought you'd want to see this," she said, her face worried.

I scanned the headlines. There was one small story about the continuing smallpox outbreak, and another about civil unrest in London. She pointed to the latter. I quickly read the short article. Fights had broken out between opposing factions regarding colonial rule and the treatment of the Native peoples in the colonies. A series of recent lectures by Reverend John Crossman to the Royal Geographical Society had ignited the violence.

"Don't worry," I said to Sarah. "I've just received his letter, and he's already left for here."

She hugged me. "I'm so glad he's away from that."

She wanted to linger and talk, but Jacob started to wail just then and she flew off to see what was the matter. I picked up the paper and scanned the rest of the headlines—I froze. "No, this can't be."

There in the blurred print was a piece of dreadful news: "Victoria's Elite Turn Out to Greet Top Parliamentarian, George Chalmers."

Chapter Forty-one

I began to regularly search the *Colonist* for any news of George and his comings and goings, and any mention of him in the society pages, but there was none. I worried that Lady Persephone had told him what I had said at the teahouse in Victoria. How could I have been so rash? *You've got some of our father's recklessness in you*, Hari told me more than once.

My spirits flagged, and I found it difficult to focus on my card dealing. Worry rooted itself deeply in my brain. I tried to reason it away. Surely George would not want to air ugly accusations about himself in public or press his point through some sort of legal action against me. I was in Barkerville, after all, and no longer a threat to him. But the words I spoke to Lady Persephone kept coming back to me. Finally, I confided in Sarah.

"I had hoped you had escaped him for good," she said. "No wonder you've been in a depressed mood lately. I think I know a way to help lift you up. Florence's play is starting Sunday night. Louis has asked me, but I'll suggest he take us both."

"I couldn't intrude. I know how much you enjoy your time with him. You're not losing interest in him, are you?"

She couldn't contain her smile. "Oh, no, not at all, quite the other way. He's kind and caring, and little Jacob loves him. I didn't expect this, as you know, but . . ." She blushed.

"Then go with him," I insisted, wanting her to have her happiness.

"I will, but I'm telling him that you're coming too. He can escort us both."

The day of Florence's debut, Sarah fussed over her clothes and her toilette. After I donned my green paduasoy gown and managed to pin my hair, I helped Sarah pin red ribbons into her bouffant hair. Her flawless skin was perfectly accentuated by the red cotton gown she wore. She had crocheted white lace around the neckline and made pretty little cuffs at her wrists. She was a vision of loveliness, and I heard Louis's breath catch when she greeted him that evening.

Quite a crowd had gathered out front of the cheerfully repainted Theatre Royal. There were scores of prospectors, looking the better for having bathed, but also some couples lingering outside, enjoying the late sunlight of one of the first really warm summer evenings. We fluttered our elegant feather-and-ivory fans and went to read the elaborate scroll on the billboard.

Florence Wilson, of the Cariboo Amateur Association, will grace our stage this evening with performances that are second to none in the colony. Witness her angelic voice bring tears to the eyes of the most hardened of old miners when she sings: "When Love Gets You Fast in

Her Clutches," "Emblems of Mem'ry Are These Tears," "My Poor Dog Tray," and the rousing "Hail Columbia."

"I'm so proud of our Florence," Sarah said, squeezing my arm.

"I can't agree more. She's achieved so much in such a short time." I took it as a sign that there was hope for the rest of us.

As I was speaking, Jack Harris appeared at my side. I could smell a mixture of talc and cigar and could feel his breath on the back of my neck. "I'll bet you're looking forward to Miss Wilson's debut, but I'll miss the Hurdy-Gurdy girls, myself."

"I'm sure your disappointment will be short-lived once Miss Wilson takes the stage," I replied. I caught sight of Louis waving at us to follow him. "Do enjoy the show, Mr. Harris."

Sarah and I followed Louis inside the theatre and took our seats at stage left. When the ushers closed the theatre doors, the room went dark for a minute until they lit the half-moon lanterns that edged the stage. The space took on a cozy, festive feel. Smells of the theatre drifted past me—oily greasepaint and the sharp tang of rosin and chalk—and music floated out of the blackened stage wings as a small string orchestra and upright piano struck up a rousing tune.

When Florence stepped out on the stage, the crowd jumped to its feet and roared its approval. She was dressed as a poor Irish country girl in a becoming bonnet, but her stage makeup made her appear larger than life with heavily rouged apple cheeks and red rosebud lips. Once the audience had taken their seats, she began to sing in a lilting soprano, and I soon settled back and relaxed, transported to another place, another time, lost in my imagination. The play was the story of a young woman who had fallen in love with the son of a rich landowner, but her father forbade their love, and the young man was forced to marry another. The first act ended with the young, heartbroken lass considering immigrating to British Columbia. I smiled at Sarah in the dusky glow of the theatre—it was easy to see Florence's influence in the playwriting.

This sort of play was all the rage, I knew, and while I loved seeing Florence in her element, I found the story itself a touch melodramatic. I suspected it was, in some ways, a catharsis for the lonely men who had left their loved ones far behind and daily risked their lives in the all-consuming quest for gold.

As the curtain came down for intermission, the ushers opened the doors to a back room and invited us to stretch our legs and take some refreshment. Sarah went to answer a call of nature while Louis searched for drinks for all three of us.

Loitering about, I soon realized the only person I recognized was Jack Harris, who spied me across the room and made his way unerringly towards me with two glasses of lemonade in his hand. I could see no escape. He came up and, taking my hand, placed a glass in it.

"It has a little something extra."

I looked around desperately for any sign of Louis or Sarah, then sniffed at the offering and wrinkled my nose at the pungent, tropical smell of rum. I could think of nothing to say, so I forced myself to take a polite sip as he watched.

He leaned in very close. "I unsettle you, don't I? You've got nothing to fear from me—or is it something else?"

I sputtered and choked on my drink, and he laughed loudly.

"I'm only teasing. You're such an easy mark, Miss Harding,"

he said, taking a step away. "How are you enjoying the show?"

I relaxed, seeing nothing malicious in his eyes. "Florence is wonderful. I honestly can't remember when I've enjoyed a performance quite so much."

"Really? You should get out more."

"You don't agree?" I raised my chin, feeling a tad offended on Florence's behalf. "Perhaps the more base fare of the dancing Hurdy-Gurdy girls is more to your liking, but I can assure you, I, for one, am charmed by Florence and am incredibly impressed by her talent."

"Oh, don't get on your high horse. I'm just suggesting that you're a bit naive."

I set my drink down with a thump on a nearby table. "I consider myself to be a woman of the world. You know that I have travelled here all the way from England by my own wits. Not many other unmarried women can boast that."

"I've offended you. I didn't mean to do that. It's just that when I saw you a while back, taking in everything Dick Canning had to say about Horsefly Creek, obviously believing every word of it, it struck me that you're an innocent."

"What in heaven's name do you mean by that?" I asked. The air in the back room suddenly felt quite close and warm.

He picked up my unfinished drink and drained it. "It's fine with me if you want to play the stock-trading game. Have at it. But there are things you need to know first, like the fact that Dick's always pumped about one claim or another. We take his stories with a grain of salt. He's not always wrong, but more often than not, he is."

"Thank you for your words of warning, but I can assure

you I am not tempted to bet on the outcome of mining ventures."

"Of course you aren't," he said with that irritating slight smile of his. "In case you are interested, though, Horsefly Creek has come up bust. I doubt you could give the shares away now."

At his words, I tried to appear nonchalant, but I felt pricks of perspiration on my brow. Thankfully, we were interrupted by a call to take our seats for the second act, and I took my leave.

For the rest of the show, I felt that my performance equalled that of Florence on the stage. I laughed when the audience laughed and enthusiastically joined in during the final singing of "Hail Columbia." After the show, Sarah and I hurried backstage to congratulate Florence, and I was most sincere in my warm wishes for her. But inside I was deflated and angry at myself.

Sarah and Louis were oblivious to my dark mood as they walked hand in hand, leaning into each other and talking in hushed tones. When she saw me straggling behind, Sarah broke away from Louis and circled back, linking arms with me. Her kindness cheered me, and I thanked the stars above that we were friends. I would somehow find a way to build my ranch, I told myself, and decided to give up fretting about it for now.

We stopped often to admire the brilliant night sky, picking out the Big and Little Dippers and the North Star. Louis described the northern lights he had seen last September, multicoloured, flickering tongues of light that snapped and crackled across the darkened horizon. Sarah professed a great desire to see them when they made an appearance in the fall, and I wondered if John would be here by then and what might come of our relationship.

Chapter Forty-two

Life took on a bit of a dull routine in the weeks that followed, but time passed pleasantly enough. It was summer, precious days of warmth and light that shouldn't be squandered in the north. And it was the time for love. Business was so brisk at the BC Express stagecoach company that they hired a second driver to spell Louis off. He had more time in town, and he spent most of it with Sarah. Seeing her happiness made me think often of John. I had started watching the calendar. Midsummer had passed, but it wouldn't be long now.

I had written Wiggles and sent along the photograph of me, Sarah, and Florence, and in her reply Wiggles had said that she had attended one of John's last lectures at the society and she had been most impressed. In spite of the aggressive hecklers, John had spoken well and with conviction. I think she guessed there was something between the two of us, as she didn't hesitate to tell me what a fine upstanding man he was.

I avoided conversations with Jack Harris as much as possible. Eventually he seemed to take the hint and left me alone. He was right about one thing, though. I was naive. Horsefly Creek shares had plummeted. My tips were slowly building into a small nest egg, but I knew I had to adjust my expectations. I would never be able to afford anything other than a small acreage, maybe thirty acres, with a modest dwelling, nothing close to the 160 acres the government was giving away for free, but I was comfortable with that. Even if I married one day, I was determined not to participate in that scheme.

It was a Saturday night and I came in to work early. The poker den was already thriving, and I was surprised to see Sarah with Jacob in her arms. She never brought him into the cardroom, as it was usually so smoky, but she was there, holding him with one hand as she carried him on her hip. He appeared mesmerized by the green Tiffany lamps. She rushed over to me and held out her left hand, fingers spread wide. Before I even saw it, I knew. There was a ring on the third finger.

"Oh, Sarah, this is so very exciting." I examined the slim gold band, an interesting creation with three small gold nuggets mounted in the middle. "I'm so happy for you," I said, embracing her.

"I couldn't wait to tell you. The wedding's going to be September twenty-fifth, just a month away. We'll have it at the church. Louis already has permission. And you, Charlotte, you must be my maid of honour."

"I will be honoured." Blinking away the tears that had come to my eyes, I focused on Jacob. "And maybe you can be the ring bearer?" I said to him. "You're still a little unsteady on your legs, but I'm sure you'll do fine."

"Of course," she said, laughing. "Won't you look handsome,

Jacob?" She twirled him around, and I smiled, her excitement infectious.

Later that night, after an exhausting shift, I readied myself for bed, thinking of the momentous day, and felt an odd sense of sorrow. I couldn't quite put my finger on the source of my melancholy until it struck me. Sarah's wedding date was September 25, a month away, so this must be August . . . I looked at my desk calendar and double-checked the date. Today was the anniversary of Hari's death.

I went over to my trunk and opened the lid, pushing my hand deep, through the stack-folded winter clothes. At the very bottom, my fingers hit something hard, and I reached for Hari's black jewellery box that I hadn't seen since that awful day on the *Tynemouth*, when Sarah helped me sort through Hari's things. I let my fingers slide across the smooth surface of inlaid mother-of-pearl. *My only memento of Hari.* I flipped it over, my fingers hunting for the hidden recessed catch that I knew was there. As children, we had thrilled at the small compartment that the depressed latch revealed and had left secret messages to each other inside, away from the intruding eyes of our mother. I smiled at the memory. I found the latch and pushed it.

Three slender gold wafers escaped from the compartment and slid onto my lap. I caught my breath, unable to believe the sight before me. They were pure gold, just as I had seen months before when the rich dandies poured a bag of nuggets on a table in the gambling den. These wafers had to have been purchased from the funds that Hari stole from Charles. *Not stole*, I corrected myself, *recovered*. They represented the dowry that Papa had set aside for me before he died, the legacy that Charles tried to keep for himself.

Slowly, I picked up the wafers, letting them slip and slide between my fingers, watching the light play off them. This gold would allow me to have my dream—ranchland and a fine home. Ironically, my dowry would ensure my ability to live the rest of my life independently. I need never marry. Then I remembered who I owed my deepest thanks to. Harriet. How I wished she were here to share this moment with me. With a heavy heart, I put the slim bars back where I had found them and pushed the latch to reset it.

A cascade of thoughts filled my head. Sarah would take her life in a new direction just as I would mine. Our friendship would change, but it could never die. I began to dream of what my new ranch and house would be like and decided I would call it *Harriet House,* in honour of my sister and the life she never had.

Chapter Forty-three

The next day, I told Mr. Roy of my plans, and he insisted he would help me. I readily agreed. I knew that I would have far greater success negotiating a land purchase and engaging a builder if I had a man with me.

It would take months for a new house to be built, but first I needed to buy the land. Mr. Roy left his business in Sarah's hands, and we took the coach south. I hoped to buy a spread on the beautiful ranchland I had heard about near a town called Lillooet.

The town reminded me of Yale, where we had caught our stage on our way north to Barkerville. Men loitered everywhere, looking lost as they tried to secure modes of transport to take them to the goldfields. My knuckles whitened as I clutched the gold-laden bag on my lap. After checking into the hotel, I made it my first order of business to purchase a small revolver at the gun and rifle shop, where the owner gave me a brief lesson on its use.

"This one's got a hair trigger, so don't point it at anyone you're not intending to shoot," he said.

I felt much easier with the little derringer tucked in my bag as Mr. Roy and I rode off to view some parcels of land that were for sale outside of town. The rolling grasslands were dotted with groves of trembling aspen and poplar trees, their leaves already starting to change from green to a canary yellow in contrast to their white-barked trunks. Mr. Roy was as taken with the landscape as I was, but his was a more practical eye, pointing out the need for plenty of water on my future property and looking for promising building sites for my house and outbuildings.

After two days of riding, we found the perfect spot: a shallow, flat-bottomed valley with a meandering stream running into a small, clear lake surrounded by trees. I could see myself living out my life there, watching the seasons come and go, tending to my animals, building the kind of existence I wanted. Surveying the gentle, undulating hills before me, smelling the dry grasses, hearing the shrill cry of the circling golden eagles overhead, I felt the first moments of true peace and joy that I had experienced in a very long time, since before Hari died and John left for England. I felt at home.

The six hundred acres were owned by a Métis widow who wanted to move to Victoria to be near her daughter. The land had originally been a gift to her husband, a Hudson's Bay factor, from Governor Douglas. With Mr. Roy at my side, we visited a land agent and made the purchase. Over the next three days, we engaged a builder and ordered a herd of cattle, arranging for them to be driven up from Washington Territory via the Okanagan Trail next year. People initially balked at doing business with a woman, but I soon saw the power of money. Once they discovered I had my own funds, they signed the contracts with a great flourish.

To celebrate, I took Henry out for the best meal I could find in town, complete with a bottle of champagne, and we toasted my new venture.

∽

When we returned, I was dying to tell Sarah all my news, but she was out with Jacob, so I headed upstairs to unpack. I put all my new paperwork neatly in my desk drawer and stowed my revolver away in my jewellery box's concealed compartment for safekeeping. I wouldn't need it in Barkerville. Coming downstairs I heard a sharp knock at the door. Opening it, I was startled to see the mail clerk standing on the stoop.

"Looks like this is your lucky day, Miss Harding. A letter from England. I was passing by on my way home and thought to drop it off."

I examined the thick envelope and thanked him profusely, even as a sense of dread swept over me. It was addressed to me in a script I didn't recognize. The return address was a law firm in London. It had to be from Charles's solicitors. I couldn't bring myself to break the seal. *What does he want now? Why can't he just leave me alone?*

I tossed the packet onto the dining table and went outside. Standing by Sarah's flower garden, I let the warm afternoon sunshine wash over me and took a moment to calm myself, feeling the gentle caress of the warm breeze in my hair, hearing the languid droning of a passing bumblebee, smelling Earth's pungent aromas, released from deep within her bosom. I breathed slowly and evenly.

The sound of a crying baby pulled me from my musings. *Sarah and Jacob must be home.* I gingerly picked up the letter and went to find Sarah. She was curled up in an old brown velvet chair, rocking her child on her lap. She smiled a warm greeting, excitement shining in her eyes.

"A letter from John?" she said softly, not wanting to unsettle her calming baby.

I shook my head. "No, it's something else."

"What, then?"

"It's from some law firm in London. You read it, please—read it out loud to me. I think it's from Charles."

Sarah raised an eyebrow and pursed her mouth. "Me? I'm painfully slow—not much of a reader. You'll be too impatient."

"No, no, slow is just what I want," I insisted. "Skip the preamble and just read the heart of the letter. Find out what he wants from me now."

She nodded, but her lower lip protruded and her brow wrinkled as she accepted the envelope. She broke the seal and took a moment to find the right place to start reading out loud.

No doubt you've heard from John Crossman's brother, Andrew, by now, so I won't repeat the sad details. We understand there have been no arrests, but the police informed me that they are investigating an extreme political group who challenged John's beliefs. Suffice it to say that the beating Reverend Crossman endured left him non compos mentis, not mentally competent.

Andrew Crossman has requested that our law firm contact John's business and personal associates to inform them that we will be taking over all John's private matters while he is incapacitated. Should John ever regain his metal capacity, we will relinquish our duty to him at that time. In the meantime, please address any future correspondence relating to John Crossman care of the undersigned.

Sarah's face flushed and she stopped reading. My heart stopped for a moment, and I felt as though I had stepped outside myself. Sarah's voice seemed far away, and I could barely comprehend what she was saying. Then the reality of the news began to sink in. *Poor John.* He had been so full of life and promise. To have endured a beating so bad that it left him unable to function. It was all too awful to contemplate.

Sarah tried to comfort me, but I gently told her that I needed to be alone. I had no appetite for dinner, so I headed up to my room, where I flopped on the bed and cried into my pillow. When I calmed and took a moment to reflect, I thought how John and I hadn't even had a chance to explore our relationship, to discover our feelings for each other. But deep down, I already knew the truth. I had loved John from the first time we met. And now he was gone from me forever.

At four in the morning, I rose, lit a candle, and wrote a letter to John's brother, Andrew. I sent him and his family my condolences and my fervent hope that in spite of John's distressing injuries, he was in fact making a full recovery. In my heart of hearts, I knew it was just wishful thinking, something one tells the family of the grievously injured in the face of a dire prognosis, but I expressed the sentiments anyway, clinging to a slender thread of hope.

Chapter Forty-four

"I've got a fitting at the dressmaker in Wells; it's two hours away and Father is busy with customers," Sarah said. "I hoped you wouldn't mind watching Jacob. The wedding's just two weeks off."

"Of course," I said. I was letting myself get swept up in the wedding preparations. Being busy was a tonic for me, and, while still grieving, I was determined not to let my personal misery ruin Sarah and Louis's special day. But more than that, Sarah needed my help. Watching Jacob was at the top of her list, since at just over a year old, he was beginning to feel the need to explore his world, taking his first tentative walking adventures.

Mr. Roy had created a carrier for Jacob out of a miner's rucksack. I strapped it to my back, so that we could walk to the stagecoach to wave goodbye. I knew the adventure would help to calm his fussing over Sarah's leaving. He was just tall enough to see over my shoulders, and the rucksack afforded him a princely view of all he surveyed.

He was getting almost too big and heavy for the carrier.

Children grow so fast, I thought with some regret. I'd dearly miss not seeing him regularly once I moved to my ranch. I had held him almost every day over the past year, and his gurgling laugh had become one of my favourite sounds. My heart had been broken and scarred in many ways, but the memory of his birth always flooded me with warmth.

On the way back, we sauntered lazily along, enjoying the warm September day. By the time we reached home, his eyes were drooping, and we were both ready for a midday snooze, me on my bed and Jacob in his little crib next to me. I threw a shawl over myself and drifted off into a deep slumber.

I didn't know how much time had passed, but I awoke with a start at the high-pitched clang of the Theatre Royal's bell. *Fire!* My heart leapt to life, thumping in my chest. Jumping to my feet, I ran to the window and saw men in the back lane drop what they were doing and run in the direction of the fire hall.

Mr. Roy called upstairs to me. "Pack a bag, Miss Charlotte, for you and Jacob, just in case," he said. "I'll be back to check on you if things get bad." Then I heard the sharp bang of the front door of the Wake Up Jake, and in less than a minute, I caught a glimpse of him racing up the street through a gap in the buildings.

Miraculously the commotion had not woken Jacob. I went to the small attic window and leaned out. While I had been asleep, the weather had changed. A hot, dry wind had picked up, and with it came a restless feel to the air—edgy, unstable, with sudden wind gusts swirling dust and grit. I didn't smell a fire, but one slender plume of white smoke hung in the air about two blocks away. I knew that with the wind, things could move fast.

I quickly but quietly sorted Jacob's things, filling a satchel with them, then went to Sarah's room and filled the bag with things I knew she'd want saved—her wedding shoes, gloves, and the red silk corsage she had made for Louis. Then I checked the window once more.

The smoke had ceased to be a slender plume. It had turned black and thickened, billowing and rising to higher and higher heights. The breeze stiffened, blowing the unmistakable smell of burning wood into the courtyard below and then up to my room.

I grabbed the bag and took it outside, hiding it in Sarah's garden. I had just started back upstairs when a loud explosion stopped me in my tracks. Jacob awoke with a cry, and I raced up the attic stairs. My chest heaving, I scanned the horizon once more. A great, thick black cloud of smoke blocked much of my view. I took a reflexive step backwards as red fingers of flames sliced skywards, dissecting the angry cloud. It was time to go. I filled another bag with my few valuables and precious papers—the deed to my property, my bankbook, my saved letters—and John's vaccination equipment. I threw Hari's and my jewellery boxes in as well. Then went to Jacob.

Jacob was fussy, protesting my attempts to dress him. He kicked his legs as I struggled to pin his fresh nappy, hitting my hand and plunging the pin painfully deep into my thumb. I sucked the oozing wound to stop the bleeding and tried to push away my growing anxiety. I talked to myself to settle my unease. *There's plenty of time—no need to panic. Mr. Roy will be here to help us soon*. But my fingers became thick and sloppy, struggling to slide buttons through holes and attach hooks to eyes.

I reached for Jacob's sweater, then thought better of it. He was dressed well enough to ward off any chill, and I didn't want to take any more time. A quick check out the open window told me that the building on the far corner of our block was on fire. *Oh my God. Florence's theatre must have gone up.* Sharp hissing and crackling noises filled the air as grey and black bits of ash floated through the open window. I grabbed my bag in one hand and scooped Jacob up with the other and made for the door, only to stop at the silhouette of a tall, slim man, dressed in all black.

"Oh my goodness, Mr. Harris, you gave me a nasty fright!" I held Jacob tight. "Are you helping with the evacuation? We're ready to go."

He didn't move.

I stepped towards him and tried to hand him my bag. "Perhaps you can carry this? I have Jacob here."

"Do you recall that day when you saw me in the mail office?" He spoke slowly, unfazed by the disaster around us. "I got a letter from Victoria, and you asked me if it was from family."

Sudden loud popping noises in the back lane made me jump, and Jacob cried, a series of long, hiccupping howls. I had to shout. "This is no time for idle chat. We can talk about it once we're outside."

"No," he said. "We'll talk now."

I swallowed hard, tasting a fine film of ash in my mouth. "I'm sorry if I offended you by prying into your business, but this is not the time or place for an apology. I'm getting out of here." I advanced towards him, ready to push past him and down the stairs, but he held up his hands.

"Stop, there's time. The fire's a ways away yet."

"Time for what?" I asked, a shiver of dread running down my spine.

"I'm a man for private hire—out of San Francisco. Folks want me to right wrongs they've suffered, real or imagined." He smiled that mocking smile of his. "I have a client who paid me to track you down."

Charles. Of course. "My former brother-in-law, Charles, has retained you to get the money, is that it?" I laid Jacob down on the bed and fished my jewellery box out of the bag. I flipped open the lid. "You see? It's empty. I spent it. It was mine to spend anyway. Tell Charles you tried." I could see smoke rising from the wood-shingled roof of the building two doors over. "For heaven's sake, the fire is getting very close. Can we please just leave?"

"Your brother-in-law is not my client. George Chalmers is. I'm here to send you a message. You know, Miss Charlotte, this fire's a gift, it helps me make my point so well."

I heard a soft thud and turned to see that Jacob had rolled off the bed and was standing unsteadily on his legs. He started a wobbly walk towards me, and to Jack.

I ran my hands along the bottom of the jewellery box until my fingers found the latch. I pressed it and felt cold, hard gun-metal drop neatly into my hand. I levelled the revolver on Jack.

"Step away from the door or I'll shoot," I said, my voice shaking

Jack almost stumbled over himself backing towards the door.

I held the gun in my damp, tremulous grip and took aim at his chest, hoping he would simply flee, and the gun exploded.

Jack flinched as if punched in the stomach, and we both stood perfectly still, watching a dark red stain grow on his shirt until he collapsed in a heap on the floor.

The hair trigger, I remembered. *I killed him.*

Jacob's hysterical cries made me focus. I had to get moving. I swept him up in my arms, grabbed my bag, then hurried to the door, avoiding Jack's blank eyes. Stepping over him, I pulled on the door, but the body blocked it from opening wide enough for me to get through. I tried again, pulling with all my might, but it was not enough.

I surveyed the room. The carrier. I quickly strapped Jacob into it so he couldn't move, then laid him on the bed. I took hold of Jack's fine leather boots and dragged him, but his dead-weight was such that he moved only a few inches. Hitching up my skirts, I straddled his waist and took hold of his suspenders, heaving the top half of his body away from the door. The door finally swung open. I moved to grab Jacob and flee, but something grasped my ankle, sharply twisting and tripping me, and I sprawled on the ground. Jack hovered over me, blood dripping from his shirt, and he reached for my throat, squeezing. I clawed at his hands, fighting for breath, but the pain in my neck was excruciating, and I felt as though I was drowning.

Blackness hovered, circling the edges of my eyes, and I could hear my heartbeat pounding in my ears as if my eardrums might burst. I could taste blood. Through it all, I heard Jacob crying.

I had to save him. With my last bit of strength, I kicked both feet wildly in all directions until I connected with something and a new shriek filled my ears. Suddenly, air gushed into my lungs. Taking great long, jagged drags of air, I struggled to my knees and drew Jacob to me, half sliding, half dragging us both across the floor, away from Jack, who lay inert by the door.

Behind him was an even more horrifying scene. Sheets of flames shot up the stairwell. Our only avenue of escape was gone. There was a sharp snap of shattering glass from the drawing room two floors below. Thick, choking smoke was funnelling up the attic stairs.

With Jacob in my arms, I ran to the window. *Thank God.* Below, Mr. Roy was climbing the wooden ladder affixed to the wall. The ladder didn't reach all the way to attic, so I leaned out the window and passed Jacob to the strong arms of his grandfather. The attic's temperature was becoming unbearable. A quick glance over my shoulder told me that flickering tongues of flame were seeping into my room. I had mere seconds until the room would be enveloped.

I tossed my bag out below, then clambered onto the windowsill. I crouched there for a brief second, facing into the room, before I gripped the edge tightly with my fingers and dropped down. My fingertips burned on the ledge as I desperately sought the top rung of the ladder with my feet before my fingers failed me. And then I felt Mr. Roy guiding my toes into position. As I let my feet take my weight, I let go of the sill with one hand and searched for something to grasp with my fingers. By holding on to bits of wooden siding that had weathered and warped, I managed to inch my feet one rung lower on the ladder.

Another explosion rocked the Wake Up Jake, and I looked up and watched in horror as flaming window curtains billowed silently towards me before wrapping themselves around my head. Needles of pain sliced my skin. I swiped desperately at my face as I lost my balance and slipped from the ladder, falling backwards, and everything went black.

When I opened my eyes, I was in a makeshift hospital tent. Both my left arm and right leg were in a brace, and there was some sort of heavy bandage on one side of my face. I became aware of dulled pain, and my entire body ached. There was a gurgling noise to my right, and I slowly shifted my head. It was Jacob, laughing and giggling in Sarah's arms, holding out his fingers to me. Sarah touched my hand lightly, and I heard her sniff.

"Thank you," she whispered. Jacob was safe. I smiled and let myself drift away.

Chapter Forty-five

Six weeks after the fire, Barkerville looked a little more like itself. Over ninety buildings had been rebuilt, including the Wake Up Jake, which Mr. Roy had worked tirelessly for four weeks to erect, taking the opportunity to modernize the restaurant with running water and gas lights. The town was bigger and better, and the main street was wider and straighter. St. Saviour's Church replaced the old church and was a much more elegant place of worship, with a steepled roof, lancet windows, and board-and-batten walls. It was the perfect place for Sarah and Louis's wedding, which had been postponed until after the reconstruction.

"Hold still," I said to Sarah as I pinned a wreath of white silk roses in her long gleaming hair. Sarah and I were getting ready in a small room at the back of the church.

"I'm trying to, but I'm just so nervous." Sarah was shivering with pent-up emotion.

The fire and its aftermath had left me emotionally fragile, but today I felt nothing but joy at Sarah's happiness. A warm

glow pulsed from my heart like gentle waves lapping a shoreline. "You are the most beautiful bride this town has ever seen,"
I said.

"Oh go on, and you are the most beautiful maid of honour."

I knew it was meant as a compliment, but my hand auto-
matically went to the angry red scar on my cheek. I wished
there was some powder or hair arrangement that could cover
it. All I could do was hope it would fade in time. The worst
of my injuries had healed fairly well. The broken arm had set
perfectly, but the leg had not yet, leaving me with a limp. The
emotional scars would take longer.

I had told no one of Jack's death and my role in it. It was a
secret I would take to the grave. The *Colonist* reported that a
Mr. Jack Harris of San Francisco was missing and presumed to
have been caught up in the Barkerville firestorm. No body had
been found in the wreckage, though. I wondered what George
thought happened to Jack, but I would never know. According
to the *Colonist*, he returned to England with Lady Persephone
and Sir Richard a week after the fire.

I'd also read that the long-discussed merger between the
colony of Vancouver Island and the colony of British Columbia had been announced, solidifying British rule. What that
would lead to, I had no notion, but what did delight me was
the news that Governor James Douglas was stepping down and
Queen Victoria was to knight him. I thought of Miss Hardcastle in the tearoom, obliged to drop a curtsey to the new
Lady Douglas, and I smiled.

I turned my attention back to Sarah, sweeping my hand
over her silk dress. Kwong Lee had received a wonderful ship-

ment of fabrics from China and offered Sarah first choice for her wedding.

"This is such a perfect dress for you, white like Queen Victoria's wedding gown," I said. "The silk makes it so special."

Sarah's smile was radiant as she admired herself in the mirror.

There was a knock on the door, and Florence poked her head in. "Everyone decent?" She was carrying a bouquet of dried roses. The real ones were long gone at this time of year.

"Oh, Sarah, you are stunning," she said, handing her the flowers.

"Thank you." Admiring the roses, Sarah said, "This is kind of you. I know the rebuilding has kept you very busy."

"Thanks to your father and his dear friends, the theatre is largely finished. We'll be opening with Dickens's *A Christmas Carol* on December first."

"How lovely," I said, remembering my run-in with that very author. "I'll look forward to seeing it."

When we heard the first stirrings of the wedding march—played on the only two musical instruments left in town after the fire, a pair of fiddles—Florence excused herself and joined the rest of the wedding guests. Sarah and I took a moment and stood facing each other.

"Thank you for being my maid of honour. You're the best friend I could have ever hoped for," she said.

"And you, mine," I answered. I thought over the events of the past year and all that Sarah had meant to me. I didn't think I would have survived those first days after Hari's death without her. She had been there for me with gentle encouragement and understanding. Then she had welcomed me into the bosom of her family here in Barkerville and had helped me build a new life. I felt tears prick the corners of my eyes and saw Sarah's well up too.

"Charlotte, I can never thank you enough for saving Jacob, not once but twice. I would be lost without him. I owe you so much. When you move to your ranch, you must remember to come and visit us as much as you can. You must never feel alone, because you will always be in my heart." She paused. "Do you still have any regrets, about coming here? About John?"

"I have absolutely no regrets about leaving England and coming to Barkerville," I said. "And John? I've made my peace with it. I've let it go. What about you? Any regrets?"

"Not a single one. Coming here is the best thing I've ever done."

An understanding passed between us. We knew we would always have each other no matter what the future brought.

I squeezed her hand. "Let's go find your father and Jacob."

They were waiting for us outside the door. When he saw his daughter, Mr. Roy looked proud enough to burst. Sarah took her father's arm and began to walk down the aisle. I gathered up Jacob in my arms and followed behind. At the altar, a nervous-looking Louis waited, but the moment he looked up and saw Sarah smile his nerves seemed to melt away. They gazed at each other with such love and I felt an ache in my heart at the thought that I would never see John waiting for me in such a place, and an ache for all that I had lost. I cuddled Jacob closer to me and scanned the faces in the crowd and reminded myself of how much I had gained. I was a pebble tossed upon a foreign shore, but I had persevered and found the life I wanted, a future of my own choosing.

Epilogue

October 30, 1864

Sarah's first wedding anniversary had been an excuse for a wonderful party, but I was happy to return to my ranch. It was a grey day in Barkerville, with the sun doing its best to peek through the clouds, and I hurried as fast as my limp would allow towards the BC Express office with my travel satchel in hand. I took the back route up the laneway just as the sun finally burst forth and flooded this little part of the world with cheerful, warming sunshine.

My route took me past the share exchange hut where a crowd had gathered. Men were shouting and waving their hands in the air. The shrill voice of the clerk stopped me cold. "Bids, gentlemen, one at a time, please—and who is offering to sell Horsefly Creek shares? Sellers, speak up!"

Had I heard him correctly? Was this frenzy over buying shares of Horsefly Creek? I still possessed ten shares, and if they were worth more than pennies now, I might as well sell them. I had never removed them from my purse, the one I was carrying now. I searched its bottom and came up with a frayed, crumpled piece of paper. I pushed my way into the crowd.

I called to the clerk and tried to catch his eye, but he ignored me. Taking my handkerchief from my purse, I waved it in the air and called to him, but to no avail. I was clearly invisible to these men. With a smile, I remembered Alice forcing her way into the ticket booth and grabbing the clerk by the collar. I needed to be a little more like her now. I pressed my way to the front until I was standing next to the clerk. He continued to ignore me. I slowly but deliberately stood on his foot.

He flinched and turned to me. "Madam, you are standing on my foot, and let me assure you, you are not a featherweight."

"I beg your pardon, but I saw no other way to get your notice. I have ten shares of Horsefly Creek, and I wish to sell them to the highest bidder as soon as possible."

His bushy eyebrows shot up and he called to the crowd, "Gentlemen, the lady here has ten shares. What am I bid?"

"Three!" someone shouted from the back.

"Four!" came another voice.

I did the math; forty dollars would be a wonderful windfall. I thought of the new smallpox vaccination supplies I could buy with the money.

"Gentlemen," the clerk said, "I hear four hundred dollars. Is there a higher bid?"

I gasped. Four *hundred*. Did I hear him right?

"Four fifty!"

"Five!"

"Anyone else?" the clerk asked. There was silence. "Sold!

Ten shares of Horsefly Creek for five hundred US dollars a share. Buyer and seller see the clerk inside."

Dazed, I entered the hut where a second clerk bade me sit next to him and sign the back of the certificate. Then he picked up the pile of United States dollars beside him and began counting. I held my breath as he counted, still not quite believing it.

"Why does everyone want these shares all of a sudden?" I asked.

"Horsefly Creek hit a big vein and they don't have a lot of shares in the public domain, miss," he answered, unfazed. He kept counting. "Five thousand US dollars minus our five percent commission." He pushed a note over to me. "Sign here."

I assumed it was a receipt for the money, but I couldn't focus well enough to read and, in fact, could barely produce a shaky signature on the note. A line had formed behind me, and the clerk asked me to move along, so I gathered up the bank notes. I pushed them into my purse, but there were so many, I struggled to close the clasp.

I wandered onwards in a fog, but once I settled in the stagecoach heading south, I started to think about what I would do with the money. I could use some to build a clinic, I realized. I could finally provide medical care, including vaccinations, to those who lived in these northern reaches, to anyone who needed medicine. I knew, in a way, that I was too late. That smallpox had ravaged the Native population already. But if I could give back to the first peoples of this land, even in a small way, I wanted to do it. After all, my windfall was a result of the harm my people had done to the land and its occupants.

I thought of John. If I was never to see him again, I wanted to remember the love we shared and to honour him and his chosen calling. I would use part of the money to build a church that opened its doors to all. I had witnessed much lawlessness and had even killed a man myself. It had been an accident, but I needed a place of solace to come to terms with my deed. Others might yearn for a similar sanctuary to find comfort. The rest of the funds I would tuck away as insurance against some future need.

∾⁗ʠ

The next day, I took my horse out riding to see where might be appropriate spots for my new plans. As I rode back, it struck me that it was a day like this that I dreamt of during my childhood, when I had imagined Hari and I growing up and living together on a farm in the country. I pulled my horse up to stand for a few moments, drinking in the vista that lay before me. From the ridge, I could see the better part of my homestead and Harriet House, a large, two-storey log house with three gables, a hand-carved double front door, and a veranda wrapping around the entire structure.

I eased my horse straight down the slope and let her find her own way to the barn. My stable manager, Garret, was there to take the reins and help me to the ground. I blessed the fact that I could simply hand my horse off to him and then head straight into the house to wash up for dinner. He would see to it that the groom rubbed her down, fed her, and put her in her stall. Harriet had made it all possible, and I would never take it for granted.

Stamping the worst of the mud and dirt off my boots, I entered the house through the kitchen door. My housekeeper Cora's head was bent over a steaming pot on the stove and snapped up the moment I entered.

"It's good you're here," she said, wiping her hands on her apron. "There's a minister here to see you—wouldn't state his business. Probably come to preach gospel or some such and then he'll be expecting a fine dinner in return."

"The minister from town? Reverend MacDonald?"

"Nay, not from town, not Reverend MacDonald. Claims he come all the way from England. Sarah told him he'd find you here. He gave me his card, he did." She fished in her apron pocket. "Reverend John Crossman."

I stood perfectly still for a moment, unsure I had heard correctly. "John Crossman—from England, that John Crossman?" I felt warm and dizzy as I gripped the back of a kitchen chair with both hands. I looked up at Cora. Her frown had deepened.

"He's in the drawing room. Should I be sending him on his way?"

"No, no, best set another place for dinner."

I heard her slap a pan down on the woodstove as I left the kitchen. Pausing in the front hall just outside the drawing room, I took a deep breath. I could hardly accept the turn of events. After all this time, John was here. Would he be the same John, the man I had fallen in love with, or someone else? I caught sight of the framed photograph on the wall in front of me, the one taken with Sarah and Florence in Barkerville before the fire. What would John think of me and my altered appearance? I hesitated, afraid to see him—to let him see me. I stepped forward.

I had forgotten how big he was. He sat in a shadow, but he stood as I entered and his presence filled the room.

"Just as beautiful as I remembered," he said. "It's good to see you, Charlotte. It's been a long time—much longer than I hoped."

I moved haltingly towards him, aware of my limp, but he kept his eyes on mine. We looked into each other's faces, discovering the ravages that our injuries had wrought. His eyes traced the outline of the burn mark on my cheek, but they didn't linger there.

His elegant Roman nose had been flattened somewhat, but most noticeable was the loss of his mass of dark locks and his facial hair and a long scar that ran from the tip of one ear all the way to the crown of his head. But the absence of his hair and whiskers only served to make his cobalt-blue eyes all the more vivid and his smile more charming.

We stood awkwardly, silently looking at each other. I wasn't sure what to say or how to greet him, so I took his hand formally and shook it.

"I sent a letter to your brother to ask how you were and wish you well. I hope you saw it."

"I wasn't able to see anything properly for months, but Andrew read it to me. It helped to know you asked after me, but then we got word of the fire and I worried about you. I asked Andrew to write and see how you made out, but the letter was returned unopened."

"I didn't get it," I assured him. "The fire—there was no post office."

"That's what I figured, so as soon as I felt up to it, I came to check on you myself." He beamed at me. "So let's hear what you've been doing since I last saw you."

We sat down, and he listened intently as I told of the recent harrowing events, expressing shock, concern, and eventually relief. When it was his turn to tell me of his injuries and recovery, he sidestepped my questions and spoke only of the opposition to his work.

"The group that opposes my views about the Natives' rights are trying to ruin my reputation and shut me up. Their movement is fed by companies with a stake in the game. They want to just grab the land and take what's there. Every day there seemed to be some new damning rumour about me. I was so happy to leave England." He paused and took a deep breath, exhaling sharply. "Though I can't help but feel that it's been for naught. So much damage has been done."

I told him about my plan for the clinic and the church. "The worst of the smallpox outbreak is over," I said, "but there is still a need, especially in the north. And there's a want for local medical care and a sense of community."

"Charlotte, that's wonderful," he said, his eyes lighting up, and I was instantly brought back to those happy days on the boat.

I reached for his hand. "I have something to show you."

I felt like I was presenting my newborn baby for the first time, such was my pride and joy as I took John around the property. After touring the barn, the horse stables, and other outbuildings, we climbed a hill to where I had placed a bench carved from a single piece of a tree trunk. We sat together, finally at ease with each other, drinking in the scene before us. From this vantage point, we could see my herd of cattle as they contentedly wandered the valley floor foraging for grass and snoozing on the cool, muddy shore of the lazy, meandering stream. Dusk descended and the crickets began their lonely, nightly lament for a mate.

"I love this place," I said.

"I can see why. Nothing in England could rival it. The perfect place to make a home."

"You really think so?"

"I do."

He withdrew his handkerchief from the breast pocket of his vest, carefully unfolding it. "My brother found these in my pocket after the beating," he said. "It was months before I was well enough to see them properly, but I was confounded when I did."

He opened his hand to reveal two gold rings: a plain gold band and an engagement ring with three small diamonds. They looked vaguely familiar, but I couldn't place them. I looked up at him questioningly.

"I hadn't the faintest idea where they came from. No memory. I didn't buy them. I would've had a record of it. My memory came back in bits and pieces, a flash here, an image there. Some of it very painful." He paused for a moment. "It took a long time, but I finally put it all together. Hortense Wiggins gave them to me."

"Wiggles?" I asked. "Were they her mother's?"

"They're from your cousin, Edward. He had asked Hortense to send them with her next correspondence to you. Seems he'd found an old trunk in the attic full of your mother's things. The rings were in it—they were your grandmother's."

I gasped and pulled his hand towards me to have a better look. Picking up the rings, I turned them over in my fingers, thrilling at their touch. They were my only link to my past, to my family.

"They're for me?"

"I wasn't planning on wearing them. They don't fit, for starters." John chuckled. "I knew Hortense had encouraged you to make the journey, so I paid her a visit to tell her how you were getting on. We had a nice chat, and she asked me to pass the rings on to you—when I told her how I feel about you."

I held my breath. "And what did you tell her?"

"That I've thought of you every single day since we parted— that I was guilty of making the worst mess of a proposal that any man has ever made, that I was going to try again, because I love you. I believe we share something that few others do, and I can't imagine spending the rest of my days with anyone else."

He took my hands, and, looking deep into my eyes, said, "Charlotte, will you marry me?"

I thought of the day I stepped aboard the *Tynemouth*, a bundle of nerves and full of trepidation over the upcoming adventure, an innocent in so many ways—naive and impulsive, a young woman with much to learn about the world, as well as herself. But I was a much different person now. I had come into my own, and I was very comfortable with myself and my place in the world. I had no need to marry if I didn't want to.

"Yes," I said, slipping the rings on. They fit instantly. "No sense in taking them off."

"Keep just the engagement ring for now. The wedding band has to wait for the actual ceremony."

I handed him back the gold band.

"It'll be a proper church wedding in town as soon as I can arrange it, and then back here to live in paradise."

I pulled him to me until my mouth found his. A tingling warmth flared throughout my body as he held me close and his soft lips closed over mine in a long, full kiss. My mind drifted to images of our future together. I imagined us spending our days in easy companionship, riding the range and sharing long evenings with fine meals by the fire. I saw myself waking in the night and feeling the warm comfort of his body beside mine.

I got up from the bench and looped my arm in his. "Let's go in for dinner."

When we set foot on the wood-planked floor of the veranda where Cora had set out dinner, we heard the strains of a fiddle striking up. Garret regularly entertained the cowboys with renditions of popular tunes, and tonight I recognized the haunting melody of a song that the Americans had brought north with them, "Weeping Sad and Lonely." From their Civil War, the deeply moving song captured the current prevailing sentiment of our generation.

We were a cohort of men and women who had left home seeking better lives—impoverished women who travelled halfway around the world for new opportunities, soldiers who chased glory in wars that others had started, and prospectors who searched for untold wealth in the sandbars of raging rivers. Some returned; many did not. A few of us found what we were seeking. But now, we yearned for something different—a home and someone to share it with.

John and I stood for a moment, gently swaying, then, as Garret picked up the tempo, John put his great arms around me and I had a clear vision of our shared future together. Leaning on each other for support, we whirled about the veranda, our steps easy and unhalting.

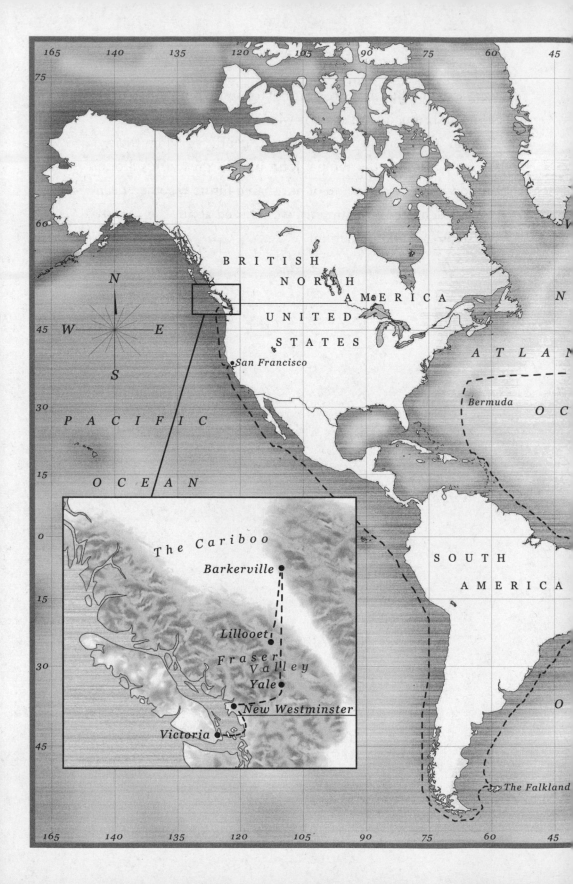

165   140   135   120   105   90   75   60   45

75

60

45   W — E

30

15

0

15

30

45

165   140   135   120   105   90   75   60   45

N

B R I T I S H
N O R T H
A M E R I C A

U N I T E D

S T A T E S

San Francisco

P A C I F I C

O C E A N

A T L A N

N

Bermuda   O C

SOUTH

AMERICA

O

The Falkland

The Cariboo

Barkerville

Lillooet

Fraser
Valley
Yale

New Westminster

Victoria

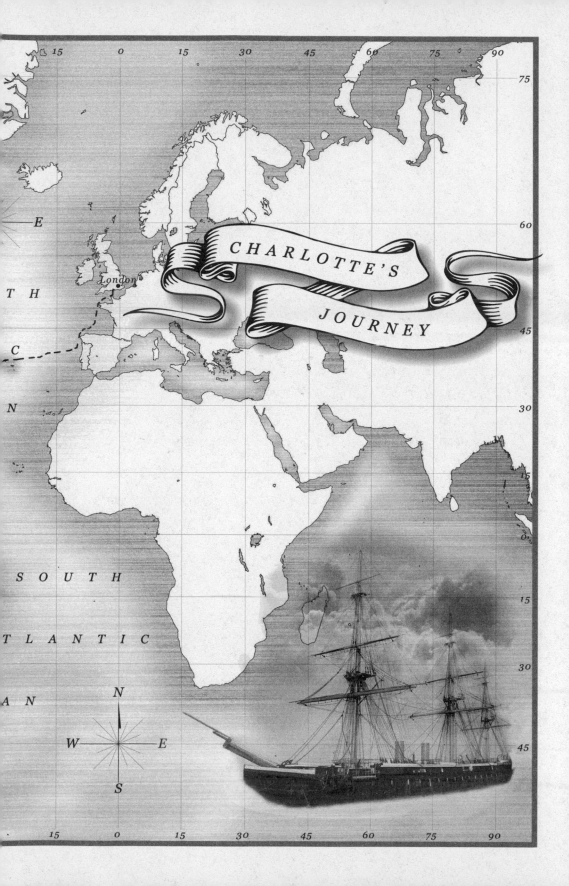

Acknowledgements

I would like to thank Simon & Schuster Canada for understanding that the story of the brideship women is an important and relatively unknown chapter of Canadian history that needed to be told. I would particularly like to thank my editors, Sarah St. Pierre and Laurie Grassi, for taking a chance with a new author. Sarah St. Pierre showed great patience and offered endless encouragement while we painstakingly worked through the editing process.

Thank you to my first agent, David Haviland, formerly with the Andrew Lownie Agency, who thrilled me by picking my manuscript out of the slush pile, and to my current agent, Andrew Lownie, for taking me on.

Heartfelt thanks to Jesse Thistle, teacher, historian, and bestselling author of *From the Ashes*. Jesse helped me develop a greater understanding of the harsh reality of life for Indigenous people in 1860s British Columbia, and I'm grateful for his insights into the role of Métis women.

I wish to acknowledge the Humber College graduate program in creative writing, where I received encouragement and guidance.

A special thanks to the founding members of my writing group, Jessica Chan, Petra Mach, Frances Fee, and Felicity Schweizer, and to my reader and editor Rowena Rae. Thank you to Allyson Latta for her structural editing advice on the first draft.

Thank you to my family: my husband, Austin; my daughter, Katherine; her partner, Colin; my son, Tom; his wife, Kat; and, of course, little Ellie.

And finally thank you to my chocolate Lab, August, who, as a puppy, chewed on my toes while I wrote the first draft and now sleeps curled up under my desk, keeping me focused and those same toes warm.

The Women of the Tynemouth

Abington, Catherine A.

Adington, Emily B.

Barnett, Hariett

Baylis, Sarah

Berry, Emily

Butten, Mary

Chase, Mary L.

Coates, Matilda E.

Cooper, Emily H.

Crawle, Margaret

Curtes, Isabel

Devilly, Mary

Duren, S. Maria

Egginton, Amelia

Evans, Eliza Jane

Evans, Mary

Faussett, Margaret

Fisher, Jane

Gilan, Minnie

Growing, Sophia

Hack, Mary Ann

Hales, Mary

Hirsch, Theresa

Hodges, Mary

Holmes, Georgina J.

Holmes, Helen

Hurst, Julia L.

Jones, Mary Ann

Joyce, Ann

King, Florence

King, Mary

Knapp, Ann

Lane, Fancy

Lovegrove, Sarah

Macdonald, Georgina

Macdonald, Jane

Macdonald, Janet

Macdonald, Mary

McGowen, Ella

McGowen, Kate

Morris, Emily A.

Ogilvie, Jane E.

Passmore, Florenece

Passmore, Welhelmina

Picken, Sophia

Pickles, Mary Ann

Quinn, Emma

Rendich, Catherine A.

Renea, Mary

Reynolds, Eliza

Robb, Jane

Saunders, Jane Ann

Sentzenich, Jane

Shaw, Sophia

Simpson, Elizabeth

Townsend, Charlotte

Townsend, Louisa

Tummage, Emma

   Helen

Wilson, Bertha R.

Wilson, Florence M. B.

Thank you to Tracy McMenemy for finding this manifest, reproduced here with its original spelling, in the British Columbia Archives and kindly sharing it with me. Tracy's art installation *The Girls Are Coming!* was featured at the Vancouver Maritime Museum in 2019.

Author's Note

When I was ten my parents took me for a summer vacation to Barkerville, which has been restored to its former gold rush glory by the British Columbia government in an effort to preserve its history. Touring the heritage buildings set in an isolated northern location and interacting with the actors portraying characters of the time was an experience I have obviously never forgotten.

After a white-knuckle drive through Fraser Canyon we arrived in time for supper at the Wake Up Jake Restaurant followed by a performance at the Theatre Royal, which advertised the famous Hurdy-Gurdy dancers. As we settled into our seats we heard the howl of the wind and rain outside, and the electricity went out. We sat in darkness while the oil lanterns that skirted the stage were lit and a single upright piano was wheeled out of the wings to replace the prerecorded music. Once the show began we were transported back to the earliest days of Barkerville, as though we had slipped back in time to the gold rush and life as it was then.

A few years later I developed a friendship with a girl named Judy, whose father spent weekends visiting ghost towns in the British Columbia interior, and I was occasionally invited to accompany them on their adventures. Judy and I dug through abandoned buildings and old garbage dumps looking for antique bottles, jars, and anything else we could find. That's where I first saw the tiny blue-green glass fingerlings that had once held opium, the same vials that I describe in these very pages.

These memories stayed with me and became quite useful when I decided to write my novel and began to research in earnest. I made my way to various museums to gather information on the voyage of the *Tynemouth* and the gold rush. While visiting the Royal BC Museum in Victoria, I took in an excellent presentation on gold and its history in British Columbia. With extra time to kill, I wandered upstairs until I found myself in an exhibit that took my breath away, but not in a good way. It was the story of the smallpox epidemic and how it had decimated the Indigenous peoples in the region. I had been ignorant of this terrible chapter in the history of my province and learning of it had a profound effect on me. I knew I couldn't write a novel about the 1800s without including this part of the story.

The smallpox epidemic was just part of the story, I later learned. With colonization came coal mines to feed burgeoning industry and pollution that destroyed salmon spawning grounds in a shockingly short period of time. The Indigenous peoples, left with decimated communities, turned to paid jobs where they were taken advantage of and forced to work in terrible conditions that fostered the spread of disease. Because of all these factors many women had no choice but to turn to prostitution in order to survive.

I visited other museums, including ones in Yale and Lillooet, looking for pictures and information that would help me paint vivid scenes for my readers. In one restored home, circa 1860, I climbed narrow wooden attic stairs to a third-floor bedroom, and that's when it struck me that the room was a fire trap. From my research I had learned how common and devastating fires were back then. This was the genesis for the scene where Charlotte is trapped by fire in her attic room.

And then, a couple of years ago, I attended a kitchen party in New Brunswick, where I learned all about the warm and lively Acadian culture, and so I couldn't resist giving Louis, the stagecoach driver, an Acadian heritage.

The Vancouver Maritime Museum featured an art installation in 2019 called *The Girls Are Coming!* It was a wonderfully evocative artistic interpretation of the story of the brideships—of which the *Tynemouth* was just one of three ships—and the women involved. Most of the news articles about the exhibit emphasized how little the story is widely known.

In the scene that takes place in the London Tavern, Charlotte is eager to understand why women are being encouraged to emigrate. I have paraphrased some of the real speeches given that day to show the prevailing concerns of the time. Prostitution, racial intermarriage, the need for English families to bolster Britain's claim to the land, and Dickens's concern for the lives of impoverished women are all brought forward. What I did not mention was the other prevailing worry of the day, homosexuality. While I did not introduce this into the narrative as I was quite certain it would not have been spoken of in polite society, the clergy's desire to stamp out what they considered to be immoral sexual activity was a behind-the-scenes driver for the resettlement scheme.

During the meeting, Charlotte ruminates on whether those who immigrate to the colony will have better futures. In spite of her doubts, history has proven that many of the brides not only led more fulfilling and financially sound lives but they also left lasting legacies, which I soon discovered.

Most days when I'm in Vancouver, I take my chocolate Labrador, August, out for a walk and pass Hastings Mill Park, home of the oldest building in the city. I have passed this building countless times and only discovered the connection to the brideships while writing this piece. One of the brideship women, Emma Alexander, née Tummage, had been a domestic servant before emigrating from England on the *Tynemouth* to Victoria. She married and moved to Vancouver. Her husband, Richard Alexander, was made manager of the Hastings Mill store and built her a fine house nearby. Over the years, Emma and Richard acquired land throughout the city and eventually became two of Vancouver's most prominent citizens. One of the only structures to survive the Vancouver fire of 1886, the Hastings Mill store was barged to its current site in 1931 from nearby Burrard Inlet and made into a museum.

Emma Lazenby, one of the emigrant women in the novel, was a real person, but in fact she travelled on another brideship, the *Robert Lowe*. Emma had seen much misery in England due to the hardships of Lancashire cotton mills and the English Poor Laws—an unsuccessful social assistance program—that led to high rates of alcoholism in northern England, which led her to become a Methodist and an advocate for temperance. In Victoria, she married David Spencer, a Welshman who shared her views. Emma worked hard to establish a shelter for destitute women while raising thirteen children. Her husband established Spencer's Department Store, became wealthy, and built a mansion for them near Governor Douglas's residence.

Another emigrant woman, twenty-year-old Jane Anne Saunders, got a job as a domestic soon after the *Tynemouth* arrived and quickly earned a reputation as a hard worker. She married a failed gold miner, Samuel Nesbitt. Together, they established a very successful bakery and eventually built Erin Hall, an elegant manor house overlooking the ocean.

Margaret Faussett started her life in Victoria as a governess but soon married a teacher, John Jessop. She also became a teacher and, with her husband, she championed a new public education system that would be nonsectarian. Their proposal for the first Public School Act was accepted by the government. As a result, and contrary to the education system in England, British Columbian schools are free and open to all.

❧

These were just some of the stories that I discovered in my research, and while little is known about many of the women, I feel optimistic that, by and large, the women had much better lives than they could have had in England.

I didn't intend that my novel be an exact portrayal of true incidents, but rather that those events inspire and inform the narrative. Other than the meeting in the London Tavern, all that takes place in part one is fiction, but part two is a blend of fact and fiction. I made the *Tynemouth* much grander than she was in real life in order to incorporate the drama that unfolds among the first-class passengers. Still, readers might be surprised to learn that the actual voyage was much more hellish than Charlotte's, with two mutinies by the seamen, one of which resulted in a fight between passengers and crew where Captain Hellyer was injured. There were a few big storms, with the worst said to have been hurricane force, causing the ship to very nearly sink.

My depiction of the colonies in part three is mostly true to time and place, and some scenes are based on stories that were widely reported at the time. There was a wild reception for the emigrant women upon arrival in Victoria, and a man named Mr. Pioneer really did propose to one of the brideship women by thrusting a handful of money towards her for a splendid gown and wedding. Apparently theirs was a long and happy union. The story of the two doctors who shot each other in a drunken dispute is also said to be true. Having found diary excerpts written by Dr. Walter Cheadle of his trip through the region, I was able to re-create some of the gold miners' slang in the scene with the two dandies in the gambling den. And the actual Barkerville fire was rumoured to have been started by a gold miner who was trying to steal a kiss from a girl in a saloon and accidentally knocked down a stove pipe in the process.

Governor James Douglas and his wife, Amelia, were real people as well. James was born to a Scottish father and a mother of Barbadian Creole ancestry. Amelia was Métis with a French-

Irish father and a Cree mother. Some historians have suggested that James's vision was to create a racially harmonious society in the colony that was inclusive of black and Indigenous peoples. However, the settlers who arrived from every corner of the world brought with them their own entrenched biases and racism. While Mrs. Douglas was reported to be rather shy, keeping a low social profile likely because of derogatory comments, many Indigenous wives of Hudson's Bay Company men were not only wealthy but also prominent and active in both the fur trade and society and thus occupied positions of power.

As a writer who loves history, I like nothing better than to create a story that weaves fact with fiction, especially when those stories are about my home province. As a woman I deeply relate to the brideship women and their struggle to find independence and a life of their own choosing. The sixty *Tynemouth* brideship women left their homeland and all that was known and familiar to them to set off for a strange land in hopes of a better future. For years, women's important stories have been ignored or glossed over in favour of those of men, but the emigrant women were brave and resilient people who deserve their place in history. It has been an honour to help place this story front and centre in the lexicon of women's collective histories. Thank you, dear reader, for joining me on this journey.

Leslie Howard

Sources

The following publications provided factual information about the story's time and place and the people involved.

BOOKS

Basque, Garnet. *Gold Panner's Manual.* Victoria, BC: Heritage House Publishing, 2012.

Bridge, Kathryn, ed. *New Perspectives on the Gold Rush.* Victoria, BC: Royal BC Museum, 2015.

Downs, Art, ed. *Cariboo Gold Rush: The Stampede that Made BC.* Toronto: Heritage House Publishing, 2013.

Illing, Thora Kerr. *Gold Rush Queen: The Extraordinary Life of Nellie Cashman.* Victoria, BC: TouchWood Editions, 2016.

Johnson, Peter. *Voyages of Hope: The Saga of the Bride-Ships.* Victoria, BC: TouchWood Editions, 2002.

Kelm, Mary-Ellen. *Colonizing Bodies: Aboriginal Health and Healing in British Columbia, 1900–50.* Vancouver: UBC Press, 1998.

Perry, Adele. *On the Edge of Empire: Gender, Race, and the Making of British Columbia.* Toronto; Buffalo, NY: University of Toronto Press, 2001.

Van Kirk, Sylvia. *Many Tender Ties: Women in Fur-Trade Society, 1670–1870.* Norman: University of Oklahoma Press, 1983.

Verney, Edmund Hope. *Vancouver Island Letters of Edmund Hope Verney 1862–65.* Edited by Allan Pritchard. Vancouver: UBC Press, 1996.

ARTICLES

Advertisement for the voyage of the *Tynemouth*. *Times of London*, May 9, 1862.

Hopper, Tristin. "Everyone Was Dead: When Europeans First Came to B.C., They Stepped into the Aftermath of a Holocaust." *National Post*, February 21, 2017. https://nationalpost.com/news/canada/everyone-was-dead-when-europeans-first-came-to-b-c-they-confronted-the-aftermath-of-a-holocaust.

Indigenous Corporate Training, Inc. "The Impact of Smallpox on First Nations on the West Coast." April 17, 2017. ictinc.ca/blog/the-impact-of-smallpox-on-first-nations-on-the-west-coast.

Museum of Health Care at Kingston. "Smallpox" in the online exhibit *Vaccines and Immunization: Epidemics, Prevention, and Canadian Innovation.* https://www.museumofhealthcare.ca/explore/exhibits/vaccinations/smallpox.html.

SOURCES

Notice of the arrival of the *Tynemouth. British Colonist*, September 11, 1862.

Ostroff, Joshua. "How a Smallpox Epidemic Forged Modern British Columbia." *Maclean's*, August 1, 2017. https://www.macleans.ca/news/canada/how-a-smallpox-epidemic-forged-modern-british-columbia/.

VIDEO

Sullivan, Sam. *Revisiting B.C. History: The smallpox epidemic of 1862. Vancouver Is Awesome*, May 10, 2018. https://www.vancouverisawesome.com/2018/05/10/smallpox-bc-1862/.

About the Author

Bopomo Pictures

Leslie Howard grew up in Penticton, British Columbia, where she developed a passion for the province's history. A graduate of Ottawa's Carleton University in economics and political science, she now divides her time between Vancouver and Penticton, where she and her husband grow cider apples. *The Brideship Wife* is her debut novel. Connect with her on Twitter @AuthorLeslieH or visit her at www.LeslieHoward.ca.

The

BRIDESHIP
WIFE

Leslie Howard

A Reading Group Guide

A Conversation with
Leslie Howard

This is your debut novel. How long has this story been with you, and what is your writing process like? Did the story change and take shape as you went along?

My writing process resembles that of building a house: first the foundation is poured, then the framing is completed, and finally all the finishing work is done. I tend to write in layers; My first draft sets out the basic plot and a broad brushstroke of characters, the second draft focuses on dialogue and setting, and the third on refining the plot and adjusting the chapter order. As this is my debut novel, the process of developing each of these drafts was lengthy. From my first one-page sketch of the premise to publication has been about five years.

During the editing process, the story ebbed and flowed as characters' conversations took the plot in new directions and I developed central themes more fully. As much as I loved some dramatic scenes, I accepted that they had to be left on the cutting-room floor once they no longer fit with the story arc. The novel didn't change so much as it matured through the process of teasing out plot threads and digging deeper into the characters' motivations and backstories.

The Brideship Wife is based on a little-known chapter of British and Canadian history—the brideships. Where did you first learn about the *Tynemouth* and the Colum-

bia Emigration Society? Did you know instantly you wanted to write a novel about this moment in time?

While waiting for a ferry that would take me from Vancouver to Victoria, British Columbia, I picked up a book in the gift shop called *Voyages of Hope: The Saga of the Bride-Ships* by Peter Johnson. I was captivated by the true story, and the seeds were planted for this novel.

Born and raised in British Columbia, I had always been interested in its history and was therefore surprised that I had never heard of this fascinating and important story. In contrast, much had been written about *les filles du roi*, the women who were brought over from France as wives for the Quebec settlers.

Charlotte is forced to leave England because of a scandal, but this event becomes the catalyst for her physical and her emotional journey. In many ways, this is her coming-of-age story. How did Charlotte's character come to you?

I was very drawn to the plight of the impoverished gentlewomen of the time. They were not employable, as they had no training, and no one would hire them anyway. Marriage was their only option, and so finding a husband was the single most important consideration in their lives.

I wanted to show Charlotte as a product of Victorian times, a young woman who tries to live up to the expectations of her family and society, but who, through a series of experiences, grows into an independent woman with early feminist views.

Which character did you identify with most, and why?
Surprisingly, John Crossman, in the way that he seizes on an idea and becomes passionate about it . . . like writing a novel about the brideships.

Throughout the novel, you explore the limited opportunities offered to women at this time and the freedom of choice. Why was it important to you to highlight these themes? Do you think these issues are still relevant today?
I believe the New World offered women the opportunity to break from the strict social confines of Victorian England and allowed them to develop and exercise their free will. In doing so, they not only benefited themselves, but also set a foundation for equality that women still fight for today. The movement of the women from the old world to the new was an inciting incident in the development of the rights of women in Canada.

You write about life in England and Canada in such vivid detail. How did growing up in British Columbia influence your writing? And how did you bring Victorian England to life?
My father was a politician who spent a lot of time driving the back roads of the province to talk to voters. As a child, I often accompanied him on those trips and came to learn a great deal about the people and the land that I love.

People joke that Victoria, British Columbia, is more English than England, and the British heritage of the province is very strong. Back in 1862, there really was a society devoted to proper tea drinking as described in the novel. When I was growing up, many of my friends' parents were British immigrants who kept the culture and traditions of their homeland strong in their adopted home.

I have always been a great fan of the historical fiction writer Georgette Heyer, whose novels are set in Regency-period England. She had a tremendous ability to bring to life the social discourse of the time, and I drew upon her writing for inspiration.

You did an extensive amount of research. While Charlotte is fictional, many of the characters and incidents in the novel are real, including Charles Dickens. What scenes in the novel might readers be most surprised to know are lifted right from history's pages?

Much of the scene in the London Tavern, where the plan to launch the brideships was discussed, is based on fact. The Lord Mayor of London spoke to the issue, as did the bishop of Honolulu, and my dialogue closely represents what they said. A letter from the Reverend Lundin Brown from Lillooet was read out, prompting someone to ask what should be done with the upper-class old maids, eliciting the response I wrote in the novel. The emigration scheme was indeed the brainchild of Charles Dickens and his friend the heiress Angela Burdett-Coutts.

The voyage of the *Tynemouth* was a hellish journey, especially for the sixty emigrant women, and the ship almost went down in a massive storm. One woman died from a suspected case of food poisoning, prompting Captain Hellyer to dump the fresh food he brought on board at the Falkland Islands. Both notices for the *Tynemouth*'s departure and arrival are word for word taken from the historical announcements.

I moved the Barkerville fire from 1868 to 1863 to serve my story. It levelled most of the town in just two and a half hours, but many of the buildings were rebuilt in six short weeks. Florence Wilson, one of the original brideship women, purchased the Theatre Royal and, with her Cariboo Amateur Dramatic Association, staged many celebrated performances as described in my novel.

Charlotte is a great reader, and she references many works of fiction that were new and popular in her time and are classics to us modern readers today, including *Little Dorrit* and *Pride and Prejudice*. Did these books influence your writing? What other books or films inspired you?
The common thread in much of Dickens's work centres on challenging the social ills of the day, and his writing influenced the themes I developed in my book. In *Little Dorrit* he satirizes the lack of a social safety net for impoverished people and the class system, two topics the characters in my book discuss. Dickens's desire to address real-life problems led him to develop and support the brideship program.

Jane Austen's *Pride and Prejudice*, set in the Regency era, is a brilliant treatise on marriage as the most important decision in any young woman's life, one that would determine her entire future. As in my novel, the protagonist feels pressure to marry for wealth all the while wishing to marry for love.

Whenever I travel, I purchase nonfiction books produced by local writers that feature people or events of that place. While in Bermuda, I picked up *The History of Mary Prince*, an autobiography of a local woman who was enslaved and suffered horrendously. But when Mary's master travelled to England with her, she escaped. There, Mary learned to read and wrote her autobiography, which was the first story of a black woman's life to be published in England. She inspired my character Henry Roy.

I got the idea for Harriet's laudanum addiction from the Aubrey–Maturin novels by Patrick O'Brian, in which the ship's physician, Stephen Maturin, becomes addicted through self-medication.

Questions for Book Clubs

1. When the novel opens, Charlotte is pressured to marry George. While she doesn't love him, she resigns herself to her fate. What does this say about the options available to women at this time?

2. Charlotte often bemoans her corset in the novel. What does the corset literally and figuratively represent?

3. When George attacks Charlotte, he threatens her into silence, saying, "Whose version do you think people will believe?" Later on, Harriet tells Charlotte that it doesn't matter what actually happened between her and George. What's really being left unsaid here about truth and reputation? Do some of these views still persist today?

4. Charlotte is rather naive at the beginning of the book. Beyond George's assault, what events show her that not everything is always as it appears?

5. Charlotte and Harriet have different ideas of what marriage should be. How is Harriet a product of her environment and her upbringing? How does she exert power within her constraints?

6. Harriet is said to have made a brilliant match with Charles, but her marriage crumbles when she can't produce an heir. Contrast her experience with the one encountered by Sarah, who is ostracized for being a pregnant widow. How does this reflect the expectations and standards for women at this time?

7. How is Charlotte's character arc a coming-of-age story? How is Harriet's a cautionary tale?

8. Brideships like the *Tynemouth* promised women the chance to have a better life in the colonies than they had in England. In what ways was this true? In what ways were women still disenfranchised?

9. Compare and contrast Charlotte's prospects with those of the other emigrant women. How do class, money, and social status limit each woman's opportunities? What different freedoms do they enjoy?

10. Consider the different marriages we see in the novel: Charlotte's parents, Harriet and Charles, Sir Richard and Lady Persephone, and the matches Sarah and Charlotte go on to make. In what ways are these couplings the same, and in what ways are they different? What does each partner get from the other?

11. How do the three decks on board the *Tynemouth* illustrate the strictures of Victorian society? How do these start to break down over the course of the journey?

12. Charlotte begins to learn about the injustices around her through the people she interacts with, especially John, Sarah, and Dr. Carson. What do each of them teach her?

13. British imperialism is a key theme in the novel. What role do women play in Britain's plans to expand its empire? Who ultimately benefits from colonization? Who suffers the most? How does the novel present inequality as synonymous with colonialism?

14. Charlotte is an avid reader. What do books offer her? How do they expand her worldview?

15. Charlotte mentions Jane Austen's *Pride and Prejudice*. In what ways does *The Brideship Wife* echo the themes of that novel? In what ways does it depart?

16. Despite her growing feelings for him, Charlotte turns down John's marriage proposal. What does British Columbia offer her that he can't?

17. Consider the gift of the emerald necklace, which Miss Wiggins says symbolizes rebirth. What does it come to symbolize when Charlotte loses it? What does the loss mean for her journey toward self-realization?

18. At the beginning of the novel, we learn that Charlotte has no dowry, but this proves to be untrue. How does the dowry take on new and different meanings throughout the story? How do Harriet's final actions subvert the patriarchal norms of the dowry?

19. Miss Wiggins doesn't marry because of the birthmark on her face, and after the fire, Charlotte has a scar on her cheek. What do these marks represent for each of them? What does this mirroring suggest?

20. In the novel, British Columbia is a symbol of freedom for the emigrant women, but many old ways of thinking persist. Discuss how different ethnicities, such as black and Indigenous peoples, are marginalized. How are land ownership and wealth at the centre of this mistreatment? What issues still linger, unresolved, at the end of the novel? What does this say about colonialism?

21. By the end of the novel, Charlotte has regained much of what she lost, and it's only then that she chooses marriage. Do you think her decision complicates this hard-won autonomy? Why or why not?
22. Discuss the significance of the title *The Brideship Wife*.

Enhance Your Book Club

1. Brideships are a little-known chapter of Canadian history. Learn more about this moment in time and the real women who came here on board the *Tynemouth*: https://www.canadashistory.ca/explore/women/crino line-cargo.

2. When Charlotte travels to Barkerville, she sees firsthand the changes made to the land because of the Cariboo gold rush, which went on from 1860 to 1863. To find out more about the gold rush, visit the Royal BC Museum learning portal here: https://learning.royalbcmuseum.bc.ca /pathways/bcs-gold-rush/.

3. Governor James Douglas and his wife, Amelia (née Connolly), were real historical figures. Read more about Amelia here: http://www.metismuseum.ca/media/db/07419.